THE CHOPPING BLOCK
GRIMM

THE CHOPPING BLOCK

GRIMM

JOHN PASSARELLA
BASED ON THE NBC TV SERIES

TITAN BOOKS

Grimm: The Chopping Block
Print edition ISBN: 9781781166567
E-book edition ISBN: 9781781166574

Published by Titan Books
A division of Titan Publishing Group Ltd
144 Southwark St, London SE1 0UP

First edition: February 2014
10 9 8 7 6 5 4 3 2 1

A CIP catalogue record for this title is available from the British Library.

Printed and bound in the United States.

TITANBOOKS.COM

To my wife, Andrea, for understanding my need to dive down the rabbit hole of odd hours, frequent distractions and occasional forgetfulness.

This novel takes place between "The Waking Dead" and "Goodnight, Sweet Grimm."

"He called them to the grand feast and gathered them in celebration, to remember and enjoy the finer things."

CHAPTER ONE

Brian Mathis wondered if he'd made a mistake bringing Tyler, his twelve-year-old son, to Claremont Park. Their little adventure had been fun and cheerful and full of father-son-bonding promise until they left behind the paved path and picnic tables, and wandered into the woods on a course prescribed by the virtual compass in the GPS app on Brian's smartphone. The overnight rainfall had turned what would have been a reasonable hiking path into a treacherous endeavor. Lagging behind his father, Tyler had already fallen twice on gentle inclines slick with mud. And now the boy was coated with the stuff—hands, knees, shoes, and a caked spot on his chin he'd rubbed the same moment his patience had expired.

Victim of his own clumsy misadventure, Brian proceeded on a twisted ankle—which continued to throb in counterpoint to his heartbeat—and reminded himself to take his eyes off the compass now and then to pay attention to his footing. Minutes later, head down and cursing under his breath, he walked right into a low-hanging branch. Hell of an example he was setting for his kid.

"You said we were close, Dad," Tyler groaned, prefacing

that indictment with a prolonged sigh.

"We *are* close," Brian said. "But I told you before. The coordinates aren't exact."

"So what's the point?" Tyler hurled a rock the size of a ping-pong ball at the nearest tree trunk. The *thwock* of the impact startled a squirrel, which scampered along one branch, jumped to another nearby and scurried out of sight.

"Don't throw rocks."

"Nothing else to do."

Ignoring the boy's complaint, Brian explained, "The coordinates take us to the general vicinity, then we look around until we find it."

"Why?"

"Because… it's like searching for buried treasure."

"I'm keeping it."

"No," Brian said. "We sign the logbook and leave the container where we found it. The honor system. If we take it, the next person will go through all this trouble for nothing."

"You said I could take something," Tyler reminded him.

"Swap something," Brian said. This particular geocache supposedly contained small toys. If you took something, you were supposed to leave behind an object of equal value. "You brought a soldier?"

"Yeah," Tyler said, rolling his eyes at his father.

It had been years since Tyler played with toy soldiers, which was why he had no qualms about leaving one behind. Tyler hoped for an upgrade, maybe a used video game or something equally unlikely. So his father had spent most of the car ride to the park trying to quash those expectations.

"The search is the fun part, not the prize at the end."

"Some fun," Tyler grumbled loud enough for his father to hear.

Secretly, Brian regretted not selecting a cache with the

lowest level of difficulty for their first attempt. Instead, he'd chosen a cache closer to home, but with the next highest level of difficulty. A cache with toys, even cheap toys, he'd thought, would appeal to the boy. Brian's second mistake was misjudging the rapid pace of Tyler's maturity. At his current age, things transitioned from "cool" to "lame" in a hurry. Since the divorce, Brian saw his son less than he would have liked. The boy's growth spurts took place in the uncompromising strobe light of his meager custody schedule.

As a bank of rain clouds passed overhead, the woods became prematurely dark. Shadows deepened like an ink spill soaking the ground around them. The odor of moist earth rose like a clinging mist, enveloping them.

Brian stopped, rubbed the back of his forearm across his damp forehead and said, "We're here."

Tyler stood beside him, turned in a circle and shrugged. "Nothing."

"It's here somewhere," Brian assured him, but worried somebody before them might have removed the cache in violation of the honor system. If they left the park without finding anything, his son would never let him forget it. *"Remember that time you dragged me through the woods in waist-deep mud for nothing?"* Because exaggeration would become a key component in this particular trip down memory lane.

"What about the clue?" Tyler asked.

"Oh—right! The clue." In his growing paternal anxiety, Brian had almost forgotten about the clue associated with the cache. He checked his phone. "It says, 'Fall up the hill.'"

They both cast expectant gazes around, as if expecting a hillside to magically rise from the surrounding forest, crowned with a glowing treasure chest like a reward in one of Tyler's video games.

"That hill?" Tyler finally asked, pointing straight ahead.

Brian looked behind them, then straight ahead. They had been following an incline for a bit, something he might have noticed if he hadn't been mesmerized by the compass on his cell phone. Ahead of them marked the top of the rise, surrounded by an irregular ring of deciduous trees in various states of decay.

"Must be it," Brian acknowledged. "So how do we 'fall up'?"

We both figured out the falling down part easily enough, he thought, with a chagrined shake of his head.

Tyler scrambled up the slope, littered with broken branches, twigs, and clumps of dead leaves well on their way to mulch that nevertheless rustled underfoot. He slipped once and caught himself on both hands before his knees touched the muddy ground again.

"Careful," Brian said, making his own way upward, mindful of his tender ankle.

Tyler picked up a stout branch the length of a cane and swung it around to disperse the leaf mounds. When he reached down to flip over a football-sized rock, Brian caught his shoulder.

"Watch out for snakes," he cautioned.

The possibility of encountering a snake, poisonous or otherwise, seemed to excite the boy's imagination, but he took extra care as he grabbed the edge of the rock and flipped it over, poised to spring away to avoid the threat of fangs. Instead, he grunted in obvious disappointment as several freshly exposed worms coiled in the dirt.

Tyler circled to the left, poking and sweeping with his branch, while Brian wandered into a tangle of dried brush and broken tree limbs at the edge of the clearing. Brushing away twigs and dried leaves, he discovered a jagged tree stump and, angling away from it, on the far side of the rise, the decaying length of the entire tree trunk, which retained only a few scattered branches.

"A deadfall," Brian whispered, then again, louder. "A deadfall."

"What?" Tyler called, glancing briefly over his shoulder.

"This downed tree," Brian called to his son. "It's a deadfall."

"So?" Tyler replied, more preoccupied with a section of tangled underbrush and loose mounds of dirt—excavated, no doubt, by some burrowing woodland creature—than his father's pronouncement.

"Don't you get it?" Brian asked. "The clue: 'Fall up the hill.' It's a deadfall—on this hill."

"You found it?"

"Not yet…" Brian pocketed his phone and swept both hands across the brittle and decaying debris piled around the deadfall. He omitted telling Tyler that this was a more likely spot for a hidden snake than the underside of a rock. Besides, if Brian had unraveled the clue to the cache's location, he wanted to find it before leading the boy to yet another disappointment. Once he unearthed it, he'd call Tyler over to claim the prize. He might just salvage the day after all.

Crouching, Brian caught a glint of color in the natural pocket formed between the tree stump and its fallen trunk; something metallic, painted bright red. *Gotcha!* he thought in an unexpectedly strong moment of satisfaction.

Before calling his son over to claim the small square tin, he leaned forward to examine the shadowy depression. He swept the ground with the beam of his keychain flashlight. Though he doubted he'd find broken glass or rusty nails or even an irritable snake, he wanted to be sure, lest their excursion end on a sour note—or a trip to the emergency room.

"Tyler, come here," Brian said. "Think I found something."

"Me too," Tyler said, his voice hushed with something akin to awe.

"No," Brian said, standing and brushing off his knees. "Pretty sure this is it over here."

He looked at his son, who was poking and prodding something with his makeshift cane. Brian's first thought was that his son had found a snake after all and that poking a snake with a stick was a very bad idea.

"Tyler," he called. "Step away!"

"No, Dad," Tyler said. "It's okay."

The boy crouched beside the tangled brush and mounds of dirt and clawed at the earth with the tip of the branch, deepening the hole and exposing a length of something white. As Brian circled around his son cautiously, a dark thought began to form. A thought that was confirmed when Tyler reached down into the hole and gripped the length of dull white in his mud-caked hands and pulled it free.

"Look," he said, eyes full of pride at his discovery. "Animal bone. A big one."

Brian was an investment accountant, not a doctor, but he'd seen enough skeleton illustrations over the years to entertain the disturbing possibility that his son was not holding an animal bone. The rational part of his brain kept suggesting and rejecting other explanations: maybe the leg bone of a large mammal… a deer or a bear or…?

Something was wrong. He could sense it at an atavistic level. Some detail that refused to register—until he was near enough to his son's outstretched hand to notice the cleanly severed end of the bone.

"Put that down," Brian said. "Drop it."

"But Dad—!"

"It might be—could be diseased—parasites," Brian muttered. But, another word came to mind. If the bone was human, with a break that clean.

Evidence.

Disappointed, Tyler dropped the bone, but he reached over to push aside some brush and said, "Look! There's more."

Brian took a hesitant step forward and looked down at a jumbled pile of bones. No flesh or organs, no muscles or tissue. Bare bones. Enough bones to make...

He noticed something rounded toward the back of the pile, with the telltale curvature of a hemisphere. Then Tyler disturbed the mass of bones with an exploratory poke with the tip of his branch. Disconnected rib bones slid aside, exposing the dark circle of an empty eye socket, twin nasal passages and a row of teeth. There could be no other explanation.

Brian was staring at a human skull. He'd led his twelve-year-old son into the woods to discover human remains. His ex-wife would never forgive him.

He fumbled for his phone and stared at the screen for a few punch-drunk moments with no idea why the display showed him a compass. Finally, he remembered how to quit the app and use his damn smartphone as a phone.

Meanwhile, the geocache search—the whole reason they'd come to the park in the first place—had become a distant, confusing memory.

Instead, two other ominous words popped into his head.

Shallow grave.

CHAPTER TWO

Detective Nick Burkhardt parked his Land Cruiser on a narrow access road overlooking Claremont Park, behind a row of official city vehicles headed by a pair of police cruisers with flashing light bars. Judging from the rest of the stalled procession, paramedics, crime scene techs and someone from the coroner's office were on site.

He turned to his partner, fellow detective Hank Griffin, and said, "Gang's all here."

"Makes us fashionably late."

They climbed out of the SUV, Hank taking a few moments longer to maneuver on his cast as he reached over the seatback for his crutches. While in Kauai on a long overdue vacation, he'd taken a bad fall—"landed a little too enthusiastically" in Hank's own words—from a zip line, tearing his Achilles tendon. In the past few weeks he'd become quite nimble on the crutches, but he left the foot chases to Nick.

Hank joined Nick at the side of the access road and frowned.

Nick understood his partner's consternation. Glancing down the irregular slope of the makeshift path delineated on either side by crime scene tape looped around tree trunks, he had the impression of facing a woodland obstacle course.

"Maybe you should sit this one out, Hank."

"I'll be fine."

"Sure?"

"I'll get there," Hank said confidently. He cleared his throat. "Eventually."

Nick started down the path, paused to look back and saw Hank prodding the ground with the tip of one crutch. Nick raised a hand to point at some overhead branches and smiled.

"I could ask them to install a zip line."

"Funny, Nick," Hank said, with a sweep of the crutch as though it was an extension of his arm. "I'm laughing on the inside."

Though Hank had joked that his doctor had told him to leave all the work to his partner, he was too proud to easily admit any limitations. Nick hoped his good-natured ribbing would keep his partner's spirits up, so he was less focused on what he couldn't do in his current condition. At the same time, he hoped Hank remained cautious enough to avoid further injury. He knew his partner was counting the days until the cast came off.

Nick turned his attention to the path ahead, noting the presence of techs and a few uniforms. Farther ahead, two paramedics stood talking to each other in low tones with an occasional glance at the techs taking measurements and photographs.

On the other side of the crime scene, Sergeant Wu spoke to the father and son who had reported the human remains. A tall, birdlike woman with a long gray ponytail, dressed in a blue denim blouse and khaki slacks, interrupted the group to speak with Wu. A forensic anthropologist who consulted with the medical examiner's office, Nick recalled. Her exact name escaped him. Yolanda Candella or Canders.

Angling toward the mound of bare bones, some of which had been laid out for measurement and photographs, Nick crouched for a better examination. More than a few of the bones had clean breaks. And that raised all sorts of questions.

He'd been a Portland homicide detective long before he discovered he was a Grimm—descended from a long line of Grimms that included his mother and his late Aunt Marie. As a Grimm, Nick had the ability to "profile" what he had always assumed were mythological creatures, most of whom were at odds with humanity. They called themselves Wesen, and in moments of stress or extreme emotion, they transformed—*woged*—and revealed their true nature. But the transformation was visible only to a Grimm. Other humans were unaware of the change in appearance—unless the Wesen chose to reveal its true face to them. Not something that happened often because the Wesen hid in plain sight, wolves in the fold of humanity.

So Nick's job description had changed. In addition to apprehending human murderers, he was, as a Grimm, uniquely qualified to find and stop Wesen killers. The only difference was that not all Wesen killers received due process. Sometimes off-book solutions were necessary.

Staring at the severed bones, Nick had to consider the possibility that the killer—and he had no doubt the victim had been murdered and buried here in a shallow grave—was not human, that the perpetrator was Wesen. He recalled the Fuchsteufelwild, a goblin-like Wesen who had slaughtered employees at the Spinner Corporation with bone blade hands that dripped acid. He'd sliced their bodies in half, cutting easily through flesh and organs and bones. Dissatisfied with his speculation, Nick shook his head. This MO was clearly different. The cuts were cleaner here, artificial, not natural or supernatural. And the flesh and blood and organs were absent, leaving only the bones.

He snapped a few photos with his cell phone, then scanned the immediate area for clothing or personal effects that might have been dumped with the remains. Out of the corner of his eye, he noticed Wu approaching, and stood.

"What've we got so far?"

"Father and son geocaching," Wu said, glancing down at his notes. "Brian and Tyler Mathis. Tyler finds the bones of the vic. Not the sort of father-son outing dad had in mind."

"Geocaching," Nick said. "That some kind of sport?"

"Mash-up of scavenger hunt with hide and seek," Wu said. "You find the item with GPS coordinates posted online."

"Somebody put human remains in a geocache and posted the location online?" Nick said.

Hank swung forward on his crutches and took up a position facing Nick and Wu, his expression one of relief at having arrived at the crime scene without incident.

"Bad coincidence apparently," Wu said. "They found the real cache over there—the little red tin box on the tree stump."

Nick said, "Don't suppose it's been dusted for prints."

Wu nodded. "But we're not optimistic," he said. "Son had his hands all over it. Father let him have it to draw his attention away from the human skeleton. Speaking of which, Doc Candelas—"

Ah, Candelas, Nick thought.

"—was none too happy the kid had been poking the bones with a stick."

"Anything she can tell us?" Hank asked.

"Looks like one vic." Wu glanced at his notes again. "Adult, female, approximately five-foot-six, possibly under twenty-five years of age. Skull features consistent with Asian ancestry." He looked up at them. "Won't know if all the bones are present until they're sorted at the lab."

"No ID?"

"No personal effects at all," Wu said. "If we're lucky, we'll get a match off the dental records."

"Witnesses?"

"We've got uniforms canvassing the area, nearby homes, structures. Maybe somebody saw something. I'll let you know if anything turns up."

"COD?" Hank asked.

"No definitive cause of death indicated. But, judging by the lack of, well, the rest of her body, she was probably killed off-site and dumped here."

"What about these breaks?" Nick asked, indicating a femur that had been removed from the pile. "They're clean. Almost precise."

Wu nodded. "Doc ruled out animal attack. Something with a fine edge, lots of force. Could be man or machine. Wounds could be pre- or post-mortem."

"Meaning our vic could have been chopped up while she was still alive," Hank said somberly.

"No matter how bad you think your day is," Wu said, shaking his head as his voice trailed off.

"Thanks, Wu." Nick turned to Hank. "Let's talk to the father and son."

When Tyler saw the detectives approaching, he unconsciously took a half step behind his father. Nick noticed something yellow, green and rubbery propped on the boy's thumb like a mutated thimble. He smiled briefly to put the boy at ease.

"What have you got there?" he asked.

"It's an alien," Tyler said, waggling his thumb from side to side so the alien's tiny rubbery hands shook up and down. "I swapped it for my soldier."

"A toy from the geocache," Brian Mathis explained with a glance toward the red tin box on the rotted tree stump. "The reason why we came here. For the geocache."

"Don't imagine you anticipated a murd—an investigation," Hank said.

"Of course not," Brian said, wrapping an arm protectively over his son's shoulders. "Geocaching… it's like a scavenger hunt. Harmless. I never thought something like this would happen."

"How did you come to this exact location?" Nick asked.

"GPS coordinates."

"From which direction? The service road?" He pointed toward the line of first responder vehicles. "Or the park?"

"The park," Brian replied. "Thought the cache would be closer to the picnic areas."

"Mr. Mathis, is it okay if I ask your son a few questions?"

After a moment of hesitation, the father nodded.

"Okay, thank you." Nick turned his attention to Tyler, flashed another brief smile to put him at ease. "Tyler, how did you locate the bones?"

"We were looking for the geocache."

"Both of you?"

"Yes," Tyler said. "My dad's GPS got us close, but not to the exact spot, so we… poked around. I searched over there. My dad was over here."

"Nothing led you to the bones?"

"No," Tyler said. "Well, it looked like an animal might have dug up some dirt, near those bushes. I pushed the bushes back, saw the white—the bone, I mean. The first one, that big one"—he pointed to the isolated femur—"and I pulled it out. That's when I saw there was more of them."

Nick wondered how much poking around the kid had done after he discovered the cache of bones.

"Anything unusual about the arrangement?" he asked.

"What?"

"Was anything odd about the bones? A pattern maybe?"

The boy pressed the rubber alien to the underside of his chin for a couple moments then shook his head.

"Except…"

"Except what?" Hank asked, leaning forward as much as his crutches allowed.

"They were all jumbled in a pile," he said. "In pieces. Not like how you see in movies and stuff. Like the person fell asleep before they died."

Nick looked at the father and pointed at the geocache tin.

"Do you know who put the geocache here?"

"I don't recall," Brian Mathis said. "The person's username is on the site. She left it over a year ago. It's been found almost a dozen times."

"How do you know?" Hank asked.

"On the site," Brian said, with a shrug, as if the information was obvious. "And there's a logbook in there."

"In the box," Nick asked.

"Yeah," the boy said. "We added our names."

Nick reached into the pocket of his black leather jacket and pulled out a pair of latex gloves, slipped them on with practiced ease and picked up the geocache tin. If father and son had both handled the box while waiting for emergency personnel to arrive, they'd probably destroyed any useful prints, and—according to Wu—the box had already been dusted for prints, but until he talked to the crime scene techs personally, he'd rather not compound any errors.

Inside the box, a plastic toy soldier bearing several juvenile tooth-etched scars sat atop a thin notebook, with a preprinted list of geocache etiquette rules. The logbook had been signed by ten people, but most had signed a first name and an initial or a nickname, "Spelunkid" scrawled in red marker stood out. One person had stamped the book with a cartoon image of an owl. A few people had written dates next to their names or aliases, the most recent "find" occurring three months ago. Finally, two stubby pencils had been provided for those without the foresight to bring a red marker. Between the logbook and the website, they might ID several suspects.

Nick glanced toward the bones, then turned to Brian Mathis.

"Where exactly did you find this?"

Brian dropped to one knee and pointed to a sheltered spot between the rotted stump and the fallen tree trunk.

"Under there," he said. "Might have missed it, if not for the bright red color."

Nick looked at Hank and gave a brief shake of his head. If the geocache and the bones were meant to be found together as some sort of macabre scavenger hunt, why not put them in the same place. More likely, the killer had no idea the geocache existed.

Nick returned to the buried pile of anonymous bones.

Unless the canvass turned up a witness to the burial or the crime scene techs discovered something not readily apparent, their best lead remained the victim herself. If she knew her killer, her identity might lead them to his doorstep.

CHAPTER THREE

If Monroe hadn't returned to Shemanski Park Market after his morning grocery shopping run—to pick up some artisanal wine and cheeses for a planned romantic evening at home with Rosalee—he probably would have missed Decker.

Reusable grocery bags once again full, Monroe turned his attention away from the outdoor farm stands sheltered under white canopies and navigated his way through the milling crowd, retracing his steps to where he'd parked his Volkswagen Super Beetle. As he stepped around a mother with her young daughter looking at a plastic container of filet beans and a wicker basket overflowing with red bell peppers, Monroe spotted a familiar face in the crowd, heading in the opposite direction, and pulled up short.

"Decker?" he called. "Is that you?"

"Monroe?" the other man said. He stopped and shook Monroe's hand in a powerful two-handed grip. Physically imposing whether in full woge or not, Decker had two inches and forty pounds on Monroe. Wearing a black knit watch cap over a riot of curly brown hair, a distressed black leather jacket, ripped jeans and scuffed work boots, he seemed a bit out of his element among the aisles of organic produce. "How the holy hell are you, brother?"

The young mother gave them both a wary and disapproving glance as she quietly steered her daughter away from the red bell peppers to the next farmer's display. Monroe gave her a little friendly wave, hoping to convey a reassuring message: *Don't worry, ma'am. I'm harmless. Mostly.*

"Actually, I'm doing well, you know," Monroe said to Decker. "Things have been sane for me. Calm. Living the straight and narrow. No complaints."

Decker looked around and seemed to realize for the first time where he was.

"Oh, man, that's right. So it *is* true, what I heard. You're living in denial."

"I guess you could say that, in a manner of speaking," Monroe said, taking Decker's arm and leading him a little farther away from any potential eavesdroppers.

Decker had never embraced the concept of discretion. He'd been a fixture in Monroe's past, before he'd reformed, before he'd given up his savage lifestyle and become a Wieder Blutbad. And just as it wasn't safe for a reformed addict to hang out with those currently using, Monroe had had to separate himself from his more fearsome brethren, lest he backslide into the old ways.

"I'm convinced—denying some things opens you up to experiencing other things," Monroe explained. "For instance, a healthier lifestyle. Less rage, bloodshed and blackouts. You should try it."

"Ha!" Decker exclaimed boisterously. "Where's the fun in that, brother? I remember when you used to run. *We* used to run. Back when you hung out with—what's her name?—Angelina! That's it. And her brother, Hap. You see them much?"

"No. Not anymore. Not for a while," Monroe said, feeling a pang of guilt over Hap's death. "That didn't end well."

"No worries, brother," Decker said, clapping Monroe's shoulder. "Eyes forward, right? Full bore, no regrets."

"Hey, man, if that works for you," Monroe said. "No judgments here. Live and let run, I always say."

Decker took in his surroundings again. "It is peaceful."

"What brings you here?"

"To Portland?"

"Yes, okay, that too, but, well, here," Monroe said. "This market."

"Passing through," Decker said. "Rolling stone, you know? Figured I'd spend a week or two and move on."

"And this market?" Monroe pressed, sensing something his old friend wasn't telling him, at least not in so many words. Decker had always talked a lot while saying little, a stream of conscious rambling that Monroe had learned to tune out now and then.

"Meeting someone."

"Someone? Really? What kind of someone?"

Decker looked at him blankly for a moment, then chuckled.

"Just someone, okay. Casual. It's not a thing."

"Do you want it to be a thing?"

"I don't know, man," Decker said. "It's always a short shelf life for me. No time to commit."

"Right," Monroe said. "Mr. Rolling Stone."

A few moments passed, and a companionable silence stretched into awkwardness, reminding Monroe that he'd taken the road less traveled and that set him apart from old friends. Most of that had been by design, to avoid temptation and opportunities to backslide into the old ways. He had no regrets about the trade-off. Besides, he had new friends now—one of them a Grimm, of all things! And Rosalee. He led a calm yet interesting life, with enough romance to keep things spicy. The call of his old life, and the friends who filled those wild days, had become little more than an indistinct echo, words in a language that no longer made sense to him. As long as he kept to his regimen of self-discipline, he could keep his eyes forward.

He clapped Decker on the shoulder and said, "Good seeing you, man. Next time you're in town, give me a call."

As he turned away—wondering if he had meant either statement, or if his own words had been rote sentiments plucked from another time and dusted off for one last insincere farewell—Decker caught his arm.

Monroe glanced back, surprised.

"Are you for real?" Decker asked.

Briefly, Monroe wondered if his old friend had sensed the insincerity in his parting words and was calling him out. He almost had to shake off the impression to see the real issue. Monroe's lifestyle.

"Of course. Why do you ask?"

"So it's not a 'go along to get along' situation?"

"It's for me," Monroe said. "My choice."

"You gave up—meat? And running?" When Monroe nodded, Decker added, "Huh! This whole time, I had a different impression. Figured it was for show, you know, an act to fool the natives or something. Like a wolf in sheep's clothing."

"Well, I'm still a—" Monroe scanned the area to make sure they were as alone as one could be in an outdoor farmer's market, then spoke in a softer voice "—Blutbad. But I've cast aside the—let's say—more extreme facets of our nature."

"Wow," Decker said, walking a few paces while shaking his head. He dropped down on a bench as if the thought of giving up the wild lifestyle was too difficult to comprehend while standing. "How? How do you change? How do you stay changed? I'd crawl out of my skin."

Monroe sat down on the bench, setting his bags down between his feet.

"Do you—Decker, are you thinking about reforming?"

"Don't see how that's possible, brother."

"It's possible," Monroe said. "I'm proof of that, right? But you can't do this for someone else." Monroe nodded in the general direction of the market stalls to indicate the "someone" with "thing" potential that Decker planned to meet here. "You have to want this for yourself."

"Okay. What if I did?" Decker said. "Then what?"

"Listen, I only know what works for me," Monroe said.

He ran his thumb and index finger down the sides of his mustache and light beard, considering whether or not he should jeopardize his own reformed status to help a friend. Spending extended time with an unreformed Blutbad presented inherent risks. His last mistake may have cost Hap his life. But Monroe had to believe in the strength of his own convictions, that he wouldn't make the same mistake twice.

"If you want to try, Decker, I'll help. Anything you need. I'll be your support system."

"You mean, like an AA sponsor or something?"

"Okay, let's go with that."

"So, if I do this, what's the first step?"

"Cold turkey," Monroe said.

"Okay, I can do turkey," Decker said, grinning. "Hot or cold."

"No meat," Monroe said.

"Brother, meat is my only food group," Decker said. "No meat is basically a hunger strike for me."

"You'll get used to it," Monroe said, then frowned.

"Someday." No sense making the transition seem easier than it was. "I've had lots of luck with veggie steaks."

"Oh, man, that ain't natural. I'm getting ill at the thought."

"It takes a lot of self-discipline."

"Not to hurl?" Decker said. "I can believe it, brother."

"Pilates works for me," Monroe said. "Every morning. Helps focus the mind. It's not easy, but it's worth it. You'll thank me. Well, not right away. First, there'll be cursing. Yeah, lots of swearing. And breakage. You'll definitely want to break things for a while. But... someday."

"I have doubts about that, brother," Decker said. "Serious doubts. And if you say the word 'tofu,' I may have to kill you." He stood and offered his hand again. "But, I'm in."

Monroe stood to shake his hand, nodding and smiling encouragingly.

"What say we start tomorrow?" Decker said.

"Sounds good," Monroe said.

But his smile faltered a moment later. Monroe wanted to help his old friend join the admittedly meager ranks of the Wieder Blutbad. He'd meant what he said: he'd help Decker, as much as possible. And yet, he had his doubts. Self-restraint was as unfamiliar a concept as discretion for the Decker he remembered. How strong was the man's motivation to change his behavior and entire lifestyle? For someone accustomed to indulging every bloody whim, adapting to a reformed life would be pure hell.

And Monroe had offered to lead the way.

CHAPTER FOUR

Long before her world had been turned upside down by her newfound knowledge of Wesen and the Grimms who hunted them—one of the latter, smaller group included her boyfriend, Nick Burkhardt—Juliette Silverton found comfort in the familiar setting of the Roseway Veterinary Hospital where she spent her days.

Sipping coffee and chatting with Zoe and Roger in the reception area, before office hours officially started, helped ease her into the workday. Checking on any animal patients who'd needed to spend the night in one of the many crates in back provided comfort to the pets while they were separated from their homes. Meeting with loving pet owners and treating their four-legged friends preemptively was the most rewarding part of her day. Even treating those with maladies or accident victims gave her a sense of satisfaction, knowing she made a difference by helping pets and their owners get back to the stress-free enjoyment of each other's company. But some maladies had no prescribed treatment. Sometimes the conversation was about ending the life to end the pain. Some days were hell.

Juliette sat forward in her office chair and closed the folder that contained the printout of Roxy Bremmer's test results. When the Bremmers brought in their six-year-old yellow lab, she'd exhibited discouraging symptoms: vomiting, loss of appetite and lethargy. Now Juliette's fears had been confirmed. The blood work indicated Roxy was azotemic, with moderately elevated BUN and creatinine values, consistent with renal failure due to pyelonephritis—kidney infection—or a toxin. Consequently, she had to break the worst possible news to the family.

She sighed and pressed her fingertips to her forehead.

After a few moments to compose herself, she stood up and attempted to brush the creases out of her white lab coat. She stared down for a moment at the folder with the damning test results, then snatched it off the desk and strode from her office, down the short hallway to the examination room where the Bremmers awaited her.

When she opened the door, they stood on either side of the stainless steel examination table, Balding Barry on the left, pale Melinda on the right, both of them with a hand on Roxy, who looked miserable. She managed a solitary tail thump in greeting—and another when Juliette patted her head—but the effort seemed to drain her. Juliette had expected to see Logan, their teenage son. A small relief. Kids and teens took this kind of news the hardest. Or maybe they were less conflicted about expressing their emotions in public over the death of a pet. Roxy had been a companion for Logan for a third of the boy's life. At least he'd be spared this one detail of the painful ordeal.

Before she opened her mouth to deliver the news, Juliette felt her professional mask slip into place. A clinical detachment necessary when a doctor must tell a patient—or, in this case, a patient's owners—that she was out of answers.

"Melinda, Barry... I'm sorry," she began.

Melinda Bremmer clapped a hand over her mouth to stifle a cry of dismay.

So much for the professional mask, Juliette thought. *Unlike my emotions, I can't disguise the sting of my words.*

"What—what is it?" Barry asked, after clearing his throat.

"The test results," Juliette said. "I'm afraid they indicate kidney failure."

"But—how?" Melinda asked. "What does that mean?"

"The likely cause is a kidney infection," Juliette informed them. "Or a toxin—"

"Toxin?" Barry said, frowning. "Poison? Somebody poisoned our dog?"

"No," Juliette said. "I'm not saying that. It could have been anything. For example, ethylene glycol—antifreeze— if ingested. It's sweet and it only takes a small amount."

"Oh..." Barry turned away from them, gripping his jaw in his free hand.

Melinda stared at him, confused, glanced at Juliette to see if she understood, and then returned her attention to her husband.

"Barry...? What is it?"

"Ah, Christ," Barry said. "Logan."

"What about Logan?"

"That damned clunker of his," Barry said. "He's been fixing it up, tinkering..."

"I—yes, but how?"

"When it started raining the other day, he drove it into the garage," Barry said. "And... I'm not positive, but I think the radiator was leaking."

"But the dog—how—?"

"When I went out to check on him—" Barry's voice grew tight with suppressed emotion "—Roxy was in the garage with him."

"So Logan… he's—it's his…" Melinda pressed her hand to her mouth again, fingers clamped over her trembling lips. "Oh, no. Oh, God, we can't tell him. If Roxy—this will crush him."

Juliette pursed her lips and blew out a breath she'd been holding. She hadn't thought the day could possibly get worse. She'd been wrong. If—realistically, *when*—the dog passed, their son would blame himself. He would always blame himself.

If only they'd brought the dog in within eight hours of ingestion, Juliette could have treated the antifreeze toxicity with Fomepizole or 4-MP. Too late for that now that kidney failure had set in…

Melinda directed her tear-filled eyes to Juliette.

"How can we fix this, Dr. Silverton? What can we do?"

"If Roxy drank antifreeze," Juliette began, then started over again. No easy way to say what she had to tell them. "With kidney failure, I'm afraid the prognosis is poor. Very poor."

"What do you recommend?" Barry asked.

"Normally, for cases like this, I would recommend… euthanasia."

"Oh, my God!" Melinda cried. "Logan will…"

"There's nothing else?" Barry asked. "No treatment…? Nothing?"

Juliette took a deep breath. *Something. Maybe.*

"I can't guarantee… And I don't want to give you false hope."

"There's a 'but' in there somewhere, Doctor," Barry said, quirking a hopeful smile. "Tell us. Please. We'll take any chance. Whatever the odds."

"We can try supportive treatment for a day or so," Juliette offered. "See if her condition improves. Treat it aggressively with IV fluids, anti-nausea meds, and—"

"Do it," Barry said. "Whatever it takes. Roxy—she's a part of our family."

"Okay. I'll need you to sign a few papers."

"Anything."

Juliette mentally ticked off the indicated IV protocol: Lactated Ringer's Solution; metoclopramide, H2 blocker for nausea; antibiotics to treat the infection. Still, it was a longshot and they needed to know that.

"You should prepare yourselves, in case—"

"We'll cross that bridge if we come to it," Barry said, clinging to a buoyant optimism that the treatment would work. He'd circled the table and wrapped an arm around his wife's shoulders. "We'll get through this, Lin."

His wife nodded silently and wiped away a tear, unable to find enough hope to give it voice. Or perhaps unwilling to disturb its fragility.

After the Bremmers had gone and Juliette had started Roxy on the supportive treatment, she returned to her office and collapsed in her chair, exhausted.

Poor Roxy, she thought. *Poked her snout into something sweet, unaware of the mortal danger it represented. Even now, with her life hanging in the balance, she's too confused and miserable to understand the cause of her pain.*

Juliette worried that, despite her cautions, she'd given the Bremmers unrealistic expectations. When they returned tomorrow, the news would be bad, if not worse, because they had allowed themselves to believe Roxy would get better.

And yet, who was Juliette to deny them their hope?

Not too long ago, she had all but given up hope that she would find her way back to Nick. She caught herself rubbing her hand where Majique—Adalind Schade's cat—had scratched her. That memory was always a jolt to her consciousness. She'd fallen into a coma and had awakened with all her memories of Nick and their life together excised. For a long time, she'd tried in vain to remember him. Eventually, the memories had returned, but in an incomprehensible flood, as if a dam had burst in her subconscious. And for a while, that had been almost as bad as having no recollection of their time together.

She'd fought her way out of the darkness, reclaiming the memories one by one, until she felt whole again. Then Nick had finally told her he was a Grimm and what that entailed. No sooner had that revelation come, than Nick's friends and acquaintances revealed their true nature to her as Wesen. Suddenly her reclaimed world included Blutbaden, Fuchsbaus and Eisbibers and many more Wesen she had yet to see.

For a while, every time she looked at a stranger, or even people she had known for years, she wondered, "Is she Wesen? What about him?" She was afraid she'd drive Nick crazy with all the questions. For now, her questions represented a light that kept the overwhelming darkness at bay, stopped the strangeness from closing in on all sides of her. The world she'd known her whole life had basically woged in front of her. She wouldn't tell Nick, but that scared her and thrilled her and made her want to call a time out so she could take a deep breath, absorb it all and exhale.

I need a big red "Pause" button.

"No," she said softly, chiding herself. "That's not what I want."

Hadn't her life already been paused long enough? Sure the changes were scary and challenging, but it felt wonderful to have her life back, memories intact, and to understand why Nick had kept certain things from her.

The first time Nick tried to tell her what he was, she

thought he'd gone crazy, suffered some sort of delusion or psychotic break. But no more. No more doubting the truth of Nick's words. The facts were undeniable. Part of her relief came from knowing they could finally move forward again emotionally, after having their relationship stall and subsequently derail.

And yet, she occasionally worried that something could happen to sabotage their progress. Not another cat-scratch-borne illness, but something else unexpected from Nick's dangerous world. At those times, her recovered memories of her life with Nick seemed like a jigsaw puzzle suspended in the air by a slender thread, swaying precariously, in danger of falling with the next gust of wind into hundreds of jumbled and lost pieces.

CHAPTER FIVE

After the bones had been collected from the Claremont Park crime scene, Nick and Hank headed back to the precinct to await test results on the bones. On the car ride back, Hank asked Nick for his preliminary impressions.

"Strange one," Nick said. "Dismembered body without a body."

"Cold case?" Hank wondered.

"Maybe," Nick conceded. "Need to wait on the ME's report."

"Bones chopped up like that," Hank said. "Think this could be Wesen?"

"Wesen with an axe," Nick said. "Can't rule out a human monster."

"Yet," Hank said and smiled.

The ME would need time to determine cause of death and estimate how long the bones had been buried. If dental records gave them an ID for the victim, they could see where that trail led them. So far the canvass had provided no leads. No footprints or tire tracks to cast. If the killer had been accommodating enough to leave such evidence behind, the recent rain had washed it away. And the only fingerprints lifted from the geocache tin matched those of Brian and Tyler Mathis.

Back at his desk, while hoping for a more substantial lead, Nick copied the names and aliases from the geocaching logbook onto a legal pad and split the list with Hank.

With a little online digging, they tracked down some of the geocachers, along with the woman who had originally placed the cache eighteen months ago for others to find. The most recent "find" listed on the geocache page was three months old. To the surprise of neither detective, not one of the scavenger hunters they contacted had noticed a pile of bones at the site.

Nick suspected the bones had been left between the last find and the Mathis' visit to the site. Nevertheless, they started to check alibis—enough to nail down addresses and proximity to the crime scene—and faced the prospect of needing a warrant to get the IDs of the remaining geocachers. If a fellow hunter had left the bones at the site, Nick doubted he or she would have recorded the visit in the handy little logbook.

With nothing solid to go on, Nick found his mind switching gears to their other big case. They had a Cracher-Mortel in a top hat, running around Portland creating zombies for some unknown reason. Another unresolved case, and that one definitely Wesen. As a homicide detective and a Grimm, Nick had one foot in each world, and at times he felt himself pulled in conflicting directions. At the moment, however, he had nothing pulling him at all.

Frustrated, he tapped a ballpoint pen on the legal pad. He'd reached the point where he'd convinced himself to march down to the Medical Examiner's Office and camp out there until Doctor Harper gave him some answers, when the telephone rang.

Nick snatched the receiver off the cradle. Wu.

"You want to get down here."

"Find something?"

"Quarter-mile from the site," Wu said. "Found a couple bones near a dilapidated wooden shack. McCormack spotted a squatter. Large guy. Called him Bigfoot."

"You think he's dangerous?"

"Getting a flesh-mask-with-chainsaw vibe out here."

"On our way," Nick said, grabbing his jacket and signaling Hank. Hank scrambled for his crutches and swung after Nick.

"Suspect?" Hank asked as he drew up alongside his partner.

"Might be Wesen after all."

The two-story house set back in the woods had seen better days but had probably never been up to code in any sense of the word. Devoid of color, the weather-beaten planks shaping the unimaginatively rectangular dwelling clung together with the bare minimum of structural integrity, dependent upon a dwindling number of crumbling, rusted nails. The sagging roof maintained barely enough incline to shed rainwater. Two round columns supported a first-floor roof extension over a porch large enough to accommodate two rocking chairs or a porch swing, but the owner had left that space unfurnished. Along the exterior walls, irregular sections of tar paper and plywood patched long cracks and gaps with no eye for aesthetics or symmetry. More scraps of plywood obscured the small windows on the first floor, while dark cloth blocked the view through two visible second-story windows.

Fortunately, the terrain surrounding the house provided a level surface for Hank to navigate on crutches. Sergeant Wu and two other uniforms—McCormack and Harris—

had approached the house from opposite directions to cover front and back doors. Wu monitored the front approach; the patrol officers waited around back. Now and then, the suspect could be seen striding through the house, his bulk shifting past one crack in the walls after another. And even if they hadn't caught regular glimpses of him, the creak and groan of floorboards protesting under his weight were a dead giveaway that the structure was occupied.

Nick moved into position beside Sergeant Wu.

"We got one suspect," Wu said. "Super-sized."

"Name?"

"No address on this charming little cottage," Wu said. "Legally, this residence doesn't exist. Mountain man DIY special."

"Where are the bones?"

Wu nodded toward a slight depression ten feet away, a repository for what looked like a couple broken rib bones and, possibly, a human femur.

"Only those?"

"That's not enough?" Wu asked.

"Maybe," Nick said, but he had his doubts. He walked over and peered more closely at the bones. The breaks on the ribs were jagged, as if snapped in half, not cleanly cut like those of the first victim. The presence of a human skull would have removed some doubt about the find.

"Okay," Nick said. "Radio your guys. Hank and I are going in."

As Wu pressed the transmit button on his shoulder microphone to advise the uniforms, Nick strode toward the small porch, the heel of his palm resting on the butt of his Glock 17. Hank stayed back one pace, giving himself room to maneuver on his crutches. When Nick glanced over his shoulder, Wu moved away from the tree line, hand close to his holstered firearm as well.

The floorboards of the covered porch groaned in protest, sagging beneath Nick's weight as he crossed to the front door. Before knocking, he stood to the side and waited for Hank to clear the line of fire. Nick's imagination worked overtime. Too easy to picture the behemoth sitting in the house, facing the rickety door with a loaded shotgun across his knees, waiting for the first knock to blast them where they stood.

Nick exchanged a look with Hank, who nodded, hand poised over his own gun as he rested on the crutches. Taking a deep breath, Nick rapped his knuckles on the door.

"Go away!" a voice boomed inside, unnervingly close to the door.

Had he been standing there the whole time Nick approached?

"Detective Burkhardt, Portland Police," Nick said. "We need to ask you a few questions."

"Don't talk to cops," the deep voice said. "Don't talk to anyone."

"This will only take a few minutes of your time."

Silence.

"Or I could take you down to the station for questioning."

Rusty hinges squealed in protest as the suspect yanked the door open.

The man stood a foot taller than Nick. Unruly hair and a thick beard spilled over a faded red flannel shirt and suspenders holding up tattered and grease-stained jeans. Technically, he was unarmed but that hardly seemed to matter. The man looked as if he could bench-press compact cars without needing a spotter.

And he was fast.

"Go away!" he roared, and charged Nick, head lowered, but not before Nick saw him woge into the bullish form of a Mordstier, complete with horns.

Nick's hands rose to catch the lowered horns before they could gore him, but the inertia of the charging Wesen drove him back into one of the porch's support posts. The wood split in half against Nick's back and head, momentarily stunning him.

The roof of the porch sagged, its creaking punctuated by popping sounds as nails broke loose.

His bell rung, Nick dropped to hands and knees and tried to shake it off.

Hank sprang forward, raised the tip of one crutch and attempted to shove the Mordstier back, but the Wesen caught the crutch and swung it, along with Hank, around, slamming the injured detective into the wall.

As the Mordstier drew back a booted foot to strike Nick in the ribs, Wu shouted, "Stop!" He had his X26 Taser trained on the suspect.

Grunting, the Mordstier ignored Wu's command and swung his foot forward.

Nick heard the crackling discharge of the Taser.

Roaring, the bull Wesen staggered back into the doorjamb but, incredibly, he fought off the effects of the paralyzing 50,000-volt charge and ripped the needle-tipped darts from his chest.

Instead, Wu was the one who looked stunned.

But Nick's head had cleared. He rose from his knees and drove the Wesen against the wall, their combined weight cracking several planks along the front of the house. The Mordstier gripped the front of Nick's jacket, lifted him up, spun him around and slammed him against the wall. Part of the wall caved in, catching Nick's elbow.

He saw the flash of recognition—but not fear—in the Wesen's eyes as he realized Nick was a Grimm. Some species of Wesen feared Grimms more than anything, viewing them as monsters or bogeymen. Others were simply wary of them, aware of the threat they represented. But some Wesen—usually the strongest among them—had little fear and maybe only grudging respect. The Mordstier, clearly, belonged to the last faction. He tugged Nick free and attempted to slam him into the cracked wall again.

But McCormack and Harris had abandoned their posts at the rear door. They rushed the porch on either side of the suspect, extendable batons raised and—in near-perfect choreography—clubbed the Mordstier across the shoulders.

Releasing Nick, the Wesen yanked McCormack's baton out of his hand and swept the back of his legs with it, dropping him in an instant. With a backhanded whipping motion, he caught Harris across the cheek with the baton, snapping his head sideways. He raised a booted foot and kicked Harris in the chest with enough force to hurl him through the remaining porch support post.

Harris fell off the porch, unconscious, his momentum sweeping one of Hank's crutches out from under him, causing the detective to fall awkwardly.

Having exchanged the Taser for his Glock 17, Wu took aim and shouted, "Drop the weapon! Now!"

Boards creaked and snapped and the porch roof ripped free and crashed between Nick and the Mordstier on the near side, Wu on the far side.

Nick covered his head to avoid the bulk of the debris, while the Wesen used the diversion to duck inside his crumbling house.

Rising in pursuit, Nick glanced back at Wu.

"Call for backup!" he called. "And somebody cover the back door."

CHAPTER SIX

Nick entered the dilapidated house alone, his Glock 17 held in a Weaver stance as he scanned the dark, musty interior. Narrow shafts of light hosting a multitude of dust motes sliced through the gaps in the walls and boarded-up windows, revealing a warped interior and a sparse collection of tattered and torn furniture, no doubt salvaged on curbside bulk trash pickup days. Though Nick would have preferred a good old-fashioned flashlight directed along the barrel of his handgun, he'd found that his other senses had improved dramatically after he'd suffered temporary blindness from a Jinnamuru Xunte attack. Surely a benefit of his Grimm heritage—and not the only one. His strength, stamina, coordination and injury-recovery time had also improved.

Through an archway straight ahead, he saw a small kitchen. Slightly to his right, against the far wall, a staircase provided access to the second floor. And to his extreme right, an archway led into a third room on the ground floor. The Mordstier could have fled out the back door, but if the hinges were a match for the front door, Nick thought he would have heard them squeal in protest.

For the same reason, Nick believed the Mordstier hadn't ascended the stairs. That left one option.

Turning right, gun level at shoulder height, Nick eased across the creaking floor toward the archway that led into the third room. He approached the opening from the side, then pivoted into the room, sweeping left to right with the barrel of his Glock. First he noticed a single row of more than two-dozen sets of mounted antlers spaced along three walls in the room, like a wallpaper border made out of bone. Not that the walls had been papered, painted or even stained. A moldy wingback chair, two ladderback chairs and a wooden bench were arranged to face a battery-powered radio sitting on a small rectangular table centered along the far wall. A ratty, stain-spotted throw rug filled the open space in the middle of the room.

No sign of the Mordstier.

Nick retreated, intending to take the stairs to the second floor. If the Wesen had fled through the back door, Hank, Wu or McCormack would have spotted him and sounded an alarm—or he was long gone.

Nick's gut—aided or not by his Grimm abilities—told him the suspect hadn't fled his home. The Wesen's presence felt as palpable to him as the mildew and decay. He couldn't hide forever in a confined space, nor was he likely to—

Something creaked. Wood thumped against wood— behind him.

Nick spun around to face—the bare wall separating the rooms.

"What the—?"

In the blink of an eye, the wall erupted toward Nick.

Instinctively, he shielded his eyes, but couldn't ignore the rush of movement behind the split planks tumbling all around him. A massive shape, almost doubled over, twin horns lowered to gore him.

Sidestepping, Nick escaped the worst of the impact, but caught what felt like a knee or an elbow to the gut and tumbled over backwards, losing his gun in the process. He sprang to his feet, scanning for the gun while keeping the bulk of the Wesen before him. What he hadn't noticed during the bull rush attack through the wall, was the long-handled axe in the Mordstier's hands.

Nick dropped to a crouch as the blade of the axe whistled overhead.

The Mordstier stomped forward to press his attack.

But Nick was ready for the reverse swing, and caught the wooden handle in both hands. He lashed out with a side kick to the Wesen's abdomen, eliciting a grunt of pain.

The Wesen yanked the axe back in the other direction, attempting to wrest it from Nick's grip, but Nick countered with his right foot, striking the inside of Mordstier's left knee.

Wu charged into the dark room and attempted a low diving tackle, his shoulder plowing into the back of the suspect's right knee.

Finally, the Wesen lost his balance.

Driving forward with the axe handle still clutched in both hands, Nick toppled the behemoth, who crashed to the floor with wood-splitting impact. But not before the Wesen caught Nick in the midsection with a boot and hurled him toward the near wall.

Though Nick lost his grip on the axe, he spun in mid-air to avoid a nasty collision, hitting the wall with the soles of both feet to kill his momentum, then sprung forward with a quick double-hop to land upright. While flipping end over end, he'd spotted his dislodged Glock in the corner, near the door.

He scrambled for the gun while, in the periphery of his vision, the Wesen sat up, shaking off the cobwebs, the axe beside his left hand. Wu, fighting some cobwebs of his own, climbed to hands and knees and tried to bring his gun to bear, but caught a vicious elbow to the ribs and fell on his side.

With a grunt, the Mordstier placed his palms on the floor, wrapping his left hand around the axe handle. He started to push himself up, but only had time to brace himself before Nick pressed the muzzle of the Glock to the back of his head, directly above the spine.

"Flinch—and I ventilate your skull."

"I know what you are."

"Then you know I'm not bluffing."

The Wesen grunted. But dropped his woge.

The entire battle inside the house had taken less than a minute.

"Slowly, shove the axe away," Nick said. "Try to pick it up and—"

"You ventilate my skull."

"Good. We have an understanding."

The Mordstier slid the axe away from his body and released it. With a quick swipe of his foot, Nick kicked it to the base of the stairs.

"Wu," Nick said. "You okay?"

Wu nodded as he climbed to his feet, but winced as he pressed a hand to his sore ribs.

"Nothing broken," he said. "If I'm lucky."

"I'll cover him," Nick said. "You cuff him."

Reluctantly, Wu holstered his sidearm. He popped open a flap on his belt and tugged out his handcuffs.

Nick backed away while keeping his gun trained on the suspect's head, positioning himself with a clear line of fire if the Mordstier tried anything.

"What's your name?"

"None of your damned—!"

"Name!" Nick barked, stepping forward menacingly. "Shame I had to shoot your kneecap while you resisted arrest."

"Guerra," the Wesen rasped, as if giving up the information pained him. "Carlos Guerra."

"Rise, Carlos," Nick said. "Slowly."

Guerra climbed to his feet, stumbling a bit as one boot split a cracked floorboard in half.

Wu jumped back, reaching for his gun again.

"Relax!" Guerra said. "Rotten floor's falling apart."

"Some place you got here," Wu said. "Supermarket Dumpster all out of cardboard boxes?"

"I don't bother nobody," Guerra said. "You got no business here."

"Yeah, well, this could have gone a whole lot easier," Nick said, unwavering in his stance. The situation was definitely not contained. "Hands behind your neck."

As soon as Guerra complied, Wu slapped a cuff over one wrist, then cuffed the other one.

Hank navigated his way through the front door on his crutches, mindful of the debris from the collapsed porch roof.

"Everything under control?" he asked.

Wu called McCormack in with his shoulder mic. Harris was still out of commission, probably concussed.

"Check upstairs," Nick told the uniform.

"I live alone," Guerra said.

"Don't hold it against us," Wu said, "if we don't take your word for it."

Hank crossed the room, giving the damaged floor a wide berth, and peered through the shattered wall.

"Trapdoor," he said, looking back at Nick.

"Of course," Nick said. "Hidden under the damn throw rug."

McCormack came through the kitchen, eyes wide as he looked around.

"Raw meat and blood on the table out there."

"I hunt," Guerra said. "To eat."

McCormack pulled out his automatic and ascended the stairs.

"Open up here," he called. "Like a loft."

A short while later, he called down, "Clear."

Wu checked the antler room and, through the damaged wall, Nick saw him descend a ladder into the underground room where Guerra had hidden. McCormack came down the stairs. A moment later, Wu joined them.

"Root cellar down there," he said. "Salted meats, mason jars, pelts and bones. Plus a couple shotguns, hunting knives and lots of bloodstains."

"Sorry," Guerra grumbled. "No maid service this week."

"Real talkative now," Nick commented to Hank. Gun still trained on Guerra's back, Nick gave him a motivational shove toward the door. "Let's go."

An hour later, back at the precinct, Guerra sat slumped in a chair in the interview room, his handcuffs looped around a metal bar bolted to the table, and denied any involvement in a murder.

"You've never been to Claremont Park?" Hank demanded.

"Of course, I have," Guerra said. "Doesn't mean I murdered anyone."

"We found bones outside your… dwelling," Nick said. "Raw meat, bones and blood in your house."

"Animal meat, animal bones, animal blood," he said. "Deer, rabbit, squirrel. You arresting me for hunting without a license?"

"No," Nick said. "Assault with a deadly weapon, attempted murder, resisting arrest and a half-dozen other charges, maybe, but not hunting without a license. We'll give you a pass on that one."

"I told you to leave me alone," Guerra grumbled. "You were trespassing."

"You don't own that land," Hank pointed out. "Building a house—I'm using that term generously—on land you don't own is a problem."

"I told you to leave me alone."

"Right now, guys in the lab are testing the blade on your axe to see if it matches the cuts on the human remains we found in Claremont Park," Nick said. "You want to get ahead of this? We tell the DA you cooperated, maybe you get life instead of the death penalty."

"You got nothing."

"You better hope so," Hank said, shaking his head in disgust.

The detectives rose to leave the interview room. As Nick was about to close the door behind him, Guerra called out.

"On second thought," Guerra said. "I got something to say."

"Yeah?" Nick asked, waiting for it.

"I want a lawyer."

Nick rapped on Captain Sean Renard's open door.

Renard looked up from a file he'd been reading. "Come in."

Nick entered, followed by Hank, slowed by his crutches.

"Anything?" Renard asked.

Nick had already informed his boss that Guerra was a Wesen and violent. Communication between the two had become simpler after they had disclosed some of their mutual secrets. Renard was a half-Hexenbiest—technically, Zauberbiest—bastard, related by blood to one of the seven Royal Houses, but not allied with his family.

For his part, Renard knew Nick was a Grimm.

The two had an uneasy truce, but not complete trust. Nick couldn't be sure of Renard's ultimate loyalties. But he had returned to Nick one of the six-hundred-year-old keys that, together with six others, would construct a map leading to something so powerful that many had died to protect its secret. Legends had arisen about the exact nature of that secret, but nobody knew for certain. The Royal Families currently had four of the keys and were desperate to get their hands on the others. With that one act—returning the key to Nick, rather than delivering it to his family—Renard had forged the tentative alliance with Nick.

"Well, he has rage issues," Nick began. "And we have more than enough to charge him."

"But?"

Hank sighed. "But not for the chopped-bones murder."

"Have the lab results come in?"

"No," Nick admitted. Though they had a powerful Wesen in custody with rage issues and a lethal axe swing, something seemed off. Hank sensed it too. If Guerra was guilty of the murder, shouldn't he look at least somewhat worried about the charge? Instead, the guy craved isolation more than anything. He lived in a rundown shack without heat or running water. Out back, they'd found a crumbling well and a rust-mottled Ford F-1 pickup truck circa 1951, complete with bald tires and a muffler dangling by a coat hanger. Considering his prodigious size and dubious mode of transportation, Guerra would be anything but inconspicuous. "Sometimes you get a sense about these things."

"All the same," Renard said. "Let's wait for the lab results before we assume he's not our guy."

"Right," Hank said.

"Keep me posted."

* * *

As Nick and Hank returned to their desks, Wu intercepted them.

"Talked to the ME," he said. "Guerra's axe is not the murder weapon—assuming the bone-chopping was the COD. Something about the angle of the cuts not matching the angle of the axe blade. They're testing the other weapons confiscated from the root cellar. So far, no matches." Wu looked down at his notebook. "None of the blood or bone evidence collected is human."

"What about the bones outside the shack?"

"Most likely deer," Wu said.

"Looks like Guerra's not our guy," Hank said.

His desk phone started ringing.

"Here's where it gets weird," Wu continued. "Harper examined the original set of human bones and, based on discoloration, softening, brittleness and smell, she believes they were boiled."

"Boiled?" Hank asked, incredulous. He sat on the edge of his desk, propped his crutches against it and reached for the telephone receiver with his free hand. "Like—in a pot?"

Wu nodded. "Or a witch's cauldron."

Hank answered the phone, his voice hushed.

"Cooked," Nick wondered. A disturbed human might be responsible, but in Nick's mind, the scales had started to tip toward a Wesen perpetrator.

Hank's posture stiffened, his hand gripping the telephone receiver a little tighter. "Yes. Thanks. We'll be right there." He hung up, looked from Wu to Nick and said, "Claremont Park canvass turned up a second shallow grave," he told them. "With another complete set of chopped up human bones."

CHAPTER SEVEN

The second crime scene, in the opposite direction from Guerra's shack, resembled the first in most details: a chopped-up skeleton buried in a single mound. Except this time, Yolanda Candelas, the forensic anthropologist who'd consulted on the first scene, determined that the victim was male, middle-aged, Caucasian or possibly Hispanic.

Peralta, a junior patrol officer assigned to the canvass detail, had spotted a partially exposed rib cage—at least according to his original statement. After Nick had noticed dirt stains on the knees of the officer's uniform, the man admitted that his left foot had made the discovery. He first *saw* the bones after tripping over them.

Also, as with the first site, the detectives had little to go on.

By mutual agreement, Hank and Nick left the crime scene to the techs who specialized in collecting what little evidence they could find there. Hank headed home. But Nick had another stop to make.

When Nick arrived at Monroe's house—its distinctive front door featured a stained-glass coat of arms with an upright red wolf—he found the Blutbad peering at his work table as if to examine his handiwork. On a square of green felt, he'd disassembled an antique gold pocket watch, its tiny wheels and springs and screws laid out like an art project. A careful arrangement of watchmaker's tools bracketed the antique watch parts, including a head-worn magnifier, a series of precision screwdrivers, tweezers and a few tools Nick couldn't identify.

"Oh, hey, Nick," Monroe said, distracted.

"One of yours?" Nick asked.

"What? No. Bud dropped this off for me to repair. 1887 Elgin hunter case pocket watch, fourteen-karat gold. Family heirloom. Finally decided to have it fixed." He looked up, eyes widening. "You're having dinner with Juliette tonight, right? Because Rosalee and I are—unless something happened with your—?"

"No change of plans," Nick said. "Shower. Fresh set of clothes."

"Good," Monroe said. "So things are still on the upswing? No complications?"

"We're taking it one step at a time," Nick said. "No new complications." Changing the topic, he said, "I wanted to get your opinion on something."

"By 'something,' I'm guessing not related to watch repair?"

"Not remotely."

With the death of Nick's Aunt Marie, he'd been thrown into the deep end of the Grimm pool. She'd left behind her trailer filled with an arsenal of medieval weapons, potions and remedies, and books of Grimm lore—a lot of material to review, but not all the answers Nick needed could be found in the trailer. Monroe had proven a valuable resource on various Grimm-related subjects and often helped Nick solve cases involving Wesen.

Monroe had once referred to himself grudgingly as Nick's "personal Grimmopedia." While Nick couldn't find fault with that assessment, he couldn't justify bypassing a valuable resource when lives were at stake. At the same time, he was confident his friendship with Monroe had progressed to the point where the Blutbad no longer felt as if Nick took him for granted. For evidence of that change, Nick needed to look no further than Monroe's invitation to Nick to stay at his house after Juliette's Nick-specific memory loss made living together awkward and uncomfortable.

Nick wanted to give her time and, more importantly, space to remember him, and he couldn't do that living under the same roof. They were through the worst of it now. Yet even though Juliette had her memories back and had started to understand the Grimm and Wesen side of Nick's life, he was still crashing at Monroe's. But not, he hoped, for too much longer.

"Didn't think so."

Nick described the two sets of bones the police had recovered along with Guerra, the Mordstier, who denied any involvement in the murder and whose viability as a suspect had diminished since his arrest.

"Lone bull, huh?" Monroe mused. "Odd behavior for a Mordstier. Those guys usually travel in packs."

"He could be our guy," Nick said. "Rage issues. Root cellar stocked with nasty gear. But, so far, no match for the murder weapon."

"Maybe he tossed it off a bridge."

"Maybe."

"Sorry I can't help, man."

"I left out one thing about the bones," Nick said. "ME believes they were boiled."

Monroe's eyebrows rose. He exhaled and sat down at his work table chair.

"Chopped and cooked. That's what you think?" he asked.

"Why else boil the bones?"

"Right," Monroe said, nodding. "I'm sure you know—of course you know, you're a Grimm—that some Wesen have been known to partake in, let's say, non-FDA approved meats. There's the Schakal, of course."

"The baby eaters."

Monroe nodded. "You got your Wendigos, Mauvais Dentes, Coyotl—they strip their victims down to the bone. Geiers harvest human blood and organs. A Rissfleich tends to go for the abdomen. Then there's the Lowen and Lausenchlangen and—"

Nick interrupted Monroe's disturbing litany with a question.

"Any with this particular MO?"

"Dude, they don't follow rule books," Monroe said. "Let me just say, it's usually an impulse. A nasty impulse. But what you've got here is way beyond nasty, man. That's some seriously sick premeditation."

After a shower and change of clothes, Nick drove to Juliette's house for a home-cooked meal. Just as well, since the topics of their conversations lately might raise more than a few eyebrows at the local restaurants. Nick tried to leave his work at the precinct, but some cases proved harder to shake off than others. That, coupled with Juliette's newfound curiosity about all things Grimm and Wesen, dictated that they should keep private conversations as isolated as possible.

Juliette kissed him the moment he walked through the door, which somehow still came as a pleasant surprise after dealing with the alienation caused by her memory loss. Adalind Schade's spell—delivered via Majique's claws after she'd fed the cat a potion—had literally wiped

Nick from Juliette's memories. Nothing else gone. Just Nick. Even memories where Nick had been part of a group were altered so that Nick was no longer there. Overnight, he'd become a stranger to her. The road back had been long and difficult and fraught with complications, but they were better than ever now, because Nick no longer had to keep Grimm and Wesen secrets from her. She had recovered and was adapting to his bizarre world. Even so, they remained cautious as they resumed the intimate part of their relationship.

For dinner, they enjoyed a chicken risotto Juliette had whipped up. She talked a bit about a difficult case she was treating, a labrador suffering kidney failure with a grim prognosis. But he sensed her unwillingness to darken the mood and wasn't surprised when she batted the conversational ball over to his side of the net. Unfortunately, a homicide detective's topics of conversation also veered into doom and gloom or frustrations with bureaucracy and paperwork. When you investigated murders for a living, you had to look elsewhere for source material for light-hearted banter.

Juliette, naturally, wanted details about the Wesen aspects of the case. There remained a chance the killer was not Wesen, as unlikely as that seemed to Nick at the moment. And he had his doubts about the Mordstier's involvement, although the Wesen's rage, combined with hunger and opportunity, provided sufficient motives to make the case against him. And yet, without a murder weapon or an approximate time of death, the case might prove difficult to prosecute.

That's when Juliette suggested they visit Aunt Marie's trailer.

"The trailer?" Nick asked. "Really?

"Yes. Why not?"

"Not exactly my idea of a romantic evening."

"This stuff is fascinating," she said, smiling across the table.

"Fascinating?" he said. "That's all?"

"Okay. A little scary," she admitted. "But we fear what we don't understand, right? So, I want to… understand."

A short while later they sat in the trailer, Juliette leafing through some of Aunt Marie's journals, tracing her index finger over some of the sketches, while Nick's gaze mostly lingered on Juliette's face. She had asked him to show her some of the Wesen he'd encountered in person. She'd paused to read the notes on those—at least the ones that weren't in German. And she'd spent several minutes scanning entries for the Wesen she'd seen woge: Blutbad, Fuchsbau and Eisbiber.

"It's strange," she said.

"Other than the obvious?"

"Other than that, yes," she said with a wry smile. "These Wesen were here all along, walking among us, and nobody knew." Off Nick's look, she added, "Well, almost nobody."

Nick leaned forward. "And you're all right with"—he spread his arms to encompass everything in the trailer and everything it represented—"with all of this?"

She closed the book and stood, and Nick stood with her, facing her.

"It's definitely a lot to absorb."

"It is," he agreed.

"But…" She took his face in her hands. "This is a part of your life now, Nick. Part of who you are. It's a package deal. And I want to be in your life too."

More hopeful than he'd been in a while, Nick slipped his arms around her waist and said, "You do?"

His life seemed almost... normal again. Well, the new normal, considering he was a Grimm. He'd had to make a lot of adjustments to cope with his own nature and his role as a balancing force between Wesen and humans. His only option was to face challenges head on, to forge ahead and hope his mistakes, byproducts of trial and error and learning on the fly, were recoverable. And Juliette had had to overcome a lot of collateral damage because of her relationship with him, but she was back to normal and adjusting admirably herself. It felt as if they'd torn down a flawed structure and were now in the process of building something stronger on a solid foundation.

"Yes," she said, flashing an inviting smile. "I do."

This time, he kissed her.

CHAPTER EIGHT

Padlocked around his neck, a crude iron collar chained Gino Parisi to the basement wall. The short length of chain from collar to wall plate allowed him to kneel, sit or lie down on the hard cement floor, but not stand. He hadn't stood in at least two days.

Two pairs of equally crude shackles bound his wrists and ankles together, and they had rubbed his flesh raw. He squirmed atop the clumps of matted straw scattered across the floor, his focus entirely on dislodging the saliva-damp gag that muffled his voice. So far, he'd managed to bite into his tongue and bottom lip until they bled. Over the past two days—*had it really been that long since his abduction; so easy to lose track of time in the dark*—his eyes had adjusted to the darkness enough to distinguish at least ten other huddled and frightened abductees. A few remained blindfolded. He'd shed his by rubbing the side of his face against the rough stone wall. Since Gino's arrival, two of his fellow prisoners had been taken away by their jailer. None of those remaining knew how much time they had left.

A woman at the far end of the basement, her features

unreadable in darkness, occasionally whimpered in pain and, apparently, she'd been a prisoner longer than any of them. But she had no fight left in her. When she was coherent enough to speak, she told each new arrival— almost by rote, in a voice raspy from discomfort—what had transpired in the days since her capture. Her name was Alice. She said she'd fallen down the rabbit hole. And that statement triggered a recurring dry chuckle tinged with madness.

Though she'd been there the longest of the survivors, she had trouble keeping track of the days. She thought weeks might have passed since they'd slipped the collar around her neck. But she couldn't say much about those taken in the days that followed.

"We all look the same in the dark," she said, again with that dry chuckle.

Many days before Gino arrived, she'd rid herself of her gag and screamed her voice raw. But no help came. Wherever they were, the location was isolated, beyond hope of rescue. Unless they found a way to escape, they were doomed. Gino didn't want to believe the woman, but feared the truth in her words.

Eventually, her screams had an unintended consequence. Annoyed by her insubordination, their jailer returned to the communal cell to mete out punishment. He'd kicked her into quiet submission, leaving her with several broken ribs. By the time Gino arrived, her spirit was as broken as her bones.

Though she no longer screamed, she could not remain silent. She told them the man would kill them all. No ransom demands. No bargaining. No reasoning with the madman. When their time came, he would drag them away, one by one. Sometimes he took two in one night. Each time, she'd heard bloodcurdling screams—and then silence.

Hours after he took one of the prisoners away, sounds of a party would drift down from the upper reaches of the house. A party every night. And Alice wondered: How could these partygoers celebrate in such close proximity to the monster tormenting and killing them and yet remain unaware of what was happening right under their noses?

For two nights, Gino had heard those sounds of merriment. But rather than presuming ignorance, he assigned them guilt, not by association, but by participation. Whatever was happening to the prisoners in the basement, the party people upstairs were part of it. If he'd been able to speak in more than a mumble, he might have revealed his suspicions to Alice and the others. Then again, he might have kept silent on that count. For some of them, terrified in the dark, their last shred of hope might cling to the idea that the partygoers would somehow find out about them and call the police or rush to their aid.

No, Gino didn't want to believe Alice's hopeless prediction, but he couldn't shake it. Unless they escaped, they really were doomed, picked off one by one until they were all dead—or worse.

Clumps of straw shifted beneath him, host to a foul mixture of blood and urine, along with dollops of gruel that had slopped over the wooden buckets with which their jailer fed them every two or three days. He'd eaten once— less than a ladleful of the cold, lumpy gruel that tasted like wet cardboard—hours after he'd been shackled, still dazed from the blow that had rendered him unconscious, and shortly before he'd been gagged. Even if they hadn't been chained to the wall, most of them would have been too weak to put up much of a fight.

Finally, he tore his gag loose, spitting the lump of bloodied cloth from his mouth. His body streaked with dried sweat and fresh blood. Gino's muscles trembled with exhaustion. But he had one small victory, his first since the nightmarish ordeal had begun.

"What—what time is it?" he croaked, his voice sounding strange to his own ears. How long had he been awake? *Too long,* he thought, *time's running out.* Soon their jailer would come to collect one of them.

At first nobody answered his question. Maybe they couldn't. Hours on a clock had become meaningless. Only one time of the day mattered to them.

Finally, Alice spoke. "Too late."

That's when he heard the heavy footfalls.

The click of the deadbolt lock in the steel door.

More creaking footfalls on each of the four wooden steps that led down to the long basement room.

Gino found himself afraid to look at the hulking figure who peered at his hostages through dark holes cut in the cloth hood he wore to hide his identity. At first, Gino thought the hood was a good sign. If the man hid his face from them, he must believe they would be freed—at least some of them—and they wouldn't be able to identify him as their captor. But then Gino came to understand the man wore the hood to instill fear into his prisoners. Looking at the man's eyes was like staring into an abyss. They were the eyes of a soulless demon who basked in their misery and torment.

Slowly his inhuman gaze traveled from one side of the basement to the other, examining each of them in turn before making his selection. Nobody knew how he made the decision. And if some secret existed to avoid selection, nobody had shared it with Gino.

Some of the prisoners froze, almost as if playing possum. If he enjoyed their screams, then death offered one form of escape. Maybe feigned death would work as well. Others whimpered. Were the pitiful unworthy of consideration? Some huddled in a fetal position, withdrawing into their own minds. Ignore the danger at all costs and maybe it would pass. Several squirmed as if the weight of his attention were physically painful and, if endured, would eventually release them from its grip. A final few prayed, hurried voices in hushed tones, even those still gagged. Gino could tell which ones continued to believe in salvation, even if he couldn't make out the details of their faces in the darkness.

Silent, but not a possum, Gino found he fit none of these categories. Though weakened by his ordeal, rage and defiance fueled him. Though religious, prayer eluded him. And even with his mouth finally unencumbered, he could not find his voice. More than anything, he wanted to lash out at the hooded man, but the collar chain and manacles made rebellion impossible. So he knelt on the concrete floor, muscles taut and trembling, and directed his hate-filled glare downward, submissively, avoiding the abyss of the eyes.

"Which little piggy is next?" their hooded jailer asked in amusement, his voice a basso profundo that had already crept into Gino's nightmares and refused to leave.

The man took two steps away from Gino and grabbed the jaw of a young woman with long wavy hair, a light color that caught and reflected the wan light cast down the stairs from the hallway above. Gino remembered Alice calling her Cherise once.

Cherise had been a possum, but now she began to whimper, "Please don't, please, no, please don't, don't…" She tried unsuccessfully to pull her face free of his cruel grip.

"Leave her alone!"

Gino had finally found his voice.

His reaction had been a reflex—a paternal impulse—

and horribly dangerous, considering his circumstances. The young woman reminded him of his daughter, a twenty-year-old sophomore in college, living in a dorm on the other side of the country. A fleeting thought of her—chained in this basement, awaiting torture and death—had overwhelmed him.

The hooded man shoved the young woman's face aside and turned toward Gino. Soulless eyes hidden within the darkness of the cloth hood seemed to stare at him, as if noticing him for the first time.

"This piggy squeals."

"Go to hell, you sick bastard," Gino shouted, grimacing as bile rose in the back of his throat. "The quicker the better."

He couldn't undo his outburst. His fifteen-year-old son played video games all the time and most of those games had save points, places in the game located right before a difficult challenge where you could save your progress. If you died facing the big bad menace, you could restart the game from your last save point without losing everything you had worked so hard for. Unfortunately, real life had no save points. What was done, was done, for better or worse. And sometimes forever. Some choices had fatal consequences.

The large man strode toward Gino, reached into his pocket and withdrew a ring of keys.

"You, little piggy, go to hell before me."

As the man towered over him, Gino finally noticed that he wore a white apron, a butcher's apron, discolored—no, stained... stained with dried blood. Not a stretch to believe the blood was human. The butcher dropped to one knee beside Gino and reached for the heavy iron collar around his neck.

Gino pulled away from the man, as far as the chain

would allow, which wasn't far enough. The butcher grabbed Gino's hair in one hand, knuckles pressing painfully into Gino's scalp as the man's other hand fitted a key to the padlock dangling above his clavicle. He fought to overcome his paralyzing fear, grasping for the rage that had infused him only moments ago. Free of his collar and chain, he would have a chance to escape. He tensed, waiting—

—and felt the cold metal fall away from his chafed throat, the hinge at the nape of his neck uttering a single squeal of protest as the collar fell away.

Gino lunged at the much larger man, desperation providing the brief spark of adrenaline needed to fire his muscles.

But the butcher growled, a sound that couldn't have come from a human throat, and a meaty fist snapped out and struck Gino across the jaw. Gino imagined it felt like a right cross unleashed by a heavyweight boxing champ in his prime. One moment he was lunging forward with deadly intent, ready to wrap the chain connecting his wrists around the butcher's throat, the next he was staring up at the ceiling, not quite sure how he had fallen.

He gasped for air, like a fish tossed on the deck of a boat, helpless to avoid the club. Rubbery-limbed, he tried to protest as the butcher looped one fist around the wrist chain and dragged him across the floor and up the wooden stairs, his head awkwardly striking each step on the way up.

Once through the open doorway, the butcher dropped him to the floor and locked the door behind them. Gino tried to speak but the words came out jumbled.

"Don't—you do—don't have to do this—you can end this."

"Quiet," the butcher said, grabbing the wrist chain again. "This will be over soon."

At the end of the hall, another door awaited them.

That's where he takes them, Gino thought, terrified, his mind racing. *The place where they scream.*

Gino's iron chains rattled against the cement floor, and clanked together as he rolled onto his stomach and tried to stand. But the butcher moved so fast that Gino's hands and feet could gain no purchase.

The door swung open, revealing an uneven cement floor angled toward a drain in the corner. Though the butcher had apparently hosed the floor, some streaks of blood remained. A long metal countertop stood in front of the far wall next to a large walk-in cooler in the corner, large enough to hang several sides of beef.

Before he had time to dwell on what the walk-in unit might contain, his attention turned to a metal crossbar on the floor, attached to a cable that rose to the ceiling and came down again at an angle to a winch with a hand crank.

"What—what is that?" he asked, his mouth almost too dry to speak.

But he didn't need to ask. He knew. The question was merely a stall for time, to slow down the process, for him to think of a way out of his current predicament. He just needed some time to think. A little more time—

The butcher released Gino's wrist chain so he could close the door. He strode to the counter and strapped on a thick leather belt slotted with knives in various sizes. Lastly, he picked up a leather sap and slapped it against his palm, as if testing its weight.

Gino scrambled to his hands and knees a moment before the blow came down on the back of his head. With a groan he collapsed, managing to roll onto his back but unable to control his arms or legs. He watched helplessly, his vision shifting in and out of focus, as the butcher fitted a hook attached to the crossbar through a link in his ankle chains.

Time seemed to stutter, jumping ahead in irregular intervals, with moments of lucidity interspersed between fear and confusion. Gino's bare feet rose in front of him, followed by his legs, dragging him closer to the center of the killing room.

In one dizzying moment, he turned his head and spotted the butcher now standing in the corner, effortlessly turning the winch's crank, lifting Gino into the air inch by inch, his weight dangling by his raw ankles. Finally, his head cleared the floor. Upside down, he tried to thrash, to pull himself free of the hook, but his weakness and the weight of his body betrayed him.

"No! Stop! You son of a bitch!" Gino yelled. "Stop it now!"

He rose higher still, until his hands waved inches above the floor.

"Please! You can stop this before it's too late!"

Again, the butcher reached for Gino's hair to expose his throat.

Gino batted at the man's hands, whipping his chains defensively at the butcher's face. His whole body swayed beneath the crossbar. Incredibly, the butcher backed away and walked out of his line of sight.

Gino sucked in great gasps of air, trembling with this apparent reprieve.

"Good! You can stop this," he said. He twisted his body, trying to see where his captor had gone. The sap worried him. "I won't tell. I can't. I haven't seen your face."

Chains rattled behind him, yanking his arms up and behind his back, pulling his shoulders painfully. A moment later a lock snapped and his wrists were pulled tight against the small of his back, effectively hogtieing him upside down. The butcher came around to face him again, black eyeholes offering no human connection at all, nothing he could appeal to for mercy.

"What will happen to me?" he asked. "Will they—the people upstairs—eat—?"

"In time, piggy," the butcher said. "After I bleed you, gut you and put you in the cooler to dry-age, your time will come. Tonight, they want the French girl."

Cherise!

"No," he said, pitifully. "Don't. Not her."

He'd thought at least he'd saved the girl, given her a chance. But he'd only given her false hope, a few hours before the end.

His own hope gone, only morbid curiosity remained. "Why?" he asked.

The butcher pulled a thin knife from his leather belt and placed the sharp tip against Gino's throat, under his right ear.

"Time to show my face, piggy."

With that, the butcher pulled the cloth hood from his head with his free hand. As his face appeared, something strange happened. His features shifted, bones rippling and reforming beneath the flesh into a shape completely inhuman. Gino had been right all along. The butcher of men *was* a demon.

Gino couldn't stop himself. He screamed at the top of his lungs.

The butcher waited, enjoying the moment to its fullest, and then he sliced Gino's throat open from ear to ear.

CHAPTER NINE

As she had an early morning appointment with a potential rental client scheduled for the next day, Sheila Jenkins decided to leave Kim's bachelorette party at *La Porte Bleue* earlier than the rest of the ladies. Truth be told, in the short amount of time she'd been in the private party room they'd hired for the occasion, she'd had her fill of fondue and wine. She couldn't recall if her headache had been simmering earlier in the day or if the revelry had triggered it, but she was no longer having fun. She felt guilty for cutting out early, but if she stayed, she feared she'd become a wet blanket on the festivities. Besides, she barely knew the other women—all close friends of the bride-to-be—with the exception of Kim's older sister, Lisa.

They had graduated high school together, followed by a two-year encore as BFFs at Mount Hood Community College before going their separate ways. For Lisa, that had meant a business degree, a husband and two children—a boy and a girl, naturally; for Sheila, the intervening years featured a real estate license and an ill-advised marriage, followed by a why-the-hell-did-she-wait-so-long divorce.

Although Sheila had no issues with Kim—their

interactions were pleasant and polite rather than chummy—she felt she was really there to catch up with Lisa rather than celebrate the upcoming nuptials. But, as host of the party, Lisa had little time to spare for Sheila, and before long, Sheila felt she had become conspicuous by her outsider status. The others sent her furtive glances, then she overheard whispered questions, all amounting to the same thing: "Who is she again?" "Oh, right, the sister's friend."

When Lisa informed Sheila it was a little black dress party, where only the bride wore another color—Kim chose an electric fuchsia—Sheila had thought she might blend in, another face in the crowd. But she had little in common with the other women, coworkers or long-time friends with shared jobs and clubs and routines, with their own private little verbal shorthand, honed over the years. On another night, without commitments hanging over her head, Sheila might have made the effort to crack the code, but she chose the path of least resistance instead.

With the legitimate excuse of a budding headache and an early morning appointment, she tapped Lisa on the shoulder and whispered her intention to leave. Lisa flashed her a sympathetic face, but the gesture was fleeting, almost perfunctory, and the offer to walk her out of the restaurant vanished without a trace as another moment of head-pounding hilarity erupted around the table. So Sheila slipped out, depressingly certain that no one would miss her.

She picked up her linen jacket on the way out, crossed the street and tried to remember where she'd parked her five-year-old silver Camry. Parking had been at a premium when she arrived and she'd managed to find a spot on a side street a few blocks away from *La Porte Bleue*. As she walked on her two-inch heels along the uneven asphalt, she felt a little wobbly.

Should've had more fondue, she thought, *and less wine.*

Lightheadedness on top of the building headache lent the streets around her a surreal quality, as if she'd stepped out of one world into another. A shroud of mist caused surrounding streetlights to glow eerily. A chill in the air made her shudder. Then she wondered if the chill had been responsible, or her sudden isolation. Reaching into her clutch purse, she pulled out her keys.

Down a narrow side street, she spotted her Camry in front of a white Ford Econoline van with a THOMAS ELECTRIC sign on the side, the lower case L taking the form of a stylized lightning bolt. As she passed the van, she glanced through the driver's side window, a quick peek, not wanting to attract a stranger's attention when she felt a little tipsy and vulnerable. Not when the world seemed to have skipped off its track. But nobody sat in the van.

She exhaled suddenly, unaware until that moment that she'd been holding her breath as she approached the van.

With the tension gone, she mentally kicked herself for not switching on her business persona at the party. She should have passed out her Forrester Cade Realty business cards, asking for referrals, mentioning available properties. But even as she entertained the idea, envisioning that alternate reality where she shamelessly promoted the business—which had seen better days—she rejected the notion. She couldn't be that person, making the event all about her, grabbing the bride's spotlight and shining it on herself. Of course, that kind of behavior would ensure she'd never receive invitations to any social gatherings ever again.

So there's a positive, she thought, laughing at her self-pitying, misanthropic mood—and promptly dropped her keys.

Crouching down to scoop up the plastic key fob, she caught movement out of the corner of her eye. A car door squeaked behind her. She stood up straight—without her keys—and backed away as a dark shape rushed her from the van.

She squealed in fright, as if jolted with electricity.

The driver must have been hiding below the window line of the van, waiting for her to pass before jumping out. He pointed down to her keys.

"Let me help you with that."

"No! I don't need any—"

Instead of reaching for the keys, his gloved hands came at her face.

His own face began to transform into something hideous, as if he were becoming evil incarnate. Too startled to scream, unable to find her voice, she stared in horror. An instant later, strong hands wrapped around her neck and clutched her jaw, twisting violently. Something snapped, a sharp spike of pain overwhelmed her, and then nothing—

With practiced efficiency, he carried the woman's body back to the van, slid the unlocked side door open, tossed her in, and slammed the door shut. Five seconds from start to finish. He fetched her car keys, stuffed them in his trouser pocket and returned to the van.

After starting the engine, he swung the van around her Camry and drove down the side street, unnoticed. Later, he'd remove the large magnetic Thomas Electric signs he'd slapped on each side panel of the van and replace them with one of the other half-dozen signs he carried in order to confuse witness descriptions of his vehicle. And, later still, he'd come back and dispose of the car to muddle the trail for the police. But first he needed to dump the body. The car could wait.

In a few days, none of it would matter anyway.

CHAPTER TEN

Despite a late and interesting night with Juliette, Nick Burkhardt arrived at the precinct before Hank, who dealt with the all-day challenge of getting from points A through Z on a pair of crutches. Only fair to cut him some slack. Wouldn't have been so bad if either of his two biggest cases had some forward progress. Too much to hope the two cases might be somehow related, but they couldn't have been more dissimilar.

The Cracher-Mortel menacing Portland brought his victims back from apparent death, for some unknown endgame. Meanwhile, the bare bones killer had gone out of his way to make sure his victims were definitively dead, removing tissue and organs, chopping the bones into manageable pieces and, according to the ME, boiling them either with or without the flesh attached.

They knew the identity of the Cracher-Mortel's victims: Lilly O'Hara and Richard Mulpus; the bare bones killer's victims remained anonymous, pending IDs through dental records. And while they knew the "zombie" case involved a Wesen perp, the bare bones killer might be human or Wesen.

If Nick had to bet one way or the other, he'd put his money on Wesen involvement. Or maybe he was simply reluctant to assign this level of depravity to a fellow human being. Not that many Wesen weren't fine, upstanding citizens. By Grimm standards, his tolerance of most Wesen was unusual, judging by their shocked reactions when they realized he wouldn't kill them indiscriminately. Still, some of the things he had seen...

By the time he settled at his desk with his first cup of office coffee, the lab results from tests on the evidence collected from Guerra's cavern were waiting in his inbox. As he'd expected, based upon the row of mounted antlers in the Mordstier's back room, the bones outside the cabin were confirmed as belonging to a deer. None of the blood tested in the dwelling was human. And, cherry on top, none of the weapons collected was a match for the murder weapon.

He called out a greeting to Hank as his partner navigated the office on crutches and finally reached his desk, next to Nick's.

"Coffee should be hot," Nick said, nodding toward the extra mug he'd made for Hank when pouring his own. Letting Hank walk on crutches while attempting to carry a cup of coffee back to his desk, qualified as partner abuse. "Unlike our cases."

"They're too fresh to be *cold* cases," Hank said, settling in and situating his crutches so they'd be close at hand but not a tripping hazard. "We need a new word."

"Chilly?" Nick suggested. "Infuriating? Headache-inducing?"

"Lab results in?"

"Guerra's clean," Nick said, then added, "In the legal sense."

"So not the bone killer."

"Probably not."

"On the plus side, he racked up enough charges to keep him out of circulation for a while," Hank said. Softer, "That's one angry Wesen."

"Still waiting on IDs on our victims," Nick said. "No official COD or time of death."

"Something will turn up," Hank said.

Nick had a feeling the next thing that turned up would be a third victim.

Decker had told Monroe he would meet him at Portland Precision Pilates and, true to his word, he had already arrived by the time Monroe swung his VW Super Beetle into a parking space across the street from the studio. Monroe had harbored doubts his friend would show up. *Good start,* he thought. But then he noticed the unreformed Blutbad had disregarded Monroe's advice to wear comfortable, non-restrictive clothing. He'd swapped the knit watch cap for a battered leather Confederate hat. A subtle message to Monroe that Decker was a rebel at heart? He still sported the black leather jacket, over a flannel shirt, ratty jeans and work boots.

Easily removed, the hat, jacket and boots weren't a problem, but Monroe had doubts about the flannel shirt and jeans. He worried that an early failure would discourage Decker from continuing down the reformed path. If Monroe planned to mentor Decker, he needed to model patience without downplaying the difficulty of achieving and maintaining a reformed lifestyle.

With that in mind, Monroe had scheduled a beginner mat class at a studio. Seeing others make natural mistakes, learn from them and work toward proficiency, even at a basic level, should provide motivation to stay the course. In theory.

Monroe climbed out of the car, slipped two coiled foam floor mats under his arm, and crossed the street, flashing an encouraging smile.

"Hey, brother," Decker said, pushing himself off the wall against which he'd been leaning to shake Monroe's hand vigorously. "Ready and waiting."

"How did your 'thing' work out?"

Decker furrowed his brow, shook his head, confused. "Thing?"

"Your meet-up?" Monroe prompted. "At Shemanski Park Market?"

"Oh—oh, that," Decker said, chuckling. "Not gonna lie to you, brother. Could have gone better. Rough night, but long as you hit more than you miss, you count yourself lucky, right?"

"That's a healthy attitude," Monroe said, but worried that Decker meant "hit" in a violent context. How well did he really know the man? "Plenty of fish in the sea."

"That there are," Decker said. "Now, we gonna do this or what?"

"That's the plan," Monroe said, trying to sound more positive than he felt. Sometimes theory and practice existed worlds apart. "I brought an extra mat."

Decker stared at the coiled mat Monroe extended to him.

"This for nappy time or something?" he asked.

"Hands and knees on a hardwood floor," Monroe said. "You know, after a while you'll appreciate a little cushion."

"Oh. I get it," Decker said with the hint of a smirk. "Soft, right?"

Monroe paused, waiting for Decker to finish the thought.

Suddenly the taller man burst out laughing and clapped Monroe on the shoulder.

"Holy hell, brother! I'm jerking your chain," Decker said, shaking his head in disbelief. "You should've seen your face, dude. Never would've known you were reformed."

"This is serious," Monroe said.

"As a heart attack," Decker said. "Gotcha. Full bore. You know me."

"Remember, Decker," Monroe said as they approached the glass door with three golden Ps arranged diagonally, like a mini-staircase. "Pilates is about patience, precision and breathing."

"I know how to breathe."

"Probably not the right way," Monroe said, almost to himself, but Decker's Blutbad hearing didn't miss a word.

"You mean I've been doing it wrong all these years?" Decker said. "It's a freakin' wonder I'm still alive."

"Okay, the Pilates way," Monroe amended.

"I know all about Pilates," Decker said as Monroe held the door open for him.

"Really?" Monroe said, unable to control the sudden elevation of his eyebrows.

"Yeah," Decker said, smirking again, as he entered the studio. "Can't wait to toss around that medicine ball. Bet I can knock you on your ass, Mr. Veggie Burger."

Monroe sighed. "It's not a medicine ball," he said, hurrying to catch up to Decker. "It's an exercise ball. And you don't throw it at people."

"Oh, yeah?" Decker asked. "So what do you do with the damn thing?"

"Mostly," Monroe said, unable to help himself. "You sit on it."

"Are you kidding me?" Decker asked, pulling up short. "What the ever-loving hell happened to you, man?"

Again, Monroe sighed. "Don't worry about it. We're signed up for a beginner mat class. No balls today."

"From what I see, the balls have been missing for a while, man."

"You know, as soon as I said it, I knew it was a huge mistake."

Monroe's early optimism had fled, reduced to a perfunctory sense of obligation to finish what he had started. But he chose to keep up appearances and hope that Decker would turn the corner and find some value in the class.

"Don't sweat it, brother," Decker said. "I'm ready to kick some Pilates ass."

There's no kicking. The words popped unbidden into Monroe's head, but he wisely kept them to himself.

Fearing Decker might become self-conscious in a group setting, Monroe had led him to the back row of the class. Out of a dozen students, Monroe counted eight women and four men. And, except for a middle-aged man who had "recent-divorce" written all over him, the others clearly had some experience with the postures, which exposed a flaw in Monroe's plan. If the class was like an ad hoc pack, Decker's proficiency status dropped him immediately down the dominance hierarchy, which didn't bode well.

Decker lasted all of ten minutes before the problems started. He handled the early postures well enough, even allowing for the restriction of his flannel shirt and jeans. No problems with "one leg circle" or "roll up" and "swan dive." But "double leg stretch" and "hundred" had him puffing and grunting when he wasn't muttering curses. "Teaser" gave him fits, especially near the end of the hold period. "Leg pull prone" led to him crashing onto the floor and rolling off his mat.

"Son of a motherless whore!"

"Decker," Monroe whispered, embarrassed by and for him.

"It's nothing, I'm fine," Decker said, waving his arm at

the rest of the class, which had collectively paused to gape at him. "Go on about your business."

When Decker elevated sideways in "side bend" with his arm extended over his head, Monroe wanted to close his eyes, but couldn't.

Decker teetered one way, then the other, and then toppled over with a roar, emitting a growl of frustration as he woged. For a moment, Monroe feared the Blutbad might attack the class. Some of them turned around to stare; others pointedly ignored his outburst in a way that made him angrier still.

"Decker!" Monroe hissed.

But Decker ignored Monroe's entreaties. He stood and kicked his foam mat across the floor. It spun in a half-revolution and struck a middle-aged woman two spots farther down their row.

"Hey!" the woman yelled, indignant.

The instructor, a young woman who had an otherwise calm and soothing voice, no longer had a peaceful air about her.

"Sir, you need to leave now!" she insisted.

Decker grumbled as he snatched his mat off the floor and collected his belongings from a cubby in the back of the room. As he strode past the woman, he barked, "You need to kiss my ass, lady."

Mortified, Monroe gathered his own mat and belongings and hastened after his friend. He offered a quick apology to the woman struck by the kicked mat, and repeated the apology to the instructor. Monroe usually practiced Pilates at home alone and had no investment in the class, but he didn't want to be permanently banned from the establishment.

"Bad breakfast burrito," Monroe said, with a knowing shake of his head. "He's not usually like this. But, you know, those things really knot up your insides. I'm just saying, we've all been there, right?"

Before anyone could respond, Monroe slipped out of the class, hurried down the hall and rejoined Decker outside the studio.

As he approached, Decker held up a hand, palm out.

"Listen," he began. "Before you say anything— that was on me. Okay, brother? Lost my cool. Mea freakin' culpa."

"I may not be blameless here," Monroe said. "Maybe a group class wasn't the right first step on this road, you know? Something—less crowded—might have been the way to go. We'll reschedule—at a different studio—maybe a private class..."

Monroe's voice faded the deeper Decker furrowed his brow.

"Or..." Monroe began, scrambling, "maybe Pilates is not your thing. It works for me, but not everything works for everyone, right? We'll find what works for you."

"Yeah," Decker said, nodding. "Something with punching and kicking."

"Let's keep that one in our back pocket while we explore a few options that are less bloodthirsty and destructive."

Decker clapped a hand over his abdomen.

"You hungry?" he asked. "I am well and truly famished." He smiled broadly and tugged on the distressed bill of his rebel cap. "Well, that wasn't a total waste of time. I worked up a real appetite with my rage-fest." Decker shoved the spare foam mat into Monroe's hands as if he never planned to touch it again. "Let's go," he said. "Got a craving for steak tartare."

Crossing the street, Monroe opened the Beetle's driver's side door and tossed the mats in—then paused with the door held open. For a long moment, he contemplated the idea of jumping into the car and peeling rubber on his way home. The fleeting thought brought with it a rush of relief and contentment. But he hadn't gotten this far by taking the easy road. Nobody said helping a Blutbad reform would be easy. It hadn't been easy for him and it remained an ongoing struggle to stay on the straight and narrow. So Pilates wasn't the answer for Decker. Something else might work. Right?

With a sigh, he slammed the door shut.

And rejoined Decker.

CHAPTER ELEVEN

When the Bremmers arrived at the veterinarian practice, they could not have looked more solemn. Husband Barry stood between his wife and son, his right arm around Logan's shoulders, his left hand gripping Melinda's right. Barry Bremmer gave the impression of a man imparting strength to his loved ones, while recognizing the shallowness of his own reserves. Despite their unfounded optimism the day before, the direness of Roxy's medical condition must have crept into their familial psyche. They had braced themselves that morning to say goodbye to one of their own.

Juliette had spotted them getting out of their car through an office window. She checked the examination room one last time, then hurried to meet them at the reception area. She would have called them before they left home to expedite their arrival, but she hadn't been sure at the time. Now she knew.

"We have an appointment to see Dr. Silverton... about Roxy Bremmer," Barry told Zoe, who sat alone behind the front desk. Apparently Roger had slipped out for bagels or doughnuts. He and Zoe alternated gopher days.

Zoe lifted the phone but saw Juliette approaching out of the corner of her eye and dropped the receiver back in the cradle.

"And here she is!"

Juliette stood before the Bremmers, palms pressed together in front of her.

"Okay, I should have called you earlier."

Melinda gasped before Juliette could finish.

"Oh, no... has she... already?"

Barry pressed his lips together and looked off to the side, to suppress his emotions. His son looked down, unable to meet anyone's gaze.

"No," Juliette said quickly. "It couldn't have been antifreeze ingestion."

"What?" Melinda asked.

Abruptly, Logan looked up at Juliette, his eyes wide. A brief glimpse of redemption, that whatever had happened to Roxy hadn't been his fault.

Juliette shook her head, frustrated with herself.

"I'm sorry," she said. "This isn't how I meant to tell— follow me." She couldn't help smiling. "I have a surprise."

"Surprise?" Melinda asked, confused by the expectation of bad news combined with Juliette's upbeat demeanor.

As Juliette grabbed the examination room doorknob, a dog barked.

"Is that—?" Barry asked her.

"Yes."

"But she sounds..." Melinda paused, her lips quivering. "Better."

Juliette swung the door open and led them in. But not before the yellow lab rushed over to her family, licking hands, tail wagging in nonstop excitement. Logan dropped to his knees and wrapped his arms around the dog. Melinda's eyes brimmed with tears until a few finally escaped. Barry coughed, overcome with emotion. He managed to utter a single word, "How?"

They all looked at her expectantly.

She didn't know what to say. How had the dog recovered so remarkably after yesterday? *I wish I knew,* she thought. But that's not an answer she could give them. She reached for the file on the stainless steel counter, flipped it open to glance at the lab results, which she had already memorized but found hard to believe.

"Her kidney values have returned to normal." *BUN 23, creatinine 0.9,* she mused. *Exactly the same as five minutes ago, the last time I looked.* "She's eating again. Seems fine. The IV fluids must have worked."

"After yesterday," Barry said. "What you said, the odds didn't seem great."

"Yes, it was a longshot," Juliette said, smiling as she looked down at the dog, who continued to receive pets and hugs from the entire family. "But Roxy beat the odds."

"It's—amazing," Melinda said.

"Roxy's tough," Logan said. "Aren't you, girl?"

"What now?" Melinda asked.

"Do you want to take her home?" Juliette said.

"Can we? Yes, of course!"

"Then she's all yours," Juliette said, cautioning them to let the dog take it easy. No matter how well she presented now, she'd been through a grueling ordeal and might tire easily. "Zoe has your bill. See her on your way out."

As they headed out to their car, dog in tow, Juliette watched them depart, smiling in relief. When she woke up that morning, she imagined a completely different outcome for Roxy. She'd been wrong, and that made her day.

Melinda saw her standing at the glass door and waved. Barry tooted the car horn as he drove across the parking lot. And Logan held up one of Roxy's front paws against the window in a little doggy wave. Juliette laughed and finally turned away from the door.

"Wow," Zoe said. "I never would have believed that was the same dog they brought in yesterday."

"You and me both," Juliette said as she headed back to her office.

While the dog's quick turnaround pleased her, she remained baffled by it. She couldn't explain it logically or medically. But she'd had no reason to keep an apparently healthy dog in her care any longer. The Bremmers certainly accepted at face value the dog's remarkable recovery. People always wonder why bad things happen to them, but they accept good fortune readily enough.

Don't look a gift horse in the mouth, she told herself. *Accept the win gracefully and move on.*

But something nagged at her subconscious. Nothing specific, but the uneasiness lingered. *Why can't I accept things the way they are? Am I letting my own recent history with bizarre revelations cast a pall over good news?*

Nick hung up the telephone and crossed off the last name from his half of the list he'd copied from the geocache logbook. Since all but two of them had used Internet handles, *à la* "Spelunkid," instead of their actual names, the most time-consuming part of the investigation dealt with connecting those aliases to real identities with contact details. Cyber-breadcrumbs based upon logged IP addresses and server logs from web hosts and Internet service providers revealed the connections. The PPD's computer tech guys had helped Nick and Hank obtain and sift through that information.

Cross-referencing the logbook to the online entries showed that everyone who signed—or stamped—the logbook had also recorded their "find" on the cache's web page. All of the geocachers had been local to Portland at the time they signed the logbook, with the exception of a woman who had relocated to the East Coast when her company opened a New York sales office. Without a firm time of death for either victim, he couldn't ask for or verify alibis. Nevertheless, they needed to collect information about their suspect pool.

Personally, Nick doubted the involvement of any of the geocachers in the bare bones cases, but that belief was far from a certainty. Needing to narrow the pool, Nick focused on men more than women or parent-and-child combinations, such as Brian and Tyler Mathis. And because of the "toy swap" nature of this particular cache, the parent-child combination, naturally, was most common.

Next, he tightened his solitary-man focus to those with a short history of geocaching. One of them, a college student, had only one "find" on his user history. When Nick questioned him, he discovered that he'd quit after his first cache because his bumbling around in the woods resulted in a horrible case of poison ivy. He showed Nick photos he'd taken at the time and posted to his various social media accounts. When Nick asked why he chose a "toy swap" geocache, the young man answered reasonably that the difficulty level was easy—but not too easy—and that the cache was the one closest to his home. He'd tried to block the incident from his mind, and had forgotten he still had an account on the geocache site until Nick's phone call.

Nick looked up from his computer screen to check on Hank's progress with his half of the list and heard his partner wrapping up a call.

"Anything?"

"Nothing," Hank replied. "You?"

"The same," Nick said. "No obvious suspects."

At that moment, Sergeant Wu walked purposely through the door and made a beeline toward their desks, balancing his notebook atop a couple folders with photos clipped to them. Hank turned expectantly in his chair.

"What have you got?" Nick asked.

"Tell us you got something," Hank pleaded. "Even if you don't."

"How about two missing persons?" Wu asked. "Well, not missing anymore. Since we found them. But that's it, as far as a pattern." He referred to his notebook. "We got IDs through dental records on both sets of bones. Marie Chang, twenty-year-old student at Pacific Northwest College of Art, disappeared while jogging twelve days ago. Second set of bones belonged to Luis Posada, middle-aged businessman, never returned to the office after a lunch meeting. Wife reported him missing... two weeks ago."

He placed the folders on the corner of Nick's desk, photos up.

Nick thanked him.

"Something else," Wu said. "While I was getting these copies, I talked to some of the guys down there. The number of unsolved missing person cases in the Greater Portland area has ticked up significantly in the past month."

Considering what had happened to Chang and Posada, the implication of Wu's unspoken conclusion was chilling. At the same time, Nick wouldn't automatically make that deductive leap. Not every person who went missing ended up as a murder victim. Some simply ran away from their lives. Others eventually turned up, with one excuse or another to explain their absence. Nevertheless, Nick had to consider that the beginning of a potential pattern had emerged.

"I want to be notified of any new missing persons cases," Nick told Wu, who nodded. Easier to follow a fresh trail than one that had grown cold over the course of a month. He'd want to review the other missing person case folders, but for now, they had other leads to follow.

Wu left, and Nick handed Hank the top folder—Luis Posada—while he flipped through Marie Chang's information. Both victims had disappeared at approximately the same time and their bones were discovered within a mile of each other, in similar shallow graves. Two weeks ago they couldn't have been more different, but in death, they had too much in common. Nick wondered if Occam's razor applied. If the simplest explanation is the correct one, maybe Marie knew Luis? A connection between the victims could make solving the cases easier, but first they had to establish that connection.

CHAPTER TWELVE

As Monroe entered the Exotic Spice & Tea Shop, his gaze swept the relatively dark interior—dark-wood cabinets, shelves and countertops—searching for its current owner, Rosalee Calvert. Jars of varying shapes and sizes, from vials to jugs, lined every shelf and surface area, with a few notable exceptions for reference books, scales and the occasional mortar and pestle.

Ostensibly a specialty herb and tea store, the spice shop was so much more than that. In addition to herbs, spices and teas, the shop contained rare and unusual ingredients the Wesen world had employed for centuries in the making of everything from life-saving remedies to deadly concoctions. Rosalee had become a de facto apothecary for the Wesen community in Portland. The human medical system would never understand and could never treat rare Wesen conditions and maladies. Where human medicine failed, Rosalee took over.

She hadn't always run the spice shop. Her brother, Freddy, had owned the place until two Skalengecks murdered him, at which time ownership had passed to Rosalee. Also reformed, Rosalee was a Fuchsbau, and she had become an important part of Monroe's life. They had been dating for a while and, now that she had returned from caring for her sick aunt, they were in a good place.

After spending the morning watching Decker flail around in anger and basically eat raw meat for brunch, Monroe needed to shake off his exposure to the man's very non-reformed ways and spend time with someone who shared his values. So he'd headed to the spice shop as soon as Decker left to run some errands.

Monroe hadn't given up on helping his old friend onto a new path, but Decker was like radiation exposure for Monroe, and he could only spend so much time with him before the dose became lifestyle-lethal. A big reason why he'd separated himself from so many people in his past.

The shop's lone customer—a plump, silver-haired man in a dark suit, softly humming as he perused the merchandise, hands clasped behind his back—caught Monroe's attention. Not a regular. Monroe couldn't recall seeing him in the shop before. Every few seconds the man reached for a jar, briefly reviewed its ingredients and returned it to the shelf, tucking his hands behind his back again. A spice shop lookie loo? Or somebody who wanted to consider everything in the store before making a purchase. Either way, he appeared harmless.

Rosalee stood behind the counter at the back of the shop, facing Juliette, as the two women chatted. Monroe heard something about a yellow lab and assumed the discussion concerned one of Juliette's canine patients. He had volunteered to watch the shop while the two ladies went out for lunch. Ever since Bud, Rosalee and Monroe had woged for Juliette, she had made every effort to familiarize herself with the Wesen world, along with Nick's place in it. Monroe gave her a lot of credit for handling with admirable equanimity what for her—or any human, for that matter—were shocking revelations.

Monroe joined them at the counter.

"Hi, Monroe," Juliette said brightly.

"Oh, how was your morning?" Rosalee asked. "You and your friend?"

"*Old* friend," Monroe said. "And it… could have gone better." *Couldn't have gone much worse,* he thought.

"Why? What happened?"

"Nothing that should keep you two from lunch," Monroe said breezily, but the truth was he didn't want to talk about it. He was embarrassed about some of his pre-reform actions and Decker represented a big part of those days. While he knew Rosalee had had her own troubles, he didn't want to rehash his own indiscretions—especially with Juliette present. And that would all come out if he talked about how he wanted to help Decker reform. But who was he kidding? He feared Decker's failure. The more people he told about Decker's attempt at reforming, the more he would have to tell about his eventual failure. A poor attitude for a mentor to have, but the morning's activities had given Monroe no reason to believe Decker could turn his life around. Moreover, Rosalee might worry about Monroe associating with a non-reformed Blutbad.

"Go," Monroe said, taking his place behind the counter. "We can talk about it later."

"Okay," Rosalee said, but her lingering gaze told him she suspected something was amiss. Maybe she'd forget about it over lunch. "Anyway, thanks for watching the shop." She smiled and squeezed his hand affectionately.

"No problem." Monroe indicated the rest of the shop with a sweep of his arm. "I think I can handle the rush."

"Oh, don't worry," she said, poking him in the chest with her index finger. "The lunch rush is coming."

Monroe turned to the side and indicated the elderly

humming gentleman with a slight nod of his head.

"What's his story?"

"Fairly new in town," Rosalee said. "Name's Oscar Cavendish. Recently discovered the shop. Mostly buys herbs and spices, nothing too exotic."

"Anything I should know about?" Monroe asked. "Special orders."

"Oh, right, almost forgot!" She reached under the counter for a small brown paper bag and placed it on the counter. "For Ben Dolan, his name's on the bag. Tell him to rub some of this ointment on his gums after meals and before bedtime. His condition should be cured in a day or two." In answer to the question Monroe posed with raised eyebrows, she added, "Seelengut with uncontrolled woging."

"Ah, Wesen hiccups," Monroe said. "I hate when that happens."

Rosalee leaned in for a kiss. "And we'll talk later. Okay?"

"Right," Monroe said. "Later."

But he hadn't specified how much later.

Cavendish eventually purchased an assortment of cooking spices, nothing unavailable in a regular grocery store. Maybe he appreciated the old world ambience of Rosalee's spice shop. Nothing about the place—other than an electronic scale—would have looked out of place in the late nineteenth century.

A few minutes later, a red-faced young Wesen man slipped into the shop, asking, "Is it ready?" as he hurried to the counter. Every ten seconds, he unwillingly woged into his Seelengut form, a process that would have looked like an extreme facial tic to humans. "She said it would be ready?"

"You must be Ben Dolan," Monroe said, handing him the bag with the ointment. As he rang up the sale, Monroe passed along Rosalee's application instructions. "You should be fine in a day or two."

"Thank"—Ben woged; shifted back—"you!"

The rest of the "lunch rush" produced a steady stream of light traffic, two or three people coming through the store at a time, but nothing Monroe couldn't handle alone. He'd covered for Rosalee plenty of times in the past. And the familiarity of the routine allowed his mind to wander, and poke at the Decker dilemma.

He'd told Decker that Pilates might not be the answer for him. And that was true, although he would've preferred to see his friend take another class or two before giving up. Of course, now that Decker was *persona non grata* at Portland Precision Pilates, they'd need to sign up at another studio. But knowing Decker's impatience, Monroe dismissed that idea. No more Pilates. Fine. But there was more than one way to reform a Blutbad.

Monroe picked up the phone and dialed Decker's cell.

"Hey, Decker," Monroe said. "Yes, your old buddy, Monroe... I know, I know. But, like I told you, it's a process... Right. I understand. But I had another idea if you're willing... Okay, good. That's the spirit! Now—have you ever tried t'ai chi?"

Nick and Hank had planned to meet Rebecca Miravalle at the dorm she'd shared with Marie Chang, until Rebecca told them Marie's parents had removed her belongings three days ago and taken them back to Seattle. Instead, Nick drove through the Pearl District, two blocks east of Pacific Northwest College of Art to Jamison Square, which encompassed a full city block. Rebecca had told them to look for a frizzy redhead by the fountain.

They passed a street vendor's food cart—triggering an anticipatory rumble from Nick's stomach—and followed the paved path angled to the center of the plaza. A steady stream of people strolled to and from the urban park's main attraction, the interactive fountain where water spilled from rectangular slabs of basalt rock arranged in a rough row—a flattened V shape—of tiered steps. Water gradually filled the plaza in a shallow pool before draining away, only to refill again, in a continual cycle all day long.

Parents watched as young children rushed into and out of the water, laughing and splashing each other. Some parents and teens waded in barefoot, pant cuffs rolled up. Others sat back in lawn chairs or lounged in picnic areas, enjoying an outdoor lunch break. At the far end of the fountain, a young man with sparse facial hair attempted Bob Dylan songs on an acoustic guitar plastered with decals.

Nick pointed toward the near edge of the row of tiered steps.

"There she is."

A redheaded girl wearing a wide-brimmed straw hat to shield her pale, freckled face from the sun, sat cross-legged on one of the stones set above the fountain level with a sketch pad propped up on her lap. Her attention alternated between the kids playing in the water and her drawing.

Nick led the way around to the upper level, behind the row of tiered steps. Hank followed close behind on his crutches, giving the expanding pool of water a wide berth. Seemed like everywhere the case led them, Hank had to deal with treacherous terrain.

Nick stopped a few feet from the redhead. Close enough to observe her talent with pencil art, but not so close that his sudden presence would startle her.

She wore a distressed Nirvana t-shirt with jeans and Birkenstock sandals.

"Rebecca Miravalle?" he asked.

"Ah!" the young woman cried out as her pencil line sliced a sketched child's ear.

Looking up at them, she pressed her pencil hand atop her hat when a breeze fluttered the brim and threatened to dislodge it. She had an off-center lower lip ring and a small turquoise butterfly tattooed at the base of her neck, complete with a drawn shadow to give it a 3D effect.

Nick's hand dropped to the shield clipped to his belt.

"Detectives Burkhardt and Griffin," he said, nodding to Hank, who raised the gold shield which hung from the lanyard around his neck. "We spoke on the phone."

"Yeah, right, no prob," she said, reflexively swiping a gum eraser over the errant line. "It's cool. Just me, lost in my own little world. Big surprise." She uncrossed her legs and hopped down off the stone. "Becky's fine, by the way."

"As I said on the phone, we have a few questions about Marie Chang."

"Yeah, right, Ree," Becky said. "You know, at first, I thought she flaked out on school."

"Was she under pressure?"

"From school? I don't know. Maybe. She was hyper-focused on her grades. Said a degree wasn't enough anymore in this crappy economy. You had to stand out from the crowd. Make a name for yourself—a brand. She wanted people to 'know the Marie Chang brand.' She didn't even know what that was yet, not really, but it's all she talked about. She always said, 'I need to excel, Becky. Mediocrity is not an option.'"

"What about relationships?" Nick asked.

"Not really," Becky said. "She'd hang out in group settings, but never had time—never made time to date. She'd go on her long runs. Said it cleared her head."

"You said, at first you thought she left school...?"

"For, like, a microsecond," Becky said. "Thought maybe

she dropped everything and went back home to Seattle. But the more I thought about it—I mean, who goes out for a run and leaves everything behind? Her money, her credit cards. I mean, willingly?"

"Did her running follow a pattern?" Nick asked.

"Daily," Becky said, nodding. "But the times varied. Sometimes she'd run when she needed a break. Other times, she'd wait until after she'd finished everything."

"Did she know a man named Luis Posada?" Hank asked.

"Luis—? No, not that I recall. Wait—what happened to Ree? You think she ran off with this Luis guy?"

Nick looked at the children milling around and motioned her away from the fountain, closer to the row of trees backing it.

"I'm sorry, Becky," Nick began. "Marie's remains were found yesterday, a few miles from here."

"Oh—oh, God!" The sketchpad slipped out of Becky's hands, along with her pencil and eraser. She started to sit down, as if she still stood beside one of the fountain stones, and Nick caught her arm above her elbow to support her. "I thought maybe something... she was missing but..." She wiped at tears in the corners of her eyes. "How? An accident—or... it wasn't—was it?"

"We believe somebody murdered her," Hank said, as gently as possible.

"But—Marie? Why?"

"That's what we're trying to find out."

"How—how was she—?"

"We're not at liberty to discuss the details of the case," Nick said.

From what Captain Renard had told them, and what little of the case Nick had caught on the news, the press knew skeletal remains had been found at Claremont Park, but neither the condition of the bones nor the identities of the victims had been released. Nick had called Marie's parents before seeking the meeting with Rebecca, while Hank had called Posada's wife.

"Did she suffer—much? Can you tell me that?"

Hank shook his head sympathetically. "We don't know."

"This Luis guy—? Did he—is he responsible?"

"No," Nick said quickly. "He's not a suspect."

"Did Marie have any enemies?" Hank asked to change the topic. "Rivals? Maybe competing for the same awards or something?"

"I don't think so," Becky said. "Nobody she ever mentioned. She wasn't a social butterfly or anything, never attended any parties. She called those kinds of things distractions."

Becky looked down, attempting to regain her composure. She stared down at her sketch pad and pencil before crouching to pick them up, almost absent-mindedly.

"Ree was quiet and focused. Never caused any problems. Not really. She might ask me to turn down my music when she was studying, but that's… This is so awful, you know." She pressed a hand to her mouth for a moment, trying to suppress a sudden sob. "Everything she worked so hard for, a name, a brand… and none of it matters anymore. Some creep took it all away from her."

CHAPTER THIRTEEN

After a quick lunch purchased from the street vendor cart at Jamison Square and consumed in the confines of Nick's Land Cruiser, the detectives headed across town to the Bell Cafe to interview Caitlin Stoop, who'd served Luis Posada his last meal and was quite possibly the last person—other than his killer—to see him alive.

The cafe had a light breakfast and dinner crowd, with the bulk of its business coming through the doors between 11:00 a.m. and 2:00 p.m. While colorful chalkboard messages, flyers and menu inserts touted various breakfast and dinner specials in hopes of improving business at the bookends of the day, the cafe needed the midday crowd to stay afloat. Donna, the Bell Cafe manager, impressed this fact upon the detectives when she agreed to give Caitlin—one of her most efficient and affable servers—a ten-minute break ahead of schedule to answer their questions. Nick reminded her they were investigating a homicide, but promised not to take up much of Caitlin's time.

Donna motioned Caitlin over, and told her in a quiet voice to show the detectives to the back booth where staff took their breaks. Caitlin—a young woman with blond hair pinned up, wearing a white blouse with a small name-tag and black slacks—nodded to her supervisor and led Nick and Hank to the back of the restaurant. Once they'd sat down, Nick explained why they had come to question her.

"I can't believe Mr. Posada is really dead," she said. "I mean, I knew him, saw him a couple times every week. Does his wife know?"

"His family has been notified," Hank said.

She shook her head, somber. "I talked to the police a couple weeks back. Guess it was the day after he had lunch here that last time. I figured something was wrong, but I never suspected..."

"What can you tell us about him?" Nick asked.

Posada had been a regular at the cafe, and Caitlin had been his server on several occasions, often enough to pick up that he'd been a manager at Sanderson Landscaping. He'd worked his way up the ladder from part of a crew to a manager in a few years.

"He would say 'I shoveled my way to success so I appreciate honest work,'" Caitlin told them. "So he'd always leave a big tip. He was a gentleman. Always polite."

"He ate alone that day?"

"Yes."

"Was that unusual?" Hank asked.

"He'd reserved a table for two, but said his lunch appointment cancelled," she explained. "I didn't question... but sometimes I got the feeling he wanted to eat alone and thought that might be weird or something?"

"Did he seem nervous?" Nick asked. "Upset about anything?"

"Said he was waiting to hear if they—his company, I mean—had won a bid on a big office campus job or something. Maybe it was a business park. Is there a difference? I don't—anyway, I had the feeling it was a big deal for Sanderson, because of the size of the job. But that was just like him."

"How so?" Nick asked.

"He was always thinking ahead to the next bid, the next big job," she said. "That's what motivated him. The next thing. The next challenge. Not what he'd accomplished yesterday. Like those investment commercials."

Nick and Hank exchanged a look.

"You know—something about past performance doesn't mean you'll have that same success tomorrow. You know the ones I mean, right?"

Nick nodded. "Did he ever talk about rivals? Companies he lost bids to in the past?"

"Can't recall," she said. "So, probably no. I think I'd remember something like that, even if I forgot the name of the company."

Figuring it was a longshot, but deciding he should ask anyway, Nick said, "Did he ever mention someone named Marie Chang?"

Caitlin looked puzzled. "No. Is that someone from his office?"

"No," Nick replied.

Hank jumped in. "Before he left, did he seem okay?"

"Okay?"

"Normal," Nick said. "Or different somehow?"

She exhaled, stared off into space as her mind drifted back to that last meal. After a moment, she shook her head.

"The police asked me the same thing," she said. "And I'm sorry, but I can't remember anything odd about him that day. I mean, he was alone, so he ate quietly, except when I stopped by to check on him, refill his glass, and bring him his check. When he left here, I just assumed—I assumed he'd be back in a couple days. Like always."

They thanked her for her time. Nick nodded to the harried manager—who was bouncing from table to table, checking on orders, refilling glasses—on their way out.

As they crossed the parking lot, Hank reflexively scanned the ground for any tripping hazard, and grumbled, "Random victims."

If the killer had chosen his victims at random, he would be difficult to catch through investigative leads. They'd need him to slip up at a crime scene, to leave behind DNA evidence or fingerprints, assuming he was in one of the criminal databases. Otherwise, they needed a witness to one of the abductions, and that was something out of their control.

Basically, they needed to get lucky.

Nick's cell phone rang: Wu.

"Yeah, this is Burkhardt."

So that Hank could hear both sides of the conversation, Nick put the call on speaker. Over the tinny cell phone connection, Wu said, "You wanted to be notified about any new missing person cases. One popped up this morning. Sheila Jenkins, thirty-two-year-old leasing agent. Left a bachelorette party at *La Porte Bleue* last night. Failed to show up at work this morning."

"Hangover?" Nick wondered.

"According to the bride-to-be's sister, who hosted the party, Sheila made a quick exit," Wu said. "Alone. Mentioned an early morning appointment."

"Anybody check her home?"

"After she failed to answer her cell and landline, her boss had somebody from the office swing by her place," Wu said. "No answer. And her car's missing."

"Did you get a plate number?"

"Already in the system," Wu said. "Patrol units notified."

Sheila might have left the party early to hook up with

someone, and she might have slept over and not returned home. That would explain the empty house and the missing car. But not the cell phone silence, nor the absence from work. Of course, if she had taken her own party elsewhere, she might have continued to drink throughout the night, passed out in somebody else's house or apartment. But Nick had a bad feeling that her disappearance fit the admittedly small profile of the others. They were both found weeks later. So Nick held onto the possibility that Sheila might still be alive. He asked Wu for addresses and phone numbers.

Propped on his crutches, Hank took out a pen and small notebook and copied down the details on the witness and Sheila Jenkins' place of business. More leads to follow, but Hank looked resigned.

When Nick disconnected the call, Hank said, "You know what this is?"

Nick nodded. "Another random grab."

The untended vacant lot had been home to a garment factory before a fire gutted the interior. Intending to rebuild, the owners had the factory razed. But the business had been underinsured and the flagging economy had left the project in limbo. A temporary construction fence surrounding the lot had fallen into disrepair, and, in several sections, had simply fallen. Bulldozers, backhoes and excavators had left the ground uneven, while weeds had been allowed to overrun the property. In short, the lot had become an eyesore.

None of that mattered to David Munks and Cody Kuberski. With a few hours to kill before dinner, they rode onto the lot on their mountain bikes, after effortlessly sneaking through one of the gaps in the perimeter fence. The choppy terrain gave them a training ground to test their off-road skills, their heads filled with adolescent dreams of someday competing in the X Games. They'd donned bike helmets, but not bothered with elbow and knee pads.

Cody, at fifteen almost a year older than David, took the initiative, trying jumps and spin moves that David would then attempt to replicate. The hills weren't as high nor the dips as low as they might have hoped. Mostly, the ground felt like a series of rises interspersed with potholes. At one point, after an unusually jarring drop, David yelped as he bit the tip of his tongue. Cody rose on his pedals as he navigated a section of dirt riddled with broken bricks.

Swinging around, he pedaled up an incline toward the back of the lot, the area farthest from the FOR SALE sign attached to the fence at street level. He hoped the other side of the construction mound had some slopes he could work with, a dip steep enough that he could pick up speed and grab some air off the next rise. David fell in behind him, struggling through the rough, bumpy ascent and lagging behind his older friend.

At the summit, Cody looked down the other side and noticed a smooth lane, more dirt and mud than nasty weeds and protruding rocks. He whooped in anticipation. Encouraged, David rode his pedals hard to catch up.

Too impatient to wait, Cody launched himself down the side of the mound, gripping the handlebars of the bike as tightly as possible. The ground smoothed out and he picked up speed, rose up the far incline and lunged forward for some altitude. He came down hard, his back wheel catching on an obstruction and almost dislodging him from the bike. He recovered in time, feet outstretched, his arms shaking as he spun sideways in an abrupt stop.

Cody looked back as David rushed down the hill, working his pedals overtime, gaining speed. David rose but didn't elevate as much as Cody had. His back wheel caught more of the obstruction and the bike shot out from under him. David skidded across some mud into mounds of loose dirt, while his bike tumbled away from him and dropped into a clump of weeds.

Climbing to his feet, David grumbled, "What the hell?"

A layer of mud caked the whole right side of his gray hoodie and jeans. He winced as he rubbed his right elbow, then shook it out to test it. Sore but apparently unbroken.

Cody noticed a red streak on the side of Dave's forehead. "Dude, you're bleeding."

David pressed the heel of his palm to the injury.

"Must've hit a rock," he said. "Or one of those bricks."

Cody rode his mountain bike back toward his friend.

David ignored his bike for the moment, and backtracked on foot. Something smooth and white protruded from the mud. He poked it with his toe.

"What is that?" Cody asked.

"Don't know."

"No," Cody explained. "Up there?" He pointed to the obstruction both their back tires had struck on the way down, a yard or two from the small white object that had cut David's forehead. "Whatever it is, we both hit it coming down."

David looked where his friend pointed and walked toward the object, dull white amid loose clumps of grass-tufted dirt. Dropping to his knees, David sunk his fingers into the mud and pulled clumps of it away.

"Holy crap!"

"What?"

"No—freakin'—way!"

Cody dropped his bike and rushed to his friend's side. The shape of the object David had exposed with his hands was unmistakable.

"Jesus!" he whispered. "That's a human skull."

"Think it's real?"

"No, numb nuts, people bury fake skulls all the time," Cody said. "I hear there's a bunch of them in the cemetery."

"Shut up!"

Cody kneeled beside him. "Look," he said, tugging at a long white bone partially exposed by David's hurried excavation. "That a rib or something?"

"We have to call someone."

"911?" Cody suggested.

"Is this an emergency?" David asked. "I mean, he's already dead."

"It's a human skeleton!" Cody said. "Somebody murdered this guy and buried his body here. Maybe there's a reward or something."

"All I'm saying is, you can get in trouble calling 911 when it's not a real emergency."

"So sue me," Cody said. "I'm calling."

CHAPTER FOURTEEN

By the time Nick and Hank arrived at the crime scene, the vacant lot swarmed with uniforms and crime scene techs, most congregating around the location where two teenage bikers had discovered the third set of bones.

Nick parked behind the long row of official vehicles, climbed out of the Land Cruiser and waited on the sidewalk for Hank to get out on his crutches. Together they walked toward a gap in the fence that served as the official point of entry, guarded by a uniformed officer. Crime scene tape zigzagged across other gaps in the fence like bright yellow stitches, to keep out bystanders and the crew of the first news van to arrive.

Fortunately, the place was industrial rather than commercial or residential, so foot traffic was minimal. Nick suspected that those gathered outside the fence worked in the immediate area. Of course, with the proliferation of smartphone cameras and video linked to social networking sites, it was only a matter of time before word got out. When Nick and Hank flashed their shields, the uniform waved them through.

Behind him, Nick heard Hank heave a resigned sigh.

Nick scanned the rough terrain ahead, a veritable minefield for navigating on crutches, and said, "Hank, you want to sit this one out, that's okay."

"No," Hank said. "Go ahead. I'll catch up."

Nick forged ahead, careful of his own footing. The abundance of weeds concealed dips and breaks in the ground along with other hazards. He followed the most direct path to the heart of the crime scene, where techs were excavating and gathering bones, and uniforms scanned the immediate area for any they may have missed.

Captain Renard stood out of the way of those processing the scene, but close enough for everyone to feel his oversight. Apparently a third bare bones murder had been his tipping point. The Captain might be feeling the heat from upstairs. Nick wished he had some good news to report.

Sergeant Wu spotted Nick and walked down to meet him.

"Was about to call you," he said as he approached.

"You got something?" Nick asked, looking toward the center of activity.

"Yes," Wu said. "But not about this."

"Somebody else disappeared?"

"No," Wu said. "Somebody's been found. A woman's body washed up in a tidal pool this morning. Head and hands chopped off. Killer obviously didn't want her ID'd."

"No dental records or prints," Nick said, nodding. "Effective."

"Usually," Wu said with an air of anticipatory satisfaction. "But the ME discovered she had a knee prosthesis. Got the serial number and contacted the manufacturer."

"She got an ID?"

Wu nodded. "Sheila Jenkins. Our latest missing person. Technically, former missing person."

"Different MO," Nick mused. Which meant the murder likely had no connection to the bare bones killer.

"Maybe he was interrupted," Wu suggested. "Head and hands chopped off. That's a lot of chopping already."

"Seems premeditated," Nick said. "Specifically to conceal ID."

"If you're chopping a whole body, you have to start somewhere," Wu said and shrugged. "Probably the extremities."

Wu had a point. The killer could have started with the feet. But why not bury the body again, even if the chopping ritual hadn't been completed? If it even was a ritual. The dismemberment seemed almost... practical rather than ritualistic. Digging shallow graves, while practical, also seemed sloppy.

"The angle of the cuts," Nick said. "Do they match the other murders?"

"Doubt the ME checked," Wu said. "For the same reason you mentioned. The cases appear unrelated."

"Let's do that," Nick said. "To find out one way or the other."

"I'll have her check," Wu said before striding downhill and reaching for his shoulder mic.

Nick glanced down the slope to locate Hank. His partner had taken a roundabout path up the lot's incline, favoring open spaces with fewer potential hazards. Turning back, Nick approached Captain Renard.

"Same as before?" Nick asked.

Renard nodded. "Chopped up like the others. One set of remains. But a... metacarpal—palm bone—was separated from the rest. Killer may have dropped it before burying the rest and stepped on it, partially embedding it in the ground, without even realizing it."

Renard nodded toward two teenage boys, each standing

next to a parent, mother of the shorter boy, father of the other one.

"Kids snuck onto the lot with mountain bikes. Tires hit the bones. Metacarpal cut the blond boy's forehead after he took a fall."

"You interview them?" Nick asked.

Renard shook his head. "Responding uniform's notes. I'll leave the interview to you and Hank—where is Hank?"

Nick pointed. "On his way," he said. "Walking wounded."

"Of course," Renard said. "Where are we on the other two murders?"

Nick explained that the interviews hadn't given them any leads.

"Victims did not know each other far as we can tell," Nick said. "They have nothing in common. Last people to see them noticed no unusual behavior. Going about their daily routines when they were snatched. Chosen at random."

"I don't like random," Renard said.

"Neither do I."

"Nick!"

Turning around, Nick saw Hank about twenty yards away, waving one of his crutches in the air.

"I'd better see what he wants," Nick said before rushing off.

As Nick approached, Hank directed the tip of his crutch at a loose mound of dirt beside the smooth path he'd been following.

"Tell me that's not what I think it is," Hank said.

Nick crouched and reached out to brush aside some weeds overhanging the bits of dull white amid the dirt and rocks.

"Sorry," Nick said. "It is."

"Get some techs down here," Hank called up to Renard, who had turned away from the original set of bones to see what had caught Hank's interest. "We've got more bones."

Some of the crime scene guys peeled off the first site and swooped down to photograph and catalog the newly discovered cache of bones. Hank's roundabout approach to the first site had inadvertently exposed a second one.

Renard immediately ordered the uniforms—who had begun to mill about with continued interest but diminished purpose—to spread out and check under every clump of weeds and in every loose mound of earth for more remains. Wu coordinated the effort, splitting the officers into teams and assigning quadrants.

Renard strode up to Nick and Hank and said, "I'm ordering GPR for this site and Claremont Park. No more surprises."

Ground-penetrating radar crews would have to wait for the crime scene guys to wrap up in the vacant lot, but Claremont Park was not an issue. If more victims had been buried there, they needed to find them and identify them. Hard to find a pattern with two murders, but the count had risen to four and could easily go higher.

"Find out what you can from our bikers," Renard continued. "We need to identify these bodies. The Chief is already breathing down my neck. When he hears about this…"

Nick and Hank split up to question the teenagers separately. Afterward, they compared notes and discovered they had nothing new to go on. Once the boys realized they had partially unearthed human remains, they hadn't disturbed the dismembered skeleton further. They had entered the lot on a whim, seeing the uneven terrain as an urban challenge for their mountain bikes. Dumb luck that they had stumbled upon the bones.

Hank leaned against a boulder that a construction excavator had unearthed without removing from the lot, propped his crutches against it, and massaged his underarms. Clearly, he needed a breather.

While everyone else inspected each bit of debris underfoot, anticipating the discovery of a third set of bones, Nick wandered away from the first scene and tried to see the whole location from the perspective of a killer looking for a place to dump human remains.

Isolated. Easily overlooked or ignored. Shallow graves indicated impatience or sloppiness. Or maybe the killer only needed the bones to stay hidden for a short amount of time, a few weeks or months at the outside. An itinerant killer, then. Murder several people, possibly more, then skip town and start the cycle over somewhere else. So far, the bones they had discovered had been from victims abducted weeks ago. What if the killer had already moved on? Assuming he had not, how much time remained to solve the case and capture the murderer—human or Wesen—before he skipped town?

A strong breeze buffeted him, like the harbinger of a brewing storm. He glanced upward, at a bank of dark clouds smudging the sky.

Soon the killer would be lost in the wind.

Another gust, and a flutter of movement caught his eye. A scrap of paper, trapped in a tangle of weeds, whipped free and flipped end over end. Faux parchment paper. Nick spotted some geometric shapes on one side before it rolled over again. Curious, he chased after it, pulling latex gloves from his pocket as he walked. If the paper belonged to the killer, it might offer a clue to his identity.

The scrap skipped out of reach twice when he bent to pick it up. He glanced around, hoping noone had noticed this bit of unintentional slapstick, as if a prankster had attached fishing line to a dollar bill and kept tugging it out of reach of his mark. One more step and the paper swirled upward, rising to knee height, where Nick snatched it out of the air.

On the front of the torn sheet of paper, someone had drawn a design with a thick black marker. An arc or curve with acute triangles running along the outside of the curve. Below the geometric shapes, the same hand had written a message or a line of code, but most of that line was on the missing section of the paper. Only the top remained. Four letters or numbers, with a gap between the third and fourth. The first one might have been a five or the top of a boxy S, the second an eight or the top of an O, and the third could have been a one, an uppercase I or an L. After the gap, the fourth item looked like a tiny inverted V, which seemed unlikely.

Nick looked up from the paper and noticed a man staring back at him from across the street. Wearing blue coveralls and smoking a cigarette, the man stood in front of an automotive shop that faced the north side of the vacant lot. Obviously his place of employment. But when he noticed Nick's attention, he flicked the cigarette away, turned abruptly on his heel and hurried into the open garage bay. Mildly suspicious behavior for an innocent bystander, or an average crime scene gawker.

Nick sealed the scrap of paper in a spare evidence bag he kept in his jacket, then shoved the bag and his gloves back in his pocket and crossed to the north edge of the lot. He followed the fence until he came to a gap with only an X of strung crime scene tape to block his way. He ducked between the arms of the X to leave the tape in place, crossed the street and approached the dingy white cinderblock building. Instead of employing a mounted or freestanding sign, the owners had painted the name of their business directly on one broad expanse of wall, in red script letters that had faded to near-illegibility over time: SWARTLEY BROS. AUTO REPAIR.

Nick glanced up and down the street, taking in a series of warehouses and manufacturing facilities whose fortunes seemed to have faded. Those in the immediate vicinity ran only skeleton crews, judging by the handful of cars in too-large parking lots. A few appeared to have shuttered entirely.

If not for the open garage bay and the presence of the smoking mechanic, Nick might have assumed the auto shop had also gone out of business. Riddled with potholes and broken chunks of concrete, the front parking lot presented a clear tire and axle hazard. No better way to discourage potential customers. Grime coated the windows that looked out from the back office and reception area.

Nick walked up to the open garage bay and peered inside, giving his eyes a moment to adjust to the dim interior. A rust-pocked gold Camaro occupied the single lift. Scattered around the cluttered garage, Nick spotted a couple air compressions, hanging pneumatic lines, a rolling jack, a brake lathe, a tire changer and wheel balancer, an air conditioner recharger and a headlight aimer. Some of the heavy equipment appeared out of order. Some hand tools, including an air gun, loose wrenches and a mechanic's lamp, had been left on the floor.

A mechanic wearing a camouflage-patterned trucker's hat, blue denim shirt and grimy, frayed jeans stood near a large red wheeled mechanic's tool chest stationed against the left wall, its many drawers closed—the lone exception to the prevailing rule of sloppiness in the shop.

"What can I do you for, mister?"

Nick's hand dropped to the gold shield on his belt.

"Detective Burkhardt, Portland PD." Nick said. "Like to ask you a few questions."

The man came away from the wall, approaching Nick,

but stopped beside the lift. An embroidered name tag on the breast pocket of his denim shirt identified him as Ron. He had deep-set brown eyes in a narrow face with a pointy chin covered with spotty stubble. Holding a grimy rag, he went through the motions of cleaning his hands and nodded toward the vacant lot.

"Regular party going on over there."

"Wouldn't call it a party," Nick said. "It's a crime scene."

"How about that," Ron said, nodding. "We don't get many police patrols out here."

"Don't suppose you saw anyone on that lot recently?"

"Couple boys riding mountain bikes."

"Before that," Nick said, irritated. "In the last couple weeks." He glanced toward the doorway leading from the garage bay into the reception area. "You're Ron Swartley?"

"That I am, Detective."

"Your brother here?"

"What makes you think so?"

"Saw someone standing out front, smoking a cigarette."

"That against the law now?"

"Answer the question."

"Could've been me out there," Ron said. "Can't seem to quit the filthy habit."

"But it wasn't," Nick said. "Man I saw wore blue coveralls."

"Sounds like Ray, all right," Ron said. "But I must have missed him."

Nick looked around the one-bay garage, which verged on claustrophobic with the clutter of heavy equipment in the aisles and loose tools underfoot.

"How?"

Ron shrugged. His gaze flickered up to the Camaro on the lift.

"I was cleaning up."

Worst excuse ever, Nick thought. His irritation and anxiety had reached a turning point. His hand moved toward his Glock 17, pulling it free.

A blur of movement flashed in the periphery of his vision before he could bring the gun to bear. Nick spun, instinctively raising his left forearm to shield himself from the blow before he fully registered what was happening.

Ray, the smoking mechanic in the blue coveralls, rushed him while swinging a crowbar.

Nick managed to deflect most of the blow, but the metal clipped his scalp, setting off a blinding flashbulb in his skull.

In the instant before the impact, Ray had woged into the form of a Reinigen.

Nick's foot shot out for him to catch himself but his shoe came down on a loose air gun, which slid out from under him, taking his balance with it. His Glock fell from his hand, spinning away to come to rest under the tire changer.

Ray swung the crowbar overhead like an axe.

Nick caught the shaft of the crowbar and held tight, using his weight and Ray's momentum to pull the man over him and away.

Ray slammed sideways against the air conditioner recharger. The crowbar clanged off of something metallic and skittered across the concrete floor.

As Nick scrambled to his feet, Ron charged him with a utility knife he apparently had hidden in the hip pocket of his jeans. The extended razor blade gleamed as it slashed at Nick's face.

CHAPTER FIFTEEN

Bruno Farley, the barrel-chested Wesen butcher with his own human livestock pen, crossed the slaughter room and opened the walk-in cooler. Inside, only three human carcasses remained. Beheaded, disemboweled and skinned, they hung from meat hooks on a U-shaped track. He grabbed the one Chef had chosen and tagged earlier, and lifted it off its hook. Chef had already claimed the organs and sweetbreads. Slinging the gutted carcass over his shoulder, the butcher walked to his preparation table and laid it out.

With the last week upon them, he'd have to pick up the pace to meet demand. From now until the end, he should have at least six carcasses ready for butchering at all times. That should keep him busy until it was time to move on.

He opened the large drawer under the worktable and took out his twenty-five-inch meat saw, a meat hook with a welded metal handle, his solid metal meat cleaver, and a few carving knives. Before he began in earnest, he checked the edges of the blades and sharpened two of the smaller ones, which he'd need to slice every last scrap of meat from the bone. Whatever he overlooked would come

off in soup pots and roasts. They never wasted anything—
except the bones.

Slamming the meat hook into the flesh to hold it in
place, he cut his way down the length of the carcass with
the meat saw in his right hand. He then bisected both halves
below the ribs to complete the quartering process. Lifting
a top quarter—not quite the same as the forequarter of
a beef carcass but close—he hung it from a sharp hook
on a gambrel suspended from the ceiling. He fixed the
other top quarter beside the first so he could focus on the
hindquarters. Each arm sagged down—fingers curled as
if clutching spare change—and spun independently of the
other, following the movement of the separate hooks. A
butcher's mobile.

Setting the handsaw aside, Farley picked up his largest
carving knife and sliced the top of the right leg clear of the
hip, repeating the process for the left. Then he switched to
his cleaver and, with powerful overhead swings, chopped
both legs in half. Not the best cuts of meat, he pushed
them to the back of the table. He cut off rump roasts, then
flank steaks, before sirloin steaks and the tenderloin for
filet mignon. He arranged these cuts on the back of the
table, which he would wrap later and keep refrigerated
until Chef came for them.

He brought down the right top quarter, sliced an arm
free, and chopped with the cleaver to split the arm in half.
With his strength, one blow—*whock!*—was sufficient
to sever the bone. Farley enjoyed the decisive sound the
cleaver made with each true cut.

Tossing the pieces of the severed arm to the back of the
table, he switched to a smaller knife to cut the rib meat
away from the bone—more detailed work. Hunched over
the table, he heard a quick knock on the door—unlocked
since he was alone.

A familiar voice called, "Bone pickup!"

"Fine," he grumbled as he ran the keen knife edge along a rib, stripping away the meat. Sometimes they wanted the ribs. For this carcass, Chef had requested the meat alone.

Absorbed in his work, he kept his back to Fixer, who wheeled in the hand truck with the squeaky wheel. If Farley had to ask him to oil the damn wheel one more time, he'd part the man's hair with the business end of his cleaver. *Show some damn pride in your work, man!* But he sighed and said nothing. *In a few days, I'll be free of that jackass.*

The bane of his existence began whistling an annoying tune as he buckled straps around the metal bin, securing it against the hand truck. The bones tended to accumulate during the feasts and the butcher hated clutter in his slaughter room. On balance, he was glad to be rid of them.

"This the whole shebang?" Fixer asked. "Or does Chef have a few left over in his soup pots?"

"Far as I know," Farley said, "that's everything."

"Guess I'll ask him. Just to be sure."

"You do that."

"Looks like I'll need to find a third dumping ground."

Regretting his decision to speak, he asked anyway. "Why is that?"

"Haven't you been watching the news, Butcher? Police discovered both locations. Too risky to go back."

Farley couldn't resist a dig. "Maybe if you had hidden the bones better..."

The man scoffed. "Why? Week from now, nobody here will give a crap."

This time, Farley remained silent. The man excused his sloppiness as expediency. Farley hadn't hired the poor excuse for a fixer. He certainly wouldn't waste time arguing with him. He'd much rather spend that time gutting the man. Too bad he wasn't human. Otherwise,

Farley would ask Chef to add Fixer to his menu.

"Relax, big guy. It's almost over."

Farley heard the door click shut. He paused in his work, eyes squeezed shut until the grating sound of the squeaky wheel eventually faded away. With a sigh of relief, he resumed work on the rib meat.

Though Hank's neck and shoulders ached from the grind of riding crutches all over the great outdoors of Portland, he kept the discomfort to himself. Once people in the department saw him on crutches, they cut him slack he neither requested nor wanted. Some of them probably thought he should be deskbound until the cast came off. Not that they would ever voice those opinions, at least not to his face.

On the surface, everyone was accommodating and understanding. But the last few days had made him rethink his bravado and stubbornness. Every so often, he hoped—well, *hope* was definitely too strong a word—but he certainly wouldn't complain if the next homicide they caught had gone down in a modern office building, with smooth tiled floors and elevators.

On the plus side, his crutches had led him to discover a second set of bones at the vacant lot, something the uniforms and techs had missed. In that instance, his disabil—his temporarily reduced ability—had helped move the investigation forward. And Nick had given no indication that Hank's mobility predicament had—

Nick?

Hank scanned the groups of uniforms and techs, looking for his partner.

The last time he'd seen Nick, he'd been bagging a piece of paper away from the others. Then he must have wandered off for some reason. Maybe something he'd seen on the paper. Following a lead, but not something that had raised any red flags. *Guess he decided to give me a breather.*

Supporting his weight on his good foot, Hank reached for his crutches and slid them under his arms. He headed in the direction where he'd last seen Nick, working his way methodically down an uneven slope. From his new vantage point, the only thing he saw was a white cinderblock building across the street from the side of the lot, a disreputable looking automotive shop.

Of course. He's interviewing potential witnesses over there.

Pausing, Hank took out his cell phone. Two bars—now one. Poor reception, but he speed-dialed Nick and waited through the static-filled ringing until the phone bounced to voicemail. He hung up. Dropped the phone in his jacket pocket and hurried across the lot.

Like a hobbled mother hen, Hank thought. *Probably worrying over nothing.*

Still…

Nick blocked Ron Swartley's right wrist with his left forearm, avoiding the slashing razor blade in the utility knife. Almost in the same motion, Nick drove his fist into Ron's gut, staggering him. Before the other man could recover, Nick gripped his knife hand and forearm and drove the limb against his knee, knocking the blade loose. Then he drove a shoulder into the Reinigen and shoved him hard.

Ron stumbled backward and banged into the wheeled tool chest, clutching a few of the drawer handles to stop himself from falling.

Nick moved forward to press the attack but heard Ray charging from behind him. He only had time to turn around halfway—enough to see that Ray was unarmed—before the rat-faced Reinigen leapt onto his back.

Spinning, Nick caught Ray's right arm and flung him toward his brother, using the man's own momentum to hurl him forward.

Ron had pushed himself away from the tool chest at the same moment his brother collided with him. In a tangle of flailing limbs, they both went down, one of them pulling the tool chest down on top of them with a crash of metal tools, clanging and pinging all around them like a rain of hardware hail.

The spilled collection of metal created many potential weapons, either handheld or projectile, so Nick decided, for the moment, to postpone fishing his Glock out from under the tire changer.

He was a Grimm. He could handle two obnoxious Reinigens.

As Nick strode toward them, the brothers pushed and pulled each other, shoving the overturned tool chest out of the way. Ray climbed to his feet first, and bolted toward the back door of the garage bay. Rather, he tried to bolt. Nick caught him by the collar of his coveralls and hauled him back.

"Not so fast."

Ron sprang up from hands and knees and threw himself bodily against the back of Nick's legs. Falling suddenly backward, Nick lost his grip on Ray, who, given a second opportunity, slipped out the back exit. A moment later, Nick heard a dirt-bike engine roar to life, a shower of gravel pelt the back wall of the shop, and the engine whine into the distance, fading away.

But Nick had more immediate concerns.

Looming over the detective in full woge, flashing his enlarged incisors, Ron had a long stainless steel wrench clutched in his hand. Impatient, he lunged forward.

Nick planted the sole of his shoe in the Reinigen's gut and shoved hard. Ron's body whipped backward, falling over the tumbled tool chest, and the back of his head whacked against the wall.

Nick pushed himself up on his elbows.

Ron groaned, tightened his grip on the wrench and tried to rise up from the tool chest.

"Freeze!"

Stone faced, Hank stood on the threshold of the open bay, balanced on his crutches, pointing his Glock at the sprawled Reinigen.

"Drop your weapon!"

Wincing, Ron let the wrench slip from his hand. It clanged against the concrete floor.

"You okay?" Hank asked Nick.

"Fine."

"Your head's bleeding."

Nick raised his hand to his scalp, just above the hairline where the end of the crowbar had caught him, and felt a laceration. Not too deep, but he'd probably need a few stitches.

"Flesh wound," he said with a shrug.

Rising, Nick felt a little lightheaded, hoped he hadn't sustained a concussion, but wasted no time cuffing Ron Swartley and dragging him to his feet.

"Reinigens," Nick said. "Brother Ray escaped out back, on a dirt bike. This one is Ron."

"I'll call it in," Hank said. "Got enough patrol units in the area. Maybe we'll get lucky."

"What's this?" Nick said, staring down at the overturned tool chest. Amid all the tools, screws, bolts and other metal paraphernalia, he noticed a baggie stuffed with pills. He crouched down and lifted the tool chest upright, then staggered back in a moment of dizziness.

"Nick?" Hank said, concerned, as he wrapped up his call and put his phone away. "You don't look okay."

"I'm all right," Nick said, while attempting to blink away a few spots in his vision. Blood had run down the side of his face, and big drops splattered on the floor. Scalp wounds tended to bleed a lot. He backed away from the stacked evidence to avoid contaminating it. "Looks like the Swartley Brothers had a little side business."

From one of the large bottom drawers of the tool chest, several other baggies had fallen out, along with bundled stacks of cash.

"Jackpot," Hank said.

Nick pushed the mound of baggies apart with the tip of a ballpoint pen from his pocket to examine the collection of pills.

"We got oxycodone—a *lot* of oxy—and, for variety, some Vicodin and Xanax. Different baggie for each dosage. What's oxy go for these days, Ron? Dollar per milligram?"

Hands cuffed behind his back, Ron looked away.

"I wouldn't know," he said.

"Got some buddies in Vice would love to hear about this," Hank said.

Nick lined up the stacks of cash with the tip of the pen. Mostly tens and twenties.

"Hey, Ron, maybe you can expedite my paperwork. How much cash should I report we're confiscating today?"

Ron shrugged his shoulders. "Don't know," he said softly, after swallowing several times with the effort to disavow ownership of the money. "Never saw it before."

Nick crossed the garage area to retrieve his sidearm from under the tire changer. He picked up a rag that looked as if it may have been laundered within the last calendar month, folded it twice and pressed it against his scalp to help stem the bleeding.

"Controlled substances are the least of your worries, Ron," Nick said. "We don't mind throwing Vice a bone. They can have this haul. We don't care. Because we're *homicide* detectives."

"What?" Ron asked, for the first time worried.

"Bad move," Hank said, shaking his head dramatically. "Burying the bodies across the street from your place of business."

"Vacant lot right there," Nick said. "Gotta be convenient."

"I got nothing to do with murders," Ron protested. "Not one damn thing."

"You can tell us all about it back at the precinct."

CHAPTER SIXTEEN

On the way to the precinct, the detectives changed plans. Instead of taking Ron Swartley in for questioning together, Hank drove the Land Cruiser and, after insisting his Grimm partner have the scalp laceration treated, dropped Nick off at the emergency room. While Nick waited for a doctor, Hank would continue to the precinct to interrogate the suspect alone.

Sitting in an uncomfortable chair in the ER, Nick pressed a wad of clean medical gauze to his wound, having traded in the unhygienic rag to a solicitous nurse shortly after his arrival. To kill some time, he reviewed the events leading up to his injury, Ray's escape and the confiscation of the pills and cash.

Even though the brothers were Wesen and criminals, Nick had begun to doubt either of them was the bare bones killer. Ron's suspicious behavior around a large police presence could be explained by the stash of drugs and money he had on the premises. Ray's unwarranted sneak attack raised the suspicion bar a little higher but, again, Nick thought the brothers were probably acting out of fear of the discovery of their side business.

Of course, given enough time, Nick could make the case the other way. Maybe the murder victims were involved in drug deals gone awry. Or maybe the brothers took their money and killed them. With luck, Hank would get Ron to talk, offer him a deal—assuming the prosecuting attorney cooperated—and let Ray, who had abandoned him, take the fall.

The ER nurse eventually returned and led him to a private area where a doctor could sew up his scalp. She warned him the doctor would probably advise overnight observation at the hospital.

Nick had no intention of staying overnight. True, he'd had some momentary dizziness, but he'd had no other concussion symptoms. His only concern was the injury itself, a lacerated and bleeding scalp. He'd trust in his Grimm abilities to get him through a minor head injury.

By the time the doctor saw him, Nick sensed the laceration was smaller than it had been back at the garage. Or maybe he'd imagined the improvement. Regardless, he only needed eight stitches and, once the nurse had cleaned blood off his face and hands, his injury was barely visible. His shirt and trousers, however, told a different story. The copious bloodstains made him look like an extra on the set of a zombie apocalypse movie.

Hank had contacted Juliette to apprise her of Nick's injury and ER visit. When she called Nick to tell him she was on her way, he asked her to bring a fresh shirt. As soon as she came through the emergency room, she voiced a dozen concerned questions, all of which he deferred until he had a chance to put on the fresh shirt in the nearest restroom and stuff the bloodied one in a plastic bag. Feeling a bit more human, he asked her to give him a ride home.

"Nick, you probably have a concussion," Juliette said.

"Listen to your doctor. Stay here overnight."

"Juliette, I'm fine," Nick assured her. Then, in a lower voice, "I'm a Grimm."

"And Gr—they don't get concussions?"

"Hard heads," Nick said. "One of the perks."

Lips pressed together, Juliette stared at him for several moments, a mixture of admonishment and concern, before deciding she couldn't change his mind.

"Well, you're staying with me," she insisted. "I'll observe you at home. And wake you every few hours. To make sure your head is as hard as you claim."

"It's a deal."

As they crossed the parking lot, Nick's phone rang. Hank.

"Have to take this," he said. "Hank, what have you got?"

"First," Hank said. "How's your head?"

"Stitched up," Nick said. "Sore, but no more bleeding."

"Okay, otherwise?"

"Under the watchful care of Dr. Silverton," Nick said, smiling at Juliette. Her return smile was far more fleeting. As a medical professional, she obviously disapproved of his ignoring medical advice. "Squeeze anything from Ron?"

"Had my doubts about that pair," Hank said, independently echoing Nick's early assessment. "Ron's not talking. Won't give up Ray. So I pulled phone records from the shop. Turns out the brothers made a lot of calls to one Dr. Harold Filbert. Looked into him. Doc's getting up there in years. Lost the bulk of his retirement fund when the market tanked a few years back. And his practice has been struggling for a while."

"Sounds like someone in need of a quick cash infusion."

"That's what I thought," Hank said. "Short on cash and options, Filbert turns his practice into a pill mill. The Swartleys run fake patients with fake problems through his office. Doc writes up a bunch of scripts. Then the

Swartleys deal the oxy on the street for ten times its value."

"Splitting the proceeds with the not-so-good doctor," Nick concluded. "But as far as the murders…?"

"Right," Hank said in a deflated tone. "Put out a BOLO on Ray. Those two had easy access to the disposal site, but otherwise… nothing solid."

As Nick suspected, the Wesen were criminals, drug dealers, but had probably not committed the murders.

"Anything new at the vacant lot?"

"Got an update from Wu," Hank said. "So far, four bodies at the second site. Six, combined from both sites."

Six and counting, Nick thought. Once the GPR teams scoured both sites, Nick expected the number of victims to rise.

And they were no closer to solving the murders.

Farley, the Wesen butcher, had orders from the host to pick up the pace of food processing. With three days left, the Empty Chair period was in play and the number of meals had increased. Chef had decided on various fusion cuisines to meet demand while retaining some semblance of thematic integrity.

Today had been a southwestern Tex-Mex combination. Tomorrow's menu would feature an Asian fusion. Farley would have preferred more time to dry-age the meat in his cooler, but with limited storage space and a higher than expected turnover, he had to make compromises in quality.

The true connoisseurs scheduled their visits for the early weeks in the month. By month's end, refinement gave way to a "last call" type of gluttony. Old World tradition dictated last night for the tight chain meal for a good reason. On the surface, a day to celebrate excess. But beneath that indulgence, desperation played a part. Many years stood between the participants and the next feasting month. And for some, this represented their last Silver Plate.

His father had been Butcher last time and his father before him. Farley's father trained him for this privilege during his adolescence, so Bruno could take over the family tradition when he died. A secret Farley could tell none of his classmates. A secret he had guarded, waiting for his time to come.

Six months ago, the host had called him and told him to sharpen his knives.

Farley had no son of his own yet, but he still had time to keep their tradition alive. Even without a son to take over, health willing, he'd be around to resume the role of butcher one more time. If not, he had a nephew with the right type of glint in his eye to assume the mantle. More than one way to keep the family tradition rolling.

Grabbing the old iron key ring from a top shelf, he walked down the hallway to the basement pen. As soon as he unlocked the steel door, he heard their panic spark. Crying, wailing, and whispered prayers, while others mumbled frantically around gags. These sounds, to him, were no more profound than the lowing of cows, the bleating of sheep, or the clucking of chickens.

This trip into the livestock pen, he'd left behind his hood. Early in the month, awash in the secrecy and caution that surrounded the event, he kept his human face hidden from them. The rough cloth mask had served its purpose, stoking their fear to a fever pitch that paralyzed them. Some of them thought that to survive they must simply endure the unpleasantness, like gripping the arms of the dentist's chair through a series of root canals. Eventually the discomfort and anxiety would pass. But now, he wanted to disabuse them of that notion. Survival was not an option. They must realize they had no hope. Before he descended the stairs, he woged for them to see what would not be endured.

The horned face of a Dickfellig.

As he walked among them, their chains rattled as they scurried away, huddling against the wall. A few became still as death, even holding their breath through the fateful moments of his selection.

One of the women, Alice, finally noticed his Wesen appearance and screamed, pointing. A few whispered, "Mask!" and one of those who had prayed softly, now whispered, "Demon!"

He stood in the middle of the basement, hunched over a bit to avoid bumping into the exposed joists with his head, fists clenched as he let his eyes adjust to the dim room.

"Good news," he told them. "Your suffering ends soon."

All had fallen quiet, save a prayerful few. By now, those who had been chained more than a few days knew not to trust him, expecting a trick. The recent additions remained cautious, understandably distrustful. But he hadn't lied. Their suffering would end soon. But not in the way they wanted. His vision had adjusted sufficiently to locate his selections.

"For some of you," he said, turning his gaze to a chosen one, "your confinement ends now."

"No, don't do this," the Korean woman said, staring down at her hands clasped in her lap. "Please don't do this."

He stared at an Indian boy huddled behind her, no more than twelve years old, avoiding eye contact.

Noticing his attention shift, the woman cried out.

"No!" She raised her hand, partially shielding the Indian. "He's just a boy."

Farley reached into the front pocket of his blood-stained apron and removed the lead-shot sap. With a quick backhand strike, he whacked the Chinese man sitting opposite the woman. Another woman shrieked. The blow caught the middle-aged man across the temple. Groaning, the Chinese man tumbled over, his limbs unhinged.

Quickly, Farley unlocked the dazed man's iron collar. Then, grabbing the chain between the man's wrist manacles, he dragged him out of the room, down the hall and strung him up with the winch. With a practiced motion, he slit the man's throat and let him bleed out on the floor. By now, the others would wonder why he hadn't locked the door when he left them.

Some of them knew the answer.

Farley returned with his sap and the keys.

This time, the bleating of the sheep became shrill.

Once again, he stood before the Korean woman.

"Choose," he asked her. "You or the boy?"

"No," she said, crying softly.

"Choose!"

She sobbed quietly, offering no response.

"Fine," he said. "You, then."

She screamed and thrashed violently as he unlocked her collar, but he outweighed her by over a hundred-and-fifty pounds. He wrapped an arm around her waist and flung her at the cement wall, knocking the wind from her.

As she coughed and sputtered, he grabbed her wrist chains and pulled her down the hallway, bare feet trailing behind her. Once again, he left the basement door open.

Inside the slaughter room, he lowered the Chinese man and carried his lifeless body across the room, skirting the river of blood that had flowed down to the metal drain. He dropped the man on the table for gutting. But first he must drain the Korean woman.

Some of the fire had returned to her eyes. She scrambled on all fours toward the open doorway, but not fast enough. A moderate blow to the back of the head with the sap took the fight out of her mind and the flight out of her limbs. By the time she had recovered her senses, she hung upside down in midair, and he stood aside so she could see past the open doorway down the hall to the other open doorway.

Her gaze shifted to him, terror in her eyes as she beheld his inhuman countenance. She overcame her terror long enough to gasp, "Why?"

"Because I'm not done."

"No."

"I'm going back again."

"Oh, no, please no, don't, no."

He crouched beside her, so his Wesen face loomed over hers—all the more strange to her for being inverted. "Yes."

"No, you bastard! You filthy bastard!"

"For the boy."

She squeezed her eyes shut and screamed at him—

And then the tip of his blade sliced into her throat.

Her eyes snapped open in shock. But her screaming had stopped. Her voice reduced to a string of coughing gurgles and gasps. Then, finally, her bleating stopped.

As she bled out, he strode down the hall and retrieved the boy.

CHAPTER SEVENTEEN

Nick would have had a restful night's sleep, but Juliette kept her word and woke him at regular intervals during the night, to make sure he could be roused, basically. His head injury meant he was at risk of internal bleeding and swelling around the brain. Dire stuff. Except, Nick had been confident in his recovery. He'd had no more than soreness around his stitched scalp, not even a headache really—other than the fact that his head ached because his scalp had been ripped open and subsequently stitched back together.

Despite his interrupted sleep, Nick was touched by Juliette's concern. For so long, she had been ambivalent about him. And "ambivalent" was, at times, putting it kindly. Her memory issues had created havoc in their relationship—Adalind Schade's intention, naturally—so the change in their status was a balm, almost intoxicating.

He'd proposed to her once, but she'd sensed that he kept secrets from her and had turned him down. How could she marry a man she didn't know and therefore couldn't trust? But her recovery had stripped away the secrets that separated them. Their relationship had a much better foundation now than it had had before. So he was grateful for that, and grateful for her concern.

In the morning they shared coffee and toast, heavy on the coffee to compensate for the lack of sleep. Nick pressed his fingers gently against his stitched scalp and felt no swelling at all. The soreness was nothing more than tenderness now. He felt good.

"I think you should take the day off," Juliette said as she rinsed her mug in the sink.

"That's not necessary."

"Nick, somebody whacked you over the head with a crowbar," she said. "You should take it easy."

"It was more of a glancing blow."

"With a crowbar!"

"I can take it easy down at the precinct," he said and took the last bite of his toast. He carried his mug over to the sink, where she stood with her arms crossed over her chest. Placing his hands on her hips, he leaned forward and whispered in her ear, "I'm okay."

"Promise?"

"Yes."

"Let me see," she said.

"What?" he asked. "My head?"

She nodded.

He tucked his chin to his chest so she could inspect his scalp. A few seconds passed with the light touch of her fingers on his scalp, parting his hair around the stitched area.

"Hmm... you can hardly tell it needed stitches," she said.

"Looked worse than it is," Nick said. "Or it's healing fast."

"Okay, I'll drive you to the precinct," she said. "But remember, if you have any headaches, nausea or vision problems—"

"Right. I'll see a doctor."

· * * ·

Hank had left Nick's Land Cruiser at the precinct, so Juliette had agreed to drop Nick off at work. But he wanted to change his clothes, so he asked her to drop him off at Monroe's house. Because they were taking things slowly since she recovered her memories, he hadn't moved back home yet. But soon, he hoped.

Juliette waited in her Subaru Outback while Nick ran into Monroe's house and almost crashed into Monroe and Bud, the Eisbiber refrigerator repairman and one of the few Wesen to have woged for Juliette.

"Sorry," Nick said awkwardly, not expecting Monroe to have a visitor so early.

"Oh, hi, Nick," Bud said. "No problem. I dropped by to pick up my great grandfather's old pocket watch." He held up the reassembled antique.

"That 1887 Elgin is a real beauty," Monroe said. "Runs like new now."

"Thanks again, Monroe," Bud said, and nodded deferentially to Nick on his way out. "Good day to you, Nick."

"Thanks, Bud," Nick said, and, belatedly, "same to you."

"Hey, Nick," Monroe said. "How's the noggin?"

"You know about that?"

"Juliette mentioned it to Rosalee and, well, naturally Rosalee—just in passing, you know, not that we were gossiping about—"

Nick held up a hand. "That's all right, Monroe. I'm here for a change of clothes, that's all. Juliette's waiting in the car. She's driving me to the precinct."

"Right," Monroe said. "But a concussion is serious business, Nick. Maybe you should take the day off."

"Juliette put you up to this?" Nick asked, smiling.

"No. Not at all," Monroe said quickly. "But, you know, maybe you should listen to her."

"I'm fine, Monroe. Really."

"Gonna introduce me to your friend, Monroe?"

Nick turned, startled, as a tall, muscular man wearing a black watch cap, flannel shirt, worn jeans and boots stepped into the room. He could have been a biker or a longshoreman. Nick wondered if he was also a Blutbad. He gave off a Wesen vibe. Or maybe it was simply the fact that so many of Monroe's friends were Wesen.

"Of course. Nick, this is an old friend, Decker," Monroe said. "I haven't seen him in years. We've been… catching up. Decker, Nick is a Portland homicide detective."

"You don't say," Decker said, raising his eyebrows. "Homicide detective. Wow."

"What do you do for a living, Decker?" Nick asked.

"Odd jobs, mostly," Decker said, shrugging. "Manual labor. I've done a little bit of everything and anything that requires elbow grease and determination. How do you know Monroe?"

"I helped Nick out on a case," Monroe interrupted nonchalantly. "He's been staying with me for a little while until—until some things get worked out."

"Friends helping friends," Decker said. "That's what it's all about, man."

"Right," Nick said. "Didn't mean to interrupt. I'll be out of your way in a couple minutes."

"No problem, Nick," Monroe said. "Decker and I were about to check out a t'ai chi class."

"T'ai chi," Nick wondered. "Not Pilates?"

"Turns out Pilates isn't Decker's cup of tea," Monroe said. "But, it's a process, you know, finding the right thing."

Nick sensed a story lurked beneath the comment, and a bit of unspoken frustration, but he was running late and

Juliette was waiting outside, so he simply nodded, excused himself and headed to his room. By the time he'd changed and come back downstairs, Monroe and Decker had left. Nick locked the door on his way out.

When he climbed into the passenger seat, Juliette turned to him.

"That guy with Monroe…?"

"Decker," Nick said. "Old friend of Monroe's."

"Wesen?"

"Yes," Nick said, then backtracked. "Probably. I mean, I assumed he was but I didn't see him woge."

She nodded—still adjusting to the details of Nick's life as a Grimm—and pulled away from the curb.

Before leaving Nick at the Portland Police Department building, Juliette had him promise again that he'd take care and contact his doctor if he experienced any post-concussion symptoms. But considering her examination of the wound earlier, her concern seemed overly cautious. True, the real danger of concussions lay in what could happen beneath the skull, not what presented on the scalp. And yet, after that brief examination, she had a hard time believing he'd been hit over the head with a crowbar.

Nick had insisted it was a glancing blow and scalp wounds tended to bleed a lot. He'd been lucky, that's all. It could have been much worse. But it wasn't. She had to let it go. The problem might be in her own head. Fear of losing him again. Not to memory loss this time, but to some other mishap. And really, she couldn't think that way. Nick was a homicide detective and faced potentially dangerous situations all the time. She'd worry herself sick if she dwelled on all the things that could go wrong.

She stopped at Fuller's Coffee Shop before heading to Roseway Veterinary Hospital, and ordered the biggest cup of coffee they had. Nick had grumbled about his missed sleep, but her night had been worse in a way. She'd been so afraid of falling asleep and not waking him at regular intervals, she'd progressed through the entire night on a series of unsatisfying catnaps. When she'd slept long enough to actually slip into REM sleep, she'd had anxiety nightmares which startled her awake. In them, she'd forgotten to turn off the stove, or she'd misplaced test results, or Adalind Schade's cat crept through the house, waiting to pounce on her.

Overall, a restless night, and now she had visions of giving herself a caffeine IV as soon as she arrived at the clinic. Zoe, who staffed the reception desk, would understand. That girl knew how to burn the midnight oil, leaving no after-hours club unexamined until dawn's early light. Zoe often joked she was part-vampire. Juliette idly wondered if there were vampire Wesen. She'd have to remember to ask Nick. Good thing she hadn't thought of that last night, or it would have been more fuel for the nightmare fire.

She'd been hoping for a calm, going-through-the-motions day with maybe a lunchtime nap. Could she lock her office door and disconnect her phone? That idea transformed from wistful notion to something she intended to schedule on her calendar as soon as she sat down to finish her coffee. And evaporated five minutes into her shift.

She heard a woman sobbing in the hallway and, without stepping out of her office, Juliette knew.

"Oh, no," she whispered.

She took a deep breath and returned to the reception area to greet the Bremmers.

But this time, Melinda had come alone with Roxy. Melinda crouched beside the dog, down on one knee, petting her head. Lethargic, Roxy hardly moved, barely a flutter to her closed eyes, a slight twitch of one ear.

Melinda looked up at Juliette. Tears had streamed down her cheeks, creating dark streaks of mascara. At that moment, Juliette doubted the woman cared much about her appearance. She was consumed with grief for her dog.

"She's just like before," Melinda said. "One good day, and now…"

"Roger," Juliette said. "Give me a hand."

Roger nodded, left his computer station behind the reception desk with Zoe to help Juliette carry the yellow lab back to the examination room. Melinda followed, fingers pressed to her face.

"After Barry left for work, I realized she hadn't come downstairs."

With a sympathetic look, Roger backed out of the room and closed the door behind him.

"Logan filled her bowl before he left, but she hadn't eaten anything," Melinda continued. "I found her upstairs, in Logan's room. She'd vomited on the floor. For a moment, I thought she—she was so still, I thought—but she was trembling, weak."

All of the dog's original symptoms had returned. She'd had a one-day reprieve, a complete turnaround, and now this. Juliette remembered telling herself not to question a "win" but now it seemed as if that turnaround had never happened.

"I thought it was a miracle, how she recovered," Melinda said, stroking the dog's coat over and over as she spoke. "We kept her away from Logan's car and its leaky radiator. She stayed out of the garage. We made sure of it. We were so grateful, we never wanted anything like that to happen again. But now—now, I don't know how I can tell Barry and Logan that she's… how can I tell them?"

Juliette had placed her palm on the miserable dog's head, feeling the warmth of its life against her skin. She wanted more than anything to give Melinda back her miracle and somehow restore Roxy's health. But the pragmatic part of her acknowledged the dog was running out of options, and cautioned her against offering another dose of false hope. If nothing else, she could give Melinda and her family a little more time to adjust to what was happening.

"Leave her with me," Juliette said. "Let me run some tests, so we know exactly what we're dealing with."

"O—okay," Melinda said, swiping at tears and making the mascara streaks more pronounced than before. "You'll call me…? When you know?"

Juliette nodded. "As soon as I know something, I'll call."

As the woman bowed down to kiss the dog's head and whisper in her ear, Juliette reached for a box of tissues on the nearby counter and handed them to the woman.

"Thank you," Melinda said, first blowing her nose, then wiping her eyes with fresh tissues.

"You'll be okay driving?"

Melinda nodded. "That I can manage," she said. "The rest…? I don't know."

"We'll get through this," Juliette said. "We'll do what's best for Roxy."

Melinda pressed the wad of mascara-stained tissues against her lips to stifle a sob. Then she nodded several times, a motion stiff with suppressed emotion. Juliette hugged her. Not a strictly professional response, maybe, but a human one. And, at the moment, that was all she had to offer.

CHAPTER EIGHTEEN

As soon as he arrived at the precinct, Nick checked his desk and his email inbox for any updates. The first message he read contained discouraging news. The scrap of faux-parchment paper with the geometric symbols and possible numeric sequence or code that Nick had bagged at the vacant lot came back negative for prints. Likely exposed to the elements for weeks, the paper's only evidential value— if it had any at all—was in the images printed on the paper. Proximity to the dump site was the only connection between the scrap of paper and the murders. But anyone who passed by the lot could have been the source of the litter. And, honestly, the paper could have been blowing in the wind for weeks before coming to rest in the lot.

Captain Renard had commandeered a conference room as a war room of sorts for the bare bones murder investigation. Two large freestanding corkboards stood side by side, blocking a set of windows, one for each burial site. As dental record matches came back, names and photos of the victims filled the boards. Similarly, stacks of case folders and open missing person files began to accumulate on the long conference room table.

Over a dozen sets of remains had been found at the vacant lot site—including a family of three tossed into one group mound—which appeared to predate the Claremont Park site. Bones from the vacant lot were three to four weeks old, whereas the Claremont Park victims had been buried within the past two weeks. A GPR team had located two more sets of bones at the park site.

With information accumulating quickly, Nick and Hank had, for all intents and purposes, moved into the conference room, forwarding their desk phone calls to the conference room lines. Wu continued to bring them forensic updates and missing person files, while Captain Renard appeared to demand update requests every few hours.

Wu rapped on the doorframe.

Nick looked up from a stack of folders.

"Patrol unit spotted Sheila Jenkins' car outside a twenty-four-hour pharmacy," Wu informed him. "Lot's never completely empty, so nobody reported it. But a store employee recalled seeing it there the day before. Chalked it up to car trouble."

"Don't suppose the vic's head or hands were in the car," Nick said.

"Crime scene's dusting for prints, checking for fibers, blood, bodily fluids and so on," Wu said. "But anything as large as a head or a pair of hands, they would have noticed by now."

"So that's a 'no,'" Hank said, sitting within arm's reach of his crutches but nowhere near his sense of humor. It had been one of those days.

"Any news on the other vics?" Nick asked.

"More dental record matches are coming in," Wu said, flipping through his notes. "Monica Jackson; African American female; twenty-five; on vacation from Atlanta, Georgia with three friends. Friends went whitewater rafting. Monica opted out, took a winery tour instead. Never returned to their hotel room.

"We've also got a family of three on vacation, cross-country drive from Delaware, camping, hiking, et cetera. Nikos... Kostopoulos, his wife, Sophia, and fourteen-year-old son, Stephen. Wife's sister had been feeding the son's pet guinea pigs. She reported the family missing after a week with no contact." He flipped a page. "And yet another vacationer, also recovered from the second site; Steve Phan, Vietnamese amateur nature photographer. Quite a following at some of the online photo sharing sites. Last image he posted is almost four weeks old."

Nick took the photos Wu had brought with the IDs and posted them on the second corkboard. A few others located in the vacant lot had come back as vacationers. Nick walked over to the first board, which displayed photos of Marie Chang and Luis Posada, plus two index cards with question marks for the most recent victims.

"You can replace one of the question marks," Wu said, taking another photo out of the folder he carried. "Lee Mi-Sun, forty-two-year-old unmarried Korean woman, manager of Little Shop of Gifts. She locked up the shop ten days ago. Never heard from again. Owner found her keys on the ground outside the locked door. Probably grabbed while her back was turned."

Nick took the woman's photo and placed it on the Claremont Park board, next to Chang and Posada. Then he stepped back to study the whole picture.

"Looks like the killer changed his MO," Nick said. "The older site—the vacant lot—is filled with the remains of tourists. As if the killer spent time stalking people whose absence might go unnoticed for a while."

Hank nodded. "People out of touch with work and family."

"No cause for alarm," Wu added. "Even vacation postcards take forever in the mail."

"Then two weeks ago, give or take," Nick continued, "he switches dumping ground."

"Tag team killers," Wu suggested. "First hands it off to the second."

"That's not it," Nick said. "Bones are prepared the same, buried the same way. That part stays consistent."

"He switched because he's nervous," Hank said. "Too many bodies buried in one place. Doesn't want to risk more trips there."

"Maybe somebody noticed," Wu said. "Spooked him."

"Both good reasons," Nick said. "But he's also changed victim profiles. Now he's killing locals."

"People who will be missed sooner," Hank said.

"He's impatient," Wu said, spitballing. "Accelerating his routine."

"No," Nick said. "That's not it. Too many bodies at the first site. His pace hasn't accelerated. It was fast from the start."

"Then what?" Hank asked. As Nick's partner, he could tell when Nick was working toward a conclusion.

"He doesn't care anymore."

"About being caught?" Wu asked, confused.

"That's not it," Hank said. "Is it, Nick?"

Nick shook his head. "The shallow graves bothered me," he said. "Short term concealment at best. Storms, heavy rains, foraging animals, dogs out for a walk. You name it. Those bodies would be discovered sooner rather than later." Nick tapped the Claremont Park board. "He's taking locals now because his timeframe is shorter."

"What timeframe?" Hank asked, giving Nick a curious look after a brief glance at Wu to see if he'd caught on.

Probably wondering if I have some previously

undisclosed Grimm power of psychic intuition, Nick thought. But he was spitballing as well, same as Hank and Wu.

"I don't know," Nick said. "Not exactly. But the reason why he's killing them, whatever it is, it's almost over."

Wu frowned. "What if his reason for killing is that he's a howling-at-the-moon, live-bug-eating maniac?"

Hank indicated the two boards with a sweep of his hand.

"He doesn't have a type," Hank said. "Adults, teens— even children. Male and female. Multiple ethnicities."

"An equal opportunity psychopath," Wu concluded.

Hank shook his head, deflated. "There's no pattern."

"Maybe that's the point," Nick said. "Variety."

The conference room phone rang. He leaned across the table and picked it up.

"Detective Burkhardt."

"Hello, Detective. Harper here."

Nick covered the receiver. "Medical examiner," he said to Hank. Then, "Dr. Harper. Good news, I hope."

"Got something on the bare bones cases I think you should see."

"I'll be right there."

"Give it up, brother," Decker said.

He was sitting in the Super Beetle passenger seat beside Monroe on their way to the T'ai Chi Circle Center, his knee bouncing up and down with nervous energy. Now and then he started slapping his palm against his knee, as if keeping time with a tune playing in his head.

"What?"

"How the hell long have you been bosom buddies with a genuine Portland homicide detective?"

"Not long," Monroe said. "Long enough."

"Is he...?"

"What?"

"You know. One of us?"

"Blutbad? Nick?" Monroe asked and chuckled. "No. No way."

"Not a Fuchsbau?" Decker asked. "Like that gal of yours—Rosemarie?"

"Rosalee," Monroe corrected reflexively. He'd only mentioned Rosalee in passing, accidentally, not wanting his old life to confront his new one. He didn't want to reminisce about the bad old days, and that's inevitably what would happen if his two worlds collided.

"No, Nick's not Wesen," Monroe said, preferring to end the discussion about Nick without letting slip that he was a Grimm. Decker might freak out or lapse or— Monroe had no idea how he'd react and didn't want to find out. But Decker refused to abandon the topic.

"Interesting," he said. "So your life on the wagon involves friendship with local law enforcement. That a case of keeping your enemies closer?"

"Nick's not an enemy," Monroe said, growing frustrated with Decker's us-versus-them mindset. "Look, he's a friend, simple as that. We met over a case. I didn't plan it. Just one of those random, serendipitous things, you know? You meet new people. It happens. I do have other human friends."

"Like who?"

"Well, for instance, Juliette," Monroe said.

"And she's…?"

"Nick's girlfriend."

"Ah. I see. Anyone else?"

"Sure," Monroe said, immediately drawing a blank. "Hank Griffin."

"Right," Decker said. "And this Hank guy—you met him how?"

"I—bumped into him once," Monroe said, recalling the time Hank first saw him woge in the woods.

"That's the only—?"

"Okay, he's Nick's partner."

"Another cop," Decker said. "Dude, are you some kind of informant?"

"What—? No, I'm not an informant—what would I inform about? And do cops live in the same house as their informants?"

"I wouldn't know, bro."

"Look," Monroe said, relieved. "We're here."

He pulled into the first parking space he saw in the studio's lot, and hoped management wasn't Facebook friends with the folks at Portland Precision Pilates or they'd get tossed out on their ears before the class even began.

As they approached the front door, Decker massaged his lower back with both palms, flashed a wince of pain. He caught Monroe staring at him.

"What?" he asked.

"You ready for this?"

"Sure," Decker said. "Why not?"

"Are you in pain?"

"A bit sore," Decker said. "Long nights. Not enough sleep. That's all."

Inside, they moved to the back of the classroom. Again, Monroe thought to limit Decker's exposure and potential embarrassment. Plus, he could mimic those in front of him without worrying about anybody criticizing his form.

"This is a beginner's class," Monroe said. "It's about slow movement, controlled and smooth. Okay?"

"Relax," Decker said. "No sweat. I got this."

Monroe believed him.

He should have known better.

This time, Decker lasted about five minutes. But

it wasn't the difficulty of the moves or postures that bedeviled him, it was the movement itself, the slowness and steadiness of it. He began to exaggerate the leaning and weaving, the crouching and arm motions, turning it into a mocking pantomime. The instructor tried to correct him, assuming the exaggeration was a lack of refinement or understanding rather than a direct insult to the whole process. Then Decker took it too far, lost his balance and crashed into Monroe, who staggered and bumped the woman beside him.

Everyone looked at the disturbance, briefly, before turning their attention back to the instructor. But Decker shook his head in frustration.

"Look at you people! What the hell are we doing here? Everyone prancing in slow freaking motion! You look silly, you know that, right? You look like you're dancing underwater with an itch you can't scratch."

"Decker!" Monroe grabbed his arm, tried to pull him back to his former spot on the exercise floor.

"No, Monroe," Decker said angrily. "This is some kind of joke, right? A reality show. Where are the hidden cameras? C'mon, where are they? Because I know people are watching us right now and laughing their asses off."

"Sir, you need to leave," the instructor said. "Now."

"Okay, Sensei Water-Dancer," Decker said with a mock salute as he headed toward the exit with plodding steps. "Watch me as I walk out of here in"—he dragged the last two words out like aural taffy—"*slow motion.*"

Monroe backed out of the room, at a normal pace.

"He's been off his meds for twenty-four hours, and *this* happens." He called over his shoulder, "I warned you! 'Taper off,' I said, 'Don't go cold turkey.'" Then, to the class: "I'm truly sorry about this. Please, accept my apology. Forget this ever happened and go on about your day."

Two days, two life-time bans, Monroe stewed as he hurried to the parking lot. *At this rate, I'll need to leave Portland before the week's up.*

Nick found Dr. Harper in the morgue of the Medical Examiner Office building, wearing her usual white lab coat, red hair pinned up in its usual bun. What he found unusual was the row of stainless steel gurneys holding skeletons rather than draped cadavers.

Though the skeletons were in pieces—with long bones bisected—somebody, or, more likely, a team of somebodies, had placed all the bones in the proper alignment. The process would allow the medical examiner to discover any missing bones, and likely establish probable cause of death. But the effect was eerie, reminding Nick of the skeleton army brought to life with Ray Harryhausen's stop-motion animation in *Jason and the Argonauts*. He shook off the odd feeling. These skeletons were destined for proper graves. But with their help, in the clues they provided, Nick hoped to bring their killer to justice.

Dr. Harper called him over to a computer display at the far end of the morgue.

"What have you got?" Nick asked.

"You know about the boiling of the bones," she said and he nodded, even though it hadn't been a question. "Boiled until the remaining flesh came off."

"Remaining?"

"Any flesh that didn't come off during the manual removal."

"The murderer stripped the flesh from the bones?"

"Chopped the bones, then stripped them," she said. "I'm fairly certain the chopping was done with a meat cleaver. Clean breaks."

She clicked on a computer screen and brought up a slide

show of magnified images of chopped bones, zoomed in to the point of separation.

"One blow, right through flesh and bone, no splintering or second hacks," she said, sounding clinically impressed. "Incredible force."

She switched images.

"But now that I've had more time to examine the bones—and more bones to examine—I noticed some saw marks along the spine, through many of the ribs." She tapped the screen with the tip of her index finger, pointing out the marks on the ribs. "I match those to a common butcher's meat saw."

She looked at him expectantly. "Meat cleaver, meat saw, boiling bones. You see how this adds up?"

He did. He'd discussed with Monroe the possibility of a Wesen with a taste for human flesh. Given what he'd witnessed so far as a Grimm, not a big leap of deduction to go there. Now, with the medical examiner's conclusion on record, the whole department would know; one step closer to a press leak and outside exposure. And that made a Grimm-like resolution to the problem all the more difficult.

He sighed in resignation and said, "We're dealing with a cannibal."

Her gaze traveled meaningfully down the row of skeletons on gurneys.

"By the looks of it, this cannibal has a big appetite."

CHAPTER NINETEEN

Decker was leaning against the front of the Super Beetle, arms crossed over his chest. He shook his head as Monroe approached.

"What the hell was that?" he demanded.

"I was about to ask you the same question," Monroe replied, unwilling to excuse his friend's tantrum. "Are you even trying?"

"I showed up."

"That's about all you did."

"That—in there—will never get me to reform," Decker said. "That is not me, okay? It's like exercising on Valium, all that slow motion nonsense. I need action." He made a fist and struck the open palm of his other hand. "I need to punch something, kick something."

"If you're thinking mixed martial arts," Monroe said. "I'd advise against it."

"Why not, man?" Decker asked. "Hard contact. Takedowns. I'm there!"

"You don't treat alcoholism with six-packs of beer."

Decker spread his arms and smiled. "What about light beer?"

Monroe shook his head. "That's it. I'm done."

He climbed into the driver's seat and started the car. Decker scrambled around to the passenger side door and hopped in.

"C'mon bro, I'm kidding."

"I agreed to help you reform," Monroe said, staring straight ahead. "You don't care about this and that's fine for you, to each his own path. I never asked you to do this. You asked for my help. If I have to drag you kicking and screaming, well, it won't work. You can't reform unless you want to and clearly that's not part of your agenda. So let's end this little experiment."

"Monroe," Decker said. "Brother?"

Monroe finally turned to look at him.

"What is this really about? We were friends once, but that doesn't make us friends now. We've gone our separate ways. We're different people."

"You can look me in the eye and say it wasn't hard for you?" Decker said. "Changing everything about who you really are?"

"Of course it was—*is*—hard," Monroe said. "But it's something I chose. Nobody forced me to change, and nobody has a gun to my head now. It's still my choice and I work at it every day, to be the man I prefer to be. I like my life the way it is. If you're happy with the way you are, it's not up to me to change your mind. This path has to come from within."

"No arguments here, brother," Decker said. "I dragged my ass out of bed these past two mornings to try this stuff, right?"

"Yes."

"That's me trying."

"But, honestly, Decker, that's not enough," Monroe said. "Not nearly enough." He sighed, palms pressed against the steering wheel. He sat with the engine idling, as if balanced on the precipice of a decision and shifting into drive meant an ending. "You have to want it more."

"Are you quitting on me, Monroe?"

"You haven't started yet," Monroe said. "So how can I quit on you?"

"How can you say that?"

"When's the last time you ate meat?"

"Not a bite since breakfast," Decker said with a sly smile.

Monroe failed to see the funny side.

"You know what? This was a bad idea."

He shifted the car into drive and steered out of the parking lot, placing his attention exclusively on the flow of traffic. If he'd seen a bit of himself in Decker, an attempt to change his ways, he'd imagined it. That was the only explanation that made sense. The veil of self-delusion lifted, Monroe would turn the page on the old friendship. As Decker often said: *Eyes forward, full bore, no regrets.*

After a couple minutes of awkward silence, Decker spoke. "Don't you miss it?"

"I don't dwell on it," Monroe said. "I focus on what I have now."

"Ever fall off the wagon?" Decker asked. "Or are you perfect, Monroe? Not a chink in your Blutbad chastity belt."

"Aside from the fact that you're mixing metaphors," Monroe said, "nobody's perfect. If you fall off the wagon, you have to want to get back on. That's how we're different."

"Maybe," Decker said. "What's that expression? Have the courage of your convictions?"

"Yeah, something like that," Monroe said, experiencing a wave of genuine sadness. Not easy, giving up on someone whose friendship you once valued. "Gotta have that."

Decker massaged his right hand with his left, staring down, falling silent for a couple minutes. When he spoke again, his voice was subdued, the bravado gone.

"I love it, you know. The thrill of it. I never want to give that up."

"I understand," Monroe said with a slight nod. He'd changed, but many Wesen never could or never wanted to. They thought it went against their nature. And that was hard to argue. But the right choices were often the hard ones. Otherwise, everyone would always do the right thing.

"But sometimes, I worry I'll go too far," Decker continued softly. "A point of no return. Hell, maybe I've already gone too far. Never been a choirboy."

"Are you talking about redemption?" Monroe asked. "Because if that's what this is about, you're putting way too much pressure on yourself. It's like that riddle, 'How do you eat an elephant?'" He glanced at Decker, who stared back at him as if he'd sprouted a second head. "What? You never heard that expression?"

"No. But you're making me hungry."

"The answer is, 'One bite at a time.'" Monroe said. "When the problem is too big to handle all at once, you tackle it one bit at a time."

"Baby steps?"

"Exactly."

"So, if you, for example, happened to fall off the wagon, you could climb back on the next day?"

"Uh, sure, okay," Monroe said, not sure where Decker's line of reasoning was headed. "But I don't think that way. That's not how I approach life. It's not okay to 'cheat' today because I can be good tomorrow."

"But, theoretically you could cheat," Decker said. "And that would be okay."

"Well, theoretically, maybe—in hindsight—but not in a premeditated way. But I think you're splitting hairs. What's your point?"

"I'm on the outside, looking in," Decker said. "You

wake up in the morning and see another day to stay reformed. But me? I look at each day and ask myself how I can stop being—unreformed."

"One bite at a time."

Decker chuckled. "Trying to figure out that first bite is the killer."

"What about meditation?" Monroe said. "Ever try it? No straining, no awkward postures, no slow motion. Just sit and relax and focus. You need to find a way to stay calm within yourself."

"No stupid stuff?" Decker asked. "Sitting still? That's it."

"As far as the physical aspect, yes," Monroe said. He tapped his temple. "The rest is up here."

"No more classes with a bunch of posers?"

"We could meditate in my house," Monroe said, not quite believing he hadn't shut the door on his involvement in Decker's life once and for all. "No outsiders."

"Okay," Decker said, slapping his knee. "Sounds like a plan."

"Great," Monroe said, while inwardly cringing at his inability to admit enough was enough. But he could accelerate the process. "I have some errands to run, but let's meet later. How about meditation and dinner? I'll cook. A zero-stress evening will make for a good start."

"Fantastic, brother."

Lacking Decker's enthusiasm, Monroe's thoughts skipped ahead to the inevitable disappointment to come. *Three strikes and I'm officially out. If meditation fails to make an impression on Decker, I'm the wrong mentor. One way or the other, after tonight, I'm done.*

Then, strangely, Decker's words intruded on this feeling of impending release. *"I love it, you know. The thrill of it... Theoretically, you could cheat. And that would be okay."*

Monroe had the disturbing notion that the seeds of his

own corruption had been planted: self-doubt, temptation, rationalization. And a more unsettling thought followed. Who was mentoring whom?

His grip on the steering wheel tightened.

Nick returned to the precinct and updated Renard and Hank on the coroner's findings. As Nick suspected, Renard embargoed the word 'cannibal' when dealing with the press.

"That's a theory," he'd said. "No more than that. We don't speculate on the reason for the murders."

Not that Nick or Hank planned on making any statements to the press. That was the captain's prerogative and he was welcome to it. But reporters sometimes bypassed official press conferences in favor of a well-timed ambush interview. So Renard made sure the detectives knew the party line.

Back in the conference room, Hank asked, "So, we dealing with a Wesen cannibal or a human cannibal?"

"Does it matter?" Nick said, thinking only of the end result.

"Speaking as a non-Grimm," Hank said, "yes, it matters. Wesen play by different rules. Don't want to bring a knife to a gun fight."

"Smart money's on the Wesen," Nick said, but didn't elaborate as he spotted Wu veering toward the conference room, case folders tucked under his arm.

"More dental record matches?" Nick asked the sergeant.

"No," Wu said. "This is something else."

"Go ahead."

"The rash of disappearances got me thinking," Wu said. "When did the uptick start?"

"A month ago," Hank said, glancing at Nick for confirmation. "About the time our vacant lot victims started disappearing."

"Right," Wu said. "But the trend actually began a little before that. I noticed something weird in the files from five weeks ago."

"How weird?" Nick wondered. After all, they had reports of at least two people coming back from the dead and a Cracher-Mortel on the loose. Weird was relative.

"A delivery man disappeared," Wu said. "Hauling industrial-grade restaurant equipment to a new place opening in Portland. The shipment never arrived. Truck was found lying on its side at the bottom of a ravine, abandoned and empty. No sign of the driver."

"Hijacked?" Hank asked.

"That was the theory at the time," Wu said. "Nothing else indicated. Restaurant supplier assumed the driver was killed offsite, or that the hijacking was an inside job."

"Restaurant equipment," Nick said. "Even if he split a black market sale with a single accomplice, how much could he have netted? Ten thousand? Twenty?"

"Hardly enough to retire in luxury," Hank said.

"Driver have any gambling debts?"

"Nothing that turned up," Wu said. "Financially stable, retirement accounts, manageable credit card debt."

"So back to option one," Hank said. "Hijacker murdered the driver, dumped the body elsewhere."

"Industrial restaurant equipment," Nick said, shaking his head. "Can't be easy to move that kind of stuff. And it comes back to the money. Something doesn't add up."

"Unless it does," Hank said. "Cannibal killer. New restaurant opening. Don't make me do the math."

Nick turned to Wu. "You have a name and address for that restaurant?"

"Yes, it's in the file," Wu said. "But they never received the shipment."

"Maybe not," Nick said. "But they knew it was coming."

CHAPTER TWENTY

Unfortunately, Roxy's test results came back as Juliette had expected, showing the six-year-old labrador back in kidney failure. She'd had a remarkable twenty-four-hour reprieve after the aggressive IV treatment, but that's all it had been. For one day the Bremmers had had the illusion of a miracle cure. In a way, that had made the obligatory phone call to Melinda Bremmer even crueler. To nurture hope and to have that hope rewarded, only to see it snatched away just as abruptly... Juliette wondered if it would have been kinder on her part to not have suggested the IV treatment. She'd done nothing more than postpone the inevitable heartache. Now, after throwing the Bremmers' emotions in a blender, she'd called Melinda to recommend euthanasia for the dog.

Melinda tearfully asked for a few hours to round up her husband and son. She knew they'd want to say goodbye to their dog one last time, to witness the end.

Of course, Juliette gave her that time. How could she not? But sitting around waiting for them to arrive was more than Juliette herself could handle. She told Zoe and Roger she'd be back after lunch and to keep an eye on Roxy while she was gone. Roger said, "No problem," without looking up from his computer display, but Zoe, more attuned to Juliette's mood and the ongoing situation with Roxy and the Bremmers, asked if Juliette wanted company for lunch.

"Thanks, Zoe," Juliette said, "but I'm meeting someone. Rain check?"

"Sure," Zoe said with a bright nod.

In truth, Juliette hadn't called Rosalee about having lunch together, and doubted she'd have someone available to cover the spice shop, but she hoped the other woman would make some time for her. Juliette thought talking to a fellow healer might help her ride out the dismal day. While Rosalee wasn't a doctor, per se, she certainly had experience healing Wesen of various non-human maladies. Plus, she had cured Juliette's memory loss and the unnatural obsession she'd shared with Nick's captain. Rosalee's specialty was healing that for which traditional medicine had no answer, let alone a cure.

When Juliette entered the Exotic Spice & Tea Shop, she saw the portly, grandfatherly gentleman—she remembered Rosalee had said his name was Oscar Cavendish—in one of the aisles, but no other customers. Juliette made her way to the counter, offering a little wave when Rosalee glanced up from a magazine she'd been skimming.

"Oh, hi, Juliette!" Rosalee said. "This is a surprise."

"Sorry about not calling ahead." She raised a large white paper bag. "Didn't know if you could get away, so I brought veggie wraps and salads—hope that's not too redundant—and some bottled water. Thought we could share a stand-up lunch."

"Nonsense," Rosalee said. "I've got a spare stool around here somewhere."

Rosalee disappeared for a moment in the back room and came back with a three-legged stool, tall enough for her to sit comfortably behind the counter.

"So, what brings you down my way?"

"A really awful day," Juliette said. "I had to call a family and give them some bad news."

"Oh, no, not the lab."

Juliette nodded as she reached into the bag for the wraps and plastic containers of salad.

"One good day, then they brought her back in again this morning, almost worse than before. It feels worse."

"I'm sorry," Rosalee said, accepting a water bottle from Juliette and setting it beside her portion of the food. "There's nothing else you can do?"

Juliette shook her head, dejectedly. She had her food laid out before her but no appetite.

"I ran the tests again. Same result. Kidney failure."

The older gentlemen approached the counter, carrying several jars of spices.

"I don't want to disturb your impromptu lunch, so let me pay for these and be on my way," he said.

"Find everything you need?" Rosalee asked as she stepped over to the cash register.

"Yes, thank you," Cavendish said. "I'm experimenting with different flavor combinations. With delectable results."

"Good for you," Rosalee said. She placed the jars in a paper bag and read him the total amount due.

As he removed a billfold from his jacket pocket, he said, "I'm curious, Ms...?"

"Calvert," Rosalee said.

"Yes, Calvert," he said, handing her two twenties. "I had heard that a Frederick Calvert owned this shop."

"Freddy was my brother."

"I note the past tense...?"

Rosalee nodded, and gave him his change.

"Yes, he—he's no longer with us."

"I am sorry for your loss, Ms. Calvert."

"Thank you," she said, passing his bag over the counter. "After his passing, I inherited the shop."

"Ah," the portly man said, nodding. "Well, you have a wonderful place." After she thanked him, he leaned forward and spoke softly, clearly intending that Juliette not overhear. "I've heard rumors, about certain… exotic items for sale."

Rosalee glanced awkwardly at Juliette before replying. "After Freddy's death, we stopped carrying… those particular items."

"Very good," Cavendish said. "Of course, I understand why you'd rather not follow in those footsteps. And I'm not personally in the market for such things. But some rumors provide a person of my advanced age a certain vicarious thrill to hear about."

"I understand," Rosalee said, but her body language had become stiff. "Have a great day, Mr. Cavendish."

"Thank you," he said on his way out. "Enjoy your meal."

After the door clicked shut, Juliette asked, "What was that about?"

"Freddy had a little side business going," Rosalee said. "Selling… controlled substances. Having that kind of thing in the shop resulted in his death."

"I'm sorry."

"It's okay," Rosalee said, jabbing a plastic fork into her lettuce. "I hadn't pictured Mr. Cavendish as the type who'd—maybe he was only looking for some juicy gossip." She took a bite of her wrap and a sip of water. "You were talking about the dog. Kidney failure. You made the call…?"

"Yes," Juliette said. "The whole family is coming in later. I had to get out of the office. To try and stop thinking about it. But they were so upset, I can't think about anything else."

"You've done all you can. Right?"

Juliette nodded. "I don't understand the sudden recovery. I think that bothers me the most. It seems so… cruel."

"Life isn't always fair," Rosalee said. "Sometimes it's the opposite of fair."

"I know," Juliette said, taking a bite of her own wrap and finding it flavorless. "But I have this feeling…" She groaned. "I don't know. It's like an itch I can't scratch."

Rosalee took a bite of lettuce, then pointed the empty tines of the fork toward Juliette. "Maybe there's something there that you can't see from the test results, but subconsciously you know it's… off."

Juliette raised her eyebrows. "Like what?"

"It's definitely kidney failure?"

"Yes," Juliette said, shrugging. "All the classic symptoms are present. And the tests confirm it."

"Both sets of tests were the same?"

"Yes—well, mostly the same," Juliette said. "They wouldn't be exactly the same. Some indicators were different."

"Different how?"

Juliette had read the results several times and they were imprinted in her mind. Closing her eyes, she could see the odd numbers again: sodium 128, potassium 6.9, blood sugar 56mg/dL.

"Sodium very low, potassium very high, and blood sugar quite low. Those results were new."

"And what do these different results tell you?"

"Well, there's no chance that anti-freeze ingestion was involved, which was our original concern. And there's no sign of infection."

"That part sounds good," Rosalee said. "But what does it all mean?"

"It means I'm stumped," Juliette said. "It's a bit odd,

but doesn't change the outcome."

"Unless it does," Rosalee said, before taking another bite of her wrap.

"But I keep coming back to kidney failure. That's terminal."

"Juliette, what am I?"

"You're a friend. Rosalee Calvert. Shop owner. Entrepreneur."

"And?"

"A Wesen," Juliette said, smiling. "A Fuchsbau." That revelation had been such a huge moment in Juliette's Grimm and Wesen enlightenment. And here they were, having lunch together, as if none of that mattered. And, truly, it didn't.

"Everything isn't always what it appears to be on the surface," Rosalee said. "How long did you know me before you knew that about me? And you might never have known…"

A hidden nature beneath the surface, Juliette considered. Could Roxy have a condition that presented as kidney failure but wasn't?

"I need to do some research."

"That's a good idea," Rosalee said and finished her wrap. "I wish I could help, but that's way outside my area of expertise."

"You may have helped more than you know," Juliette said. "I need to go."

"Thanks for lunch!" Rosalee called as Juliette hurried out of the shop.

On the way to her car, Juliette called Melinda Bremmer on her cell phone.

"Melinda, I'm so glad I caught you."

"Has something happened to Roxy?"

"No," Juliette said, hoping that was true. "She's the same."

"You're still going to wait for us before—before you…?"

"Yes, of course," Juliette said. "But I want to check something before we… take that course of action."

"Okay," Melinda said. "But I'm not sure what you're…"

"I need to research a few of the… anomalous test results," Juliette said, again treading the fine line between pursuing all avenues of inquiry and offering false hope.

"What are you saying?"

"I want to check some results," Juliette said. "And depending on what I find, I might need to run some more tests on Roxy."

Juliette needed to buy time so she could discover the root cause of her misgivings about the diagnosis, but without getting the Bremmers' hopes up, only to crush them again later. Even if she found something else responsible for the dog's condition, a different diagnosis might be just as deadly.

"More tests?" Melinda said. "She's suffering, though, isn't she?"

Juliette stopped short, her car key in the door lock.

"Yes," she admitted. She took a deep, silent breath, exhaling slowly. "But… I don't want to give up on Roxy until I've answered some lingering questions."

Melinda was silent for so long Juliette thought she'd lost the connection. Then she worried that Melinda would choose to end Roxy's suffering now rather than prolong her pain. She was about to ask Melinda to reconsider when the other woman spoke.

"I haven't called them yet," Melinda said. "To tell them."

"Oh."

"I couldn't do it over the phone," Melinda said. "I wanted… I wanted them safely home before…"

"Melinda…"

"No, it's okay," Melinda said. "I wanted them safe, together with me, before I told them." She made a snuffling noise on the line, like a burst of static. "We don't want her to suffer"—her voice caught—"but we'll wait for them to come home. Can you have the answers by then?"

"Yes," Juliette said, too quickly. She hadn't framed the questions yet. She couldn't know what tests to run until she understood what troubled her about the dog's condition.

The clock was ticking. She couldn't return to the clinic fast enough.

Judging by the dark windows and the empty parking lot behind the corner building, the restaurant was closed. Nick pulled the Land Cruiser into the spot closest to the side of the building.

"Sure this is the right address?" he asked.

Hank double-checked the piece of paper Wu had handed him back at the precinct.

"It's what it says here," Hank said. "Whether it's right or not, I don't know."

"Maybe Crawford's inside, waiting for us," Nick said, but had his doubts. No other cars in the lot. Unless the man had a driver drop him off or walked to the restaurant on foot, the place was deserted. "If you want to wait here, I'll check."

"Are you kidding me?" Hank said, grabbing his crutches from the back seat. "After the forest paths and hills and muddy lots? This is a paved lot and a level sidewalk."

"Knock yourself out," Nick said.

They walked to the front of the building. A sign above the broad plate-glass windows proclaimed in two-foot high letters PORTLAND & SEA TAVERN. Other than the sign, nothing else about the building indicated that it had ever functioned as a dining establishment. A notice on the Plexiglas door said CLOSED.

Nick cupped his hand around his eyes and peered

through one of the broad windows into the dim interior. A rounded archway divided the open space into two sections. A door with a porthole window set in the back right wall might or might not lead into a kitchen. Twin doors in the back left were labeled as restrooms. In the center of the open area stood a folding metal card table with two chairs, one of them lying on its side.

"Anything?" Hank asked.

"Looks empty."

"In the back?" Hank said and swung his way over to the door. He rapped on the glass with his knuckles, loud enough to be heard by anyone in the building.

"Five weeks since they ordered the hijacked kitchen equipment," Nick said. "And nothing's in there. No tables or booths. No ordering counter or bar. No sign of a restaurant setup."

Hank rapped again, louder than before.

A minute passed.

Impatient, Nick pulled out his cell phone and said, "Read me Crawford's phone number."

Lamar Crawford had agreed to meet them at the restaurant, but hadn't told them it was closed—rather, that it had never opened. And now he was a no-show.

Hank read the number to Nick, who dialed and waited for Crawford to pick up.

"Hello?"

"Lamar Crawford?"

"Speaking," the man said. "How may I—?"

"This is Detective Burkhardt, Portland PD."

"Oh, Detective, I'm sorry, we were supposed to meet at… Ah, I've lost track of the time. I'm afraid I wasn't feeling up to the drive. Perhaps we could meet here, at my office."

"Give me the address."

CHAPTER TWENTY-ONE

Monroe dreaded the conversation he needed to have with Rosalee. Not so much for what he had to say but for what he had to leave unsaid. He wandered along an aisle, feigning interest in several jars filled with glittery powders, while she rang up the purchases of an embarrassed young couple who apparently shared some sort of Wesen infection involving hives and sneezing. Judging by their furtive glances around the shop, he figured they needed a few moments of privacy.

After the couple had left the shop clutching their remedies in twin bags, Monroe joined Rosalee behind the counter. Her broad, welcoming smile warmed his heart but made the topic of discussion harder to broach. Of course, she sensed his unease immediately.

"Monroe, what's wrong?"

He reminded himself to never play poker with her.

"Oh, nothing really..."

"I know your 'bad news' look," she said. "So how bad is it?"

"About tonight..."

"Tonight, I planned to cook dinner for you. I found this

recipe for…" Her voice trailed off and she frowned. "You won't be coming to dinner tonight, will you?"

"It's just that I, that old friend of mine who dropped by, I sort of promised I'd, you know, cook for him after we…" This time Monroe's voice faded. He cleared his throat and tried to start again.

Rosalee placed a hand on his chest.

"You haven't said much about this old friend."

"No," Monroe said. "He's an old friend from, well, an old friend. Someone I never intended to see again."

"I see," Rosalee said. And Monroe believed she had intuited just how "old" a friend he meant. Before she'd met Monroe, Rosalee had her own dark period, a time she wasn't proud of, same as Monroe. They had that in common, so she probably understood better than most what it meant for Monroe to hang around with somebody he knew during his own dark phase. "Monroe, are you…?"

"No, I haven't done anything," Monroe said. "I've been trying to help him."

"Help him?"

"Be more like me."

"He's a Blutbad?"

Monroe nodded. "Hardcore," Monroe said. "But he's trying to change. At least he says he is."

"You don't believe him?"

"It's been a struggle," Monroe said. "I know I've been absent a lot lately, but…"

"Monroe, is it okay for you to be around someone like him?"

"Yes—no—I'm fine," Monroe said quickly. "I just want to say that after tonight, it's over."

"It is?" she asked, doubtful.

"I tried to help him, but tonight's the last time," Monroe said. "He is—was—a friend, so I owed him that much, right? But I've made up my mind. One last attempt to set him on a good path. Then I'm done. It's over. I have to admit to myself that I've done what I can and the rest is up to him."

"I understand."

"Good," Monroe said, nodding, as if he needed to convince himself again that he'd had a moral obligation to try to help Decker and that he should back away if meditation failed as spectacularly as had Pilates and t'ai chi. "Because, maybe you're right, you know?"

"Right about what?"

"That it might not be the best idea for me to spend a lot of time with him."

She took his hand in hers. "If I am right," she said, "maybe you should cancel your meeting tonight."

"No, I'll be fine tonight," Monroe said. "One last night. Meditation and a non-meat meal at home. Tame stuff. And tomorrow, everything will return to normal."

Again, Monroe felt as if he was trying to convince himself. His words rang hollow in his own ears and he wondered if he was simply reciting the rationalizing mantra of an at-risk Wieder Blutbad, like a child whistling past a graveyard to convince himself he's not afraid.

The LC Leasing, Inc. offices were located approximately two miles from the Portland & Sea Tavern in a one-story slate-gray building with batches of floor-to-ceiling windows at odd intervals backed by closed vertical blinds.

The detectives weren't sure what to expect, but Nick suspected Lamar Crawford had never intended to meet them at the restaurant, that he'd simply been stalling for time. To what end, Nick couldn't guess. Maybe he needed to inform his accomplices, especially if the truck hijacking had been an inside job.

Unlike the restaurant, the office was open for business. Nick held the glass door open wide so Hank could enter on his crutches. A young blond receptionist in a form-fitting red dress greeted them pleasantly.

"Welcome to LC Leasing," she said with an expansive smile. "How may I help you?"

Hank flashed the detective's badge hanging from the lanyard around his neck.

"We have an appointment with Lamar Crawford," he said.

The receptionist's smile faltered, but she rose and said, "This way."

Large photos of modern office buildings hung in thin frames mounted on the wall to their left. Nick recognized some of the buildings from the Pearl District. To the right, he peered into a row of five offices, one after the other, each one unoccupied, but with computer displays and paper-filled inboxes on glass-and-steel desks.

"Where is everyone?" Nick asked.

She gave a perfunctory reply, "Tours with potential clients." Now that she understood Hank and Nick had no interest in leasing office space, her earlier graciousness had evaporated.

The receptionist ignored the side offices and led them to the office in the rear, which looked twice as large as the others. She tapped on the doorframe.

"Mr. Crawford, these police officers say they have an appointment with you."

"Detectives," Hank corrected. "Griffin and Burkhardt."

An elderly gentleman with a sallow complexion, watery eyes and hollow cheeks looked up from his computer display and gave her a wan smile.

"It's quite all right, Nancy," Crawford said. "I've been expecting them. Please hold all my calls."

"Yes, sir," she said, turned on her heel and left the room. She avoided eye contact with the detectives on her way out, as if they no longer mattered in her world.

Hank exchanged a look with Nick, but neither commented.

"Please, have a seat, Detectives," Crawford said, indicating the two chairs in front of his own modern glass-and-steel desk. The same style as the side office desks, Crawford's appeared half again as large as the others. A definite pecking order existed. His office also featured a lion's share of the slender floor-to-ceiling windows.

Crawford's desk presented an immaculate workspace. Aside from the computer display, keyboard, mouse, and a multi-line silver telephone, the glass surface held only a framed photo of a middle-aged woman with a teenage boy, and a manila folder under Crawford's left palm. His right hand gripped a Mont Blanc ballpoint pen.

Nick took the chair to the left, farthest from the door, so Hank would require less maneuvering on his crutches before sitting. As Hank settled into the uncomfortable chair beside him, Nick assessed Lamar Crawford. His first impression had been accurate. In addition to Crawford's poor complexion and apparent ill health, his bespoke suit hung loosely on his shoulders, as if his frame had withered too quickly for his tailoring to keep up. Crawford's earlier claim of feeling too ill for the restaurant meeting seemed entirely plausible.

"I understand you have questions about the lost shipment of restaurant equipment," Crawford said, squeezing the Mont Blanc in one skeletal hand.

"Lost when someone hijacked the truck carrying the equipment," Hank pointed out.

"Yes. Assuming that is what happened," Crawford said. "The driver and equipment went missing simultaneously."

"You believe the driver was complicit in the theft?" Nick asked.

"Frankly, I don't know what to believe," Crawford said dismissively. "To this day, neither the driver, nor the equipment has turned up. The supply company filed a police report at the time—and my office cooperated fully with the investigation. But we never received that shipment. And—I might add—we had prepaid for everything. I'm still awaiting a refund from the supplier, who is, in turn, waiting for an insurance settlement."

"You purchased the equipment personally?"

"I placed the order, yes," Crawford said, tapping the Mont Blanc against the glass desktop: *bock—bock— bock!* A sign of nervousness or simply a nervous habit?

"You have purchase orders?" Hank asked.

"Of course," Crawford said, insulted. "I placed the order and paid for the equipment. This is not an attempt at insurance fraud, if that's what you're insinuating."

"Not at all," Hank said. "Just establishing your connection to the order."

"Is there a connection?" Crawford asked rhetorically. "Absolutely. I ordered the equipment. I authorized the payment."

"Anyone in your office acquainted with the driver?" Nick asked.

"No," Crawford said. His pen paused mid-tap. "We had never ordered anything from this company before, which is why we prepaid. How could any of us possibly know the driver of the delivery truck?"

"Stranger things have happened," Hank said.

"In this case, no one at this place of business had… prior knowledge—is that how you phrase it?—of the driver. At least not to my knowledge. You are welcome to interview anyone here to confirm that."

"Speaking of your business," Nick said. "LC Leasing? You lease property?"

"Office space, primarily," Crawford said. "Business to business."

"Own any other restaurants?"

"As a matter of fact, no," Crawford said. "Portland & Sea Tavern would have been our first."

"Why now?" Hank wondered.

Bock—bock—bock!

"Let's call it an attempt at diversification," Crawford said. "The real estate market has gone through some… challenges in the last few years. Business investment down. Hiring down. The tavern would have been our first restaurant."

"Restaurants have a high failure rate," Nick said. "Not exactly a safe bet for diversification."

Crawford squinted at him. "Are you questioning my business acumen?"

Nick shrugged, spread his arms. "Just thinking out loud."

"Opening the restaurant was my wife's idea," Crawford said. "Not that she wanted any direct involvement in the enterprise."

"As you know, we came from the restaurant."

"Yes," Crawford said, setting the pen down. "Again, I apologize. I intended to meet you there rather than bring police business here, but my health…"

"We couldn't help but notice the restaurant is empty."

"Except for a card table and couple folding chairs," Hank added.

"That is unfortunate," Crawford said. "As you said, restaurants are risky ventures in the best of times. With my failing health and the lost shipment, I took it as a sign to abandon the whole project. We may decide to use the rental space for some other venture. Or cut our losses."

Crawford took a deep breath, which did little to fill out his baggy suit jacket. "Well, if there are no further questions, I'd like to wrap this up." He glanced at his gold wristwatch. "I have scheduled appointments this afternoon."

Nick glanced at Hank, who returned a slight shake of his head.

They both stood, Hank propping himself up on his crutches.

"If you don't mind," Nick said. "I'd like to get a copy of the equipment purchase orders."

"Of course," Crawford said, rising unsteadily. "They're in our computer system. Give Nancy an email address on your way out and I'll have her forward copies to you."

Nick had the impression a strong gust of wind could topple the gaunt man.

They turned to leave. Nick waited for Hank to exit on his crutches, and happened to glance down. A balled-up piece of tan paper had missed a trashcan flush against the side of the desk. Nick picked up the paper, intending to deposit it in the trashcan, but paused with it clutched in his fingers. The paper was mottled, not a solid color. Faux parchment paper. Curious, Nick opened the ball of paper, revealing a hand-drawn circle surrounded by a series of acute triangles above an address printed at the bottom of the page.

His gaze flashed to Crawford.

Standing behind his wide modern desk, eyes wide with sudden fear, Crawford woged, exposing himself as a Geier. Seeing Nick's look and realizing that the homicide detective who'd been questioning him was a Grimm, the man's fear became palpable. He gasped audibly, almost a croak of pain, and dropped into his chair.

Startled by Crawford's sudden collapse, Hank glanced over his shoulder and caught the tail end of the unspoken acknowledgment between Wesen and Grimm. He shook his head.

"Should have known," Hank said.

Nick placed the creased paper printed side up in the middle of Crawford's desk.

"I know what you are and you know what I am," Nick said with the forceful tone of authority. He jabbed his index finger at the center of the circle. "So explain this to me!"

In between other appointments, Juliette had covered her desk with reference books and textbooks, each flipped open to pages dealing with kidney disease and anything relevant to the constellation of signs she had noticed in Roxy or in line with the results of her blood tests. She'd cross-referenced this information with online materials available through her various reference subscriptions.

And she'd found a possibility.

Something that would require another test to confirm. Something she couldn't share with the Bremmers because it might not pan out. Unfortunately, she only had a few hours before the family would arrive to say their final goodbyes to their beloved pet.

Roxy had been miserable and mostly unresponsive— barely a tail thump in greeting—when Juliette had drawn 3cc of blood and then hooked up an IV to give her one vial of Cortrosyn. An hour later, when she'd taken more blood, Roxy's only physical response was an ear twitch, as if this annoying medical treatment was one more small piece of a bad dream she'd been having for far too long. With the ACTH stimulation test completed, Juliette submitted the blood work to the lab.

She collapsed in her office chair, feeling wrung out after the last few hours. A low tide of energy after the adrenaline rush of research and discovery had worn off. She stared at her cluttered desk, her hands dangling off the chair arms, and felt unequal to the task of cleaning up. All the heavy lifting had been mental. Yet the physical resources eluded her. She fantasized about the nearest hit of caffeine. Coffee pot in the break room. Vending machine in the hallway.

Somebody rapped on her office door.

"It's open."

Zoe poked her head in, then did a double-take when she noticed the mounds of books on the desk.

"Final exams coming up?"

"All done."

"Pass or fail?"

Juliette frowned. "To be determined," she said. "Fingers crossed."

"You look wiped."

"An accurate diagnosis," Juliette said and sighed. "How's the lobby?"

"Empty at the moment," Zoe said.

"How's the coffee?"

"At this time of day?" Zoe said. "Like tar, I imagine. I could start a fresh pot."

"Would you?" Juliette asked, savoring the prospect of fresh, hot coffee.

"You need a hand with this stuff."

"Books go on shelves, right?" Juliette asked, quirking a tired smile. "I seem to recall a connection between the two."

Together they closed and shelved the books, in no particular order. Seeing the top of her desk reappear was its own reward. Zoe left to make the promised fresh pot of coffee. Juliette leaned back in her chair, head tilted up as she stared off into space, and hoped for good news.

That's all she could do while she awaited the test results.

CHAPTER TWENTY-TWO

"Tell me what this means!" Nick demanded, his index finger pressed to the hand-drawn circle surrounded by acute triangles.

"How should I know?" Crawford said, refusing to look at the image on the faux-parchment paper. "It's a flyer."

"Did you print it?" Nick asked, glancing at an all-in-one personal laser printer on a small stand in the back corner of the office. The original design had been hand drawn with a black marker, but it could have been scanned and printed on a laser printer stocked with novelty parchment paper.

"No, I didn't print the damn thing," Crawford said, agitated. "I picked it up in the library. On a table with a bunch of other flyers and business cards. Anyone could have left it there."

Nick glanced at the address printed below the geometric symbols. He couldn't remember any libraries in Portland at that address. Barring an online search or physically visiting the address, he couldn't know for sure.

"Why did you take it?" Hank asked.

"I don't get your meaning," Crawford said evasively.

"What was it about that symbol—or that address—that made you decide to pick up this particular flyer from that library table filled with other flyers and business cards?"

"No particular reason," Crawford said, somehow looking more exhausted than he had mere minutes ago. "I grabbed it with other flyers."

Nick glanced down into the empty trashcan.

"And where are they?" he asked. "I'd like to see the selection."

"Look, I thought it looked interesting. So I picked it up. But, as you can see, it makes no sense. So I threw it away—or tried to, anyway."

Nick tapped the address on the bottom of the page.

"What will we find here?"

"How should I know?"

"The flyer was interesting enough to take with you," Nick said. "But it made no sense to you. So you threw it out, without bothering to find out what's at that address?"

"That's right."

"You change your mind a lot."

"That's not a crime!" Crawford exclaimed, but the emotional outburst had drained him.

His phone buzzed, one light blinking insistently.

"That's Nancy," he said and grabbed the receiver before they could object. "Everything's fine, Nancy," he said. "No, of course not. They *are* the police. Just… stay out of this. It's not your concern."

The phone almost fell from his grip as he hung up. His hands were shaking.

"I don't know what any of this means," Crawford said, his voice quavering. "If you continue to harass me, I will call my lawyer."

Nick had the sense that Crawford was on the ropes, ready to come clean with the proper encouragement, his threat to call a lawyer nothing more than a last-ditch bluff.

"This flyer you seem to know nothing about," Nick said. "We found another one just like it at a vacant lot where multiple murder victims were buried in shallow graves."

"And we can tie you to another missing person and likely murder victim," Hank said. "The delivery truck driver."

"I told you," Crawford said. "I never met the man."

"Murderers kill strangers all the time."

Nick placed both hands flat on Crawford's desk and leaned forward, fully expecting his superior position and proximity as a Grimm to intimidate.

"The driver carried a load of equipment for a restaurant you had no intention of opening," he said. "The only question is: are you the ringleader in this series of murders, or are you working for someone else."

"Somebody put you up to this, Crawford," Hank said. "Give us a name and maybe you don't spend the last few months of your life rotting in jail."

Crawford clutched his expensive pen, squeezing the barrel as if it were an anchor to the comfortable and privileged lifestyle that was slipping away from him minute by minute. He took several deep, shaking breaths and finally calmed himself before he spoke.

"They promised me a cure…"

"A cure?" Nick asked.

"To this wasting sickness," Crawford said, looking down at his hollow chest. "To human medicine, it resembles cancer, but is less treatable and always fatal." He clasped his hands together, the pen trapped between them, to quell their trembling. "But they… With their experiments, and everything they collected, they told me… they offered a treatment that would prolong my life, if not cure the disease. A type of remission." He ran one hand through his thinning hair. "I am not a young man, so the promise of five, possibly ten more years... that meant everything to me! I would live to see my son graduate from high school and college, maybe even marry."

"What price for this treatment?" Nick asked.

"A simple thing," he said. "Open a restaurant, for all intents and purposes, or at least begin the process. Then order the equipment."

"Why?" Hank asked.

"At first, I thought it was a front," Crawford said. "A legitimate business to launder money from some criminal enterprise."

"But they wanted something else," Nick said.

"The equipment, obviously," Crawford said. "Untraceable back to them."

"It wasn't a front," Hank concluded. "It was a cover."

"They wanted anonymity," Nick added.

"I should have known—from the start—what they were about," Crawford said. "I participated last time, in Rio. So long ago. But it's time again, and that's what they wanted from me. Time." He shook his head. "I wanted more time *from* them. Instead, I bought time *for* them."

"Time for what?" Nick said.

"To finish," Crawford said with a resigned shake of his head. "It was all a lie. The cure. The remission. They've given me a few so-called treatments to string me along. Placebos? Maybe. I believe they whipped up some kind of energy drink cocktail, of all things. To make me feel... invigorated. To think I had hope—and more time."

He sighed, in defeat or resignation. Or so Nick imagined.

"But I know the truth now," Crawford said. "There is no cure. They bided their time with me. It's almost over and they no longer need my help. Only my silence. I'm an accomplice with a built-in expiration date. Untreated, I'll die within the month."

"Who? Who are they?"

He sighed again and exchanged his Mont Blanc for the computer keyboard.

"It's all in here," he said, tapping away on his keyboard, a look of determination on his face.

Nick glanced at the laser printer in the corner, expecting its motor to thrum into life and spew out a list of names. But after a few moments of uninterrupted sleep from the printer, Nick had a bad feeling.

"You won't find them," Crawford said.

"What—?" Confused, Hank looked to Nick.

"What have you done?" Nick leaned forward and spun the LCD monitor around to see the display. A red progress bar had appeared in the middle of the screen with one word flashing below it: "SCRUBBING…"

"He's erasing the hard drive!" Hank exclaimed.

"No 'Cancel' button," Crawford said. "Once it starts, you can't stop it."

Through the glass desktop, Nick saw the computer tower tucked under Crawford's desk, and the cord cover concealing the wires sprouting from the back. The power cords exited the cover and ran to a wall outlet opposite the trashcan. Nick jumped up and pulled the power plugs from the wall. The LCD screen went dark, the tower's fan fell silent, and the hard drive spun down.

"He stopped it," Hank said.

"Whatever information your program erased," Nick said. "You'll tell us personally. Down at the precinct. I'm placing you under arrest."

"I have a family," Crawford said, his gaze lingering on the framed portrait at the corner of his desk. A fleeting smile played across his face. "A healthy family."

He opened a side desk drawer in front of the monitor, the motion obstructed from Nick's view.

"That's all that matters to me now."

"Gun!" Hank shouted.

Reflexively, Nick's hand dropped to his Glock 17 in its belt holster. He pulled the gun free and commanded, "Freeze!"

But even as Nick spoke, Crawford shoved the barrel of his own automatic in his mouth and pulled the trigger, splattering the windows and vertical blinds behind him with blood and brain matter. The old man's body slumped in his executive chair, tendrils of smoke rising from the crater in the back of his skull.

Crawford's gun hand fell in slow motion, the barrel of the automatic clicking against his upper teeth as it pulled free of his mouth. The weapon fell from his lifeless fingers and thumped on the floor beside him. Blood oozed down the leather chair and began to drip steadily onto the floor, spattering the rug.

Nick shoved his Glock back into its holster.

Hank stared in shock at the horrific tableau before them, looked away, shaking his head, then back again, unable to speak.

Behind them, just beyond the office doorway, Nancy, the receptionist was screaming, "What have you done? Oh, God! What have you done?"

Nick shouldered past her toward the front of the building, calling in the suicide and requesting a computer forensics expert as he walked. What secrets Crawford knew had died with him, but his semi-purged hard drive might provide clues to whoever had arranged for him to order the restaurant equipment.

Juliette glanced at the clock above her office door—not long before the Bremmers arrived—and then looked back down at the ACTH stimulation test results. She smiled to herself, then clamped a hand over her mouth, as if she intended to hold that expression in place until their appointment. She double-checked the numbers. Pre-cortisol and post-cortisol results. Both listed on the printout as < 0.7.

The test confirmed the diagnosis she had anticipated— had hoped for—assuming Roxy had not experienced real kidney failure. Not an ideal situation, but not the worst outcome either.

Her intercom buzzed.

When she answered the phone, Zoe said in a solemn voice, "The Bremmers are here."

Juliette hadn't had time to tell Zoe about the test results, so Zoe assumed the Bremmers had come to witness the euthanasia. And they had! But, the ACTH test results had altered the plan.

"It's fine, Zoe," Juliette said, hoping her upbeat tone conveyed a new purpose for the visit. "Bring them to my office."

Without enough chairs for all three of them to sit, Juliette closed the folder with the test results inside and hurried around to the front of her desk to greet them standing up.

"Here they are," Zoe said, leading the way, an eyebrow arched curiously.

Juliette smiled at her and nodded.

Barry and Melinda Bremmer came first, holding hands that parted only as they stepped through the doorway then found each other again. Behind them, Logan walked with his head hanging, not willing to make eye contact. Barry appeared solemn, in control of his emotions, while Melinda's eyes were bright with welling tears, a fragile but hopeful expression on her face. She knew Juliette had been grasping at straws, but Juliette sensed she hadn't shared that information with her husband or son.

"I have good news," Juliette said, feeling the smile return

to her face. "Roxy is not experiencing kidney failure."

"But you said—? The tests—?" Barry said.

"Yes, I know," Juliette said. "The tests appeared to indicate kidney failure. But I noticed some odd results with the second test. Something bothered me about them. I had an idea—actually, a good friend suggested an idea—that maybe Roxy had a condition that, on the surface, presented as kidney failure, while underneath was something else entirely."

"But she's sick," Logan said, finally looking up at Juliette. "Really sick."

Juliette nodded. "She does have a serious condition. It's the reason why her kidney values resolved so quickly with IV fluids. She doesn't have kidney failure. She has a condition that mimics kidney failure. It's called Addison's disease."

"What does this mean for her?" Barry asked.

Melinda's question overlapped her husband's. "How serious is it?"

"Addison's is a deficiency of glucocorticoids and mineralocorticoids—that is, cortisol and aldosterone—caused by the destruction of the adrenal gland, which is located in the abdomen, near the kidneys."

"Oh, no!" Melinda said.

"I don't know what all that other stuff means," Barry said. "But 'destruction' sounds bad."

"Can she live without it?" Logan asked. "The adrenal gland?"

"Addison's is very treatable," Juliette said. "Roxy will need oral prednisone for the cortisol deficiency, and monthly injections of desoxycorticosterone pivalate—DOCP—for the mineralocorticoid deficiency. I know that's a mouthful and a half, but the important thing is that her condition is treatable."

"How long will she need the oral stuff and the injections?" Barry asked.

Juliette's smile faltered a bit. "I'm afraid she'll need both for as long as she lives. While Addison's disease won't shorten her life, treating it demands a dedication to daily medication and monthly injections."

All three family members stared at her, absorbing the information.

Melinda came forward first, wrapping Juliette in a grateful hug, her body wracked with quiet sobs of joy. After a few moments, she said, "Thank you. Thank you so much."

When she stepped back, Barry offered his hand in a more formal thank you. Logan gave a flip of his tousled hair, smiled, and said, "Yeah, thanks, Doc."

"I'm so happy for you guys," Juliette said, absently placing the somewhat crumpled test results folder behind her on her desk. "And Roxy, of course!"

Melinda looked around, as if expecting the dog to pop out of some hiding place in Juliette's office. "Where is she?"

"I'll take you to her," Juliette said. "I need to show you how to administer the daily meds and the monthly injections. Then I'll write up the scripts, and you can take her home today."

As she took them to see Roxy, Juliette thought that the day had certainly taken a turn for the better. And she'd have to thank Rosalee again, for reminding Juliette to look beneath surface impressions for the truth.

CHAPTER TWENTY-THREE

"What happened here?" Renard demanded.

Captain Renard showed up at LC Leasing, Inc. after the crime scene techs had taken their measurements and photographs, while someone from the coroner's office removed Lamar Crawford's body. One of the computer forensic techs had bagged Crawford's computer tower for examination and data retrieval, while another checked the computers in each office—after Nancy provided employee login and password information—to determine if they needed to confiscate more than just Crawford's PC.

Sergeant Wu glanced at the blood-splattered windows and blinds and shook his head.

"Not often a suspect eats a gun right in front of you," he said.

Nick had already provided Renard with the sequence of events leading to Crawford's suicide, so he assumed the captain was after some context and speculation at this point.

"Crawford is connected to the bare bones murders somehow," he began. "His direct actions triggered the disappearance of a delivery truck driver right before missing persons cases in this area spiked. Plus, I found another copy of this flyer"—he indicated the bagged flyer on Crawford's desk, which Nick had already photographed with his cell phone—"at the vacant lot where the first murder victims were found."

"Crawford got them started," Hank said. "They promised him a miracle cure for his illness in exchange for his help and silence."

"And he believed it?" Renard asked.

"He was convinced." Nick glanced at Wu, who was unaware of the Wesen aspect of many of their cases. "He was desperate, his illness was fatal, so he wanted to believe in a miracle cure. They took advantage of that."

"And yet he killed himself anyway," Renard said.

"No miracle cure for a bullet through the brain," Wu commented.

"We got the impression he killed himself to protect his family," Nick said. "If we took him into custody, they would be targets to ensure his silence."

"Or killed if he talked," Hank added.

"Let's hope forensics can pull something useful off his computer," Renard said.

"We want to talk to the wife," Hank said. "See how much she knew about the restaurant and the hijacked shipment."

"Get to her before the press," Renard said. "She needs to be notified of his death."

"I want to see where this flyer leads," Nick said. "Crawford said he picked it up at the library, but that's a different address."

"You believe it's a message?" Renard asked. "Some kind of code?"

Nick displayed the photo of the flyer on his cell phone and showed it to Renard.

"Anything seem familiar about it?" he asked pointedly.

Renard understood: Did the symbols ring any Wesen bells with him? He peered carefully at the photo, then met Nick's gaze.

"Nothing I've seen before," he said.

Hank agreed to talk to the widow, while Nick followed the trail of the flyers, which might require running around to multiple locations, starting with the library flyer table to confirm Crawford's story.

Nick pulled Wu aside and asked him to take the receptionist in for questioning, after getting a copy of any restaurant-related purchase orders. Depending on the nature of her relationship with Crawford, she might have valuable information about the restaurant cover. In addition, Nick wanted her out of circulation while Hank visited the widow and son. If Nancy talked to the press or called the family, the police would lose control of the information and Crawford's co-conspirators might have time to erase evidence to cover their tracks or interfere with the investigation.

Nick dropped Hank off at the precinct so he could take his own car to Crawford's residence, then he returned to the business district and located the closest library to LC Leasing, Inc. He parked out front, walked through the library's lobby and found the community table with small business tri-fold brochures, computer printed and photocopied flyers, and at least two-dozen business cards. After less than a minute scanning the table, Nick found a small stack of flyers—seven, by his quick count—that matched the one he'd found crumpled in a ball on Crawford's office floor.

He took one of the flyers to the front desk and asked the librarian on duty if anyone could leave flyers on the table or if they had a submission and approval process with written records of who left what.

"I'm sorry, Detective," the rail-thin woman said. "We have no records for that sort of thing. Anyone can leave a flyer or a business card there as long as the content is not obscene. We don't even check if they're members of the library."

He placed the flyer on the counter, face up, and asked, "Do you recognize this one?"

She glanced down and nodded. "I've seen it before, in passing."

"Do you know who left it? Or what it means?"

She frowned, staring at the paper, as if trying to solve a puzzle. Finally, she shook her head.

"I don't know who left it, or what it means. Maybe it's some kind of math club."

"How long do items usually stay on the table?"

She shrugged. "Until they're gone," she said. "Every couple weeks, if the table gets too cluttered, we'll get rid of some stuff, sometimes sweep it clean."

"When was the last time that happened?"

She glanced over at the table, estimating the amount of accumulated clutter, he imagined.

"At least a week. Maybe two. No more than that."

Nick glanced around the upper walls of the library, but saw no cameras mounted anywhere.

"Don't suppose you have any security footage?"

"No, I'm afraid not."

Nick returned to his Land Cruiser. The library was a dead end, but he had another obvious lead: the address on the flyer itself. He recognized the street name. The destination was several miles from the library and, with luck, might provide some answers.

* * *

Monroe had prepared his dining room for meditation. He had moved the table and chairs aside, put down the two foam mats he'd taken to the Pilates class, dimmed the lights, prepared a candle for their focus, and turned his stereo on, playing a CD of soothing electronic music without the hint of a beat and set it on repeat. *Get Decker in the right frame of mind from the start,* Monroe thought, *and maybe this will work.*

His own anxiety stayed manageable because, as he kept reminding himself, the meditation session had no downside. Either it worked and Decker found the key to his own reformed path, or it failed as miserably as the Pilates and t'ai chi classes. Either way, Monroe was off the hook. He would have legitimately tried to help Decker—*three times*—with nothing to show for his efforts.

Decker himself seemed tired of the effort involved in reforming—and he hadn't taken more than a single step. The drive to change was the key to success or failure. Without Decker's willingness to work for the change, nothing *would* change. They could part as old friends, part of a shared past. Monroe wouldn't look back fondly on those memories, but he had enjoyed himself at the time... for a time. Everything in context. He was a changed Blutbad now. Decker had, until now, remained constant, and might continue unmoved by anything Monroe had to offer. And Monroe could accept that now. If this last attempt failed, it was just that, a last attempt.

Everything ready, he checked the time and heard the rumble of a car engine, followed by the sudden stillness as the engine cut off, then the *thunk* of a car door slamming.

"At least he's on time," Monroe said to himself. "Good start. Now the fun begins. Or the not-fun."

Monroe met Decker at the front door, momentarily seeing the other man's image distorted through the stained glass window as he navigated the front walk. When Decker raised a fist to rap on the glass, Monroe pulled the door open and said, "Good to see you again."

Decker's left hand clasped Monroe's shoulder in a powerful grip while offering his right hand to shake, and subsequently applied enough pressure for the gesture to serve as a show of dominance in addition to a greeting. Monroe refused to play the game, matching pressure for pressure, without attempting to win the exchange. Decker's attention had already moved on.

"Once more into the breach, brother!"

"Unto," Monroe said quietly.

"What?"

"Nothing," Monroe said, shaking his head. "Come in. I've prepared everything so we can get started."

"Just the two of us this time."

"As promised," Monroe said. "No instructor or classmates. No judgments."

Decker cocked his head. "What's that noise?"

"What noise—oh, the music," Monroe said. "I chose something conducive to meditating."

"Got any Skynyrd?"

"I don't know. Probably, but—"

"Allman Brothers? Hell, Creedence?"

"Trust me," Monroe said. "For meditation, you want this kind of music. Or silence, really. But as a beginner, I thought you might need some aids. Just to get started."

"By meditating, I pictured us sitting on a deck, drinking some brews, blasting some old school tunes, talking about the good old days."

"Actually, meditation is kind of the opposite of everything you just said," Monroe replied. "Except for the sitting part. That's in there."

"You're the pro, bro," Decker said, performing a slight

bow and a sweep of his arm. "Lead the way, Maharishi."

"I'm no expert at this," Monroe admitted as he led Decker to the cleared dining room. "I've studied a few techniques. Enough for you to try and see if it works for you."

Though the admission was true, Monroe also thought Decker might have been intimidated by expert instructors, even if the classes they attended had been for beginners. Along with dominance displays, Decker wouldn't want to feel inferior in any public activity. And lack of knowledge or skill would definitely give him an inferiority complex. Monroe wanted his own attitude about the meditation session to be one of discovery as well.

"I've silenced the house phone and my cell," Monroe said. "It's best not to anticipate possible interruptions. So turn off or silence your cell phone and I'll put it on the table over here with mine."

Decker frowned. "What if I miss a call?"

"Voicemail," Monroe said. "Whatever it is, it can wait thirty minutes, right?"

"Probably," Decker said, pulling out a scuffed-up cell phone and powering it down. "Done!"

"Great," Monroe said. "Take off your boots. Pick a mat, sit down and get comfortable. Give me a minute and we can get started."

While Decker positioned himself on the left mat, Monroe lit the candle he'd placed on a wall shelf in their line of sight. The lights in the room were already dim, and the electronic music played softly in the background, functioning almost as white noise. Everything ready, Monroe kicked off his loafers and sat cross-legged on the mat next to Decker.

"Cross your legs, hands clasped in your lap, spine straight," Monroe instructed, his voice coming out hushed, adapting unconsciously to the environment he'd prepared in the room. He glanced over at Decker, who had mirrored Monroe's posture, but not without some low grumbling. "Good," Monroe said once the other man was ready.

"What now?"

"Look at the candle flame," Monroe said. "Focus on that and be still."

"Locked and loaded," Decker said. "What now?"

"Stay quiet and calm," Monroe said in a soothing tone. "Quiet... now take deep, measured breaths, in through your nose, out through your mouth... Think only of your breathing. Feel your body expand as you inhale, contract as you exhale."

Decker stayed quiet, which felt like progress.

"Feel the stillness of your body in between breaths."

Decker's breathing fell in rhythm with Monroe's.

"Focus on your breathing now," Monroe said. "Think of nothing else. Only your breathing. Breathe in... and breathe out."

Monroe felt the calming effects of meditation descend over him and spoke less and less, focusing on his own breath, breathing in and out, staying in time with Decker's—

—snoring!

"Dude! You fell asleep?"

Uncrossing his legs, Monroe reached over and shook Decker's shoulder. Sometime during the breathing exercise, Decker had slumped out of his straight posture position, his head lolling to the side, a thin line of drool dangling from his grizzled chin.

"Hey! Why'd you wake me?" Decker said, shaking off his lethargy. "That was totally relaxing. I can see why you do this."

"That's not why you—"

"I've never fallen asleep so fast in my life."

"Decker, you aren't supposed to sleep through

meditation," Monroe said. "You're supposed to clear your mind, let go of stress and anxiety…"

"Too short for a power nap," Decker continued, heedless of Monroe's corrections. "But that's on you, brother. Woke me too soon."

"I give up," Monroe said, shaking his head.

"Hey, it was relaxing," Decker said. "That's a good thing, right, man? But, you know, some Skynyrd would have kept me stoked."

"I should have known," Monroe said in resignation. "Of course you would fall asleep during meditation."

"Listen, this is on me, Monroe. I've been keeping late nights, not catching much uninterrupted sleep. It's an exhausting lifestyle, am I right? This—this naptime thing—was bound to happen. Don't blame yourself, man."

"I don't," Monroe said. *Only thing I blame myself for is believing any of this had a chance at success,* he thought bitterly. *"An exhausting lifestyle." That's his biggest problem. He doesn't want to give up that lifestyle. Doesn't want to change.* "Why, Decker?"

"Why'd I fall asleep? Already explained—"

"Why do you bother? To try this. Or Pilates. Or t'ai chi."

"I wanted to spend some time with an old buddy," Decker said. "Isn't that enough?"

"No," Monroe said. "This is all too much effort for—for catching up with an old friend."

"I wanted to try it on for size, brother," Decker said. "To see what makes the watchmaker tick—now. I knew, before, back when we ran together. But now? Pure, unadulterated mystery."

"So you were… curious?"

"Yep," Decker said. "And… I wanted to wrap my head around it. See if I could do what you do. Thought it would be challenging but, man, I had no friggin' idea. Like crawling over broken glass to cross the road. But this time, with the meditating, I glimpsed it, you know. For a couple minutes, at least, I felt at peace. Then it was gone."

"When you fell asleep."

"Exactly," Decker said. He held up a thumb and index finger, an inch apart. "But I made some progress, right? On the road to enlightenment."

"I suppose every long journey begins with thinking you're about to begin a long journey," Monroe said. "I have an idea. So far, it's been all about the stick. We should try the carrot first. A meal."

"I hate carrots," Decker said. "That's the stuff I feed the stuff I eat."

"I bought a pair of steaks for us earlier today," Monroe said. "Terrific veggie steaks."

"Those three words should never be so close together."

"You're gonna love these," Monroe said. "Trust me. Maybe we'll try round two of meditation after we've had something to eat."

"Yeah, something," Decker grumbled. "Say, purely as a backup plan, you got any delivery menus?"

Nick located the address listed at the bottom of the circle-with-triangles flyer. He had to double-check the number because the street address was not prominently displayed outside the Homestead Food Co-op market. With a quarter-folded copy of the flyer in his hand, he wandered through the market, looking for anything unusual, anything that raised a red flag. Not that he expected to find human body parts scattered in the produce section of the store, but if cannibals were involved, a food connection seemed plausible.

He asked the store manager—a tall woman with gray hair tied in a ponytail, wearing a blue cap with the store name embroidered across it—if the flyer with the store's address meant anything to her. She nodded.

"I've seen it before."

Without another word, she strode down the aisle away from her office, so Nick followed her. For a minute, he thought she was escorting him out of the store, but she stopped near the entrance and turned to face a cluttered corkboard hanging against a glass partition. She reached forward and pushed aside a flyer with tear-off tabs listing a car for sale and another one announcing the formation of a bowling league. Underneath those two, Nick saw several identical circle-and-triangles flyers held to the board with pushpins.

"Right there," the manager said. "Saw it before these others covered it."

Nick removed one of the flyers and stared at it. Identical.

No—not identical! The address written below the circle and triangles was different from the address on the flyer he'd brought with him—and the address on the new flyer was not the library's address.

"Do you know who posted these?" he asked.

"Not a clue, Detective," she said, then chuckled. "Sorry. No pun intended. People come in, tack the stuff up, and leave."

"When did you first notice this on the board?"

She exhaled forcefully. "Maybe... a week ago? No longer. I only noticed because of the parchment paper. Everything else is either plain white paper or neon colors."

Nothing helpful, but he had another address to check.

As he climbed back into his Land Cruiser, he wondered if he'd fallen victim to a prank, someone's idea of a wild goose chase or a snipe hunt. Possibly, but he had to play along for now.

Before driving to the new address, Nick texted Monroe

the photo he'd taken of the Crawford flyer. Though Captain Renard was unfamiliar with the geometric image, Monroe might have seen it before. If not, he might have some old books or records that explained it.

If the addresses led nowhere, Nick planned to check Aunt Marie's trailer. Though most of her journals dealt with the nature of the various types of Wesen, she might have information about the design and its significance, especially if it had been distributed before, which seemed likely. He recalled Crawford's words: *"I participated last time, in Rio. So long ago."*

So far, he had nothing to show for his efforts. He hoped Hank had had better luck with Crawford's widow.

CHAPTER TWENTY-FOUR

The Crawford residence—traditional English style, dark-gray roof, white siding—stood at the back of a circular, tree-lined driveway, on a three-acre lot, isolated from road noise and curious neighbors. A separate driveway led to the three-car garage. Propped on his crutches, Hank rang the doorbell and admired the almost-rustic surroundings. From certain viewing angles, the house seemed totally isolated from those nearby.

Crawford's widow—an attractive woman who introduced herself as Ellen after Hank flashed his detective's shield—invited him inside. After meeting her in person, Hank decided the photo on Crawford's desk had been taken recently. He guessed her age—late forties to early fifties—at twenty years younger than her husband's, although his advanced illness had done his appearance no favors.

Ellen Crawford led him through the open, airy house to an expansive living room with hardwood floors, a wide bay window and a large walnut fireplace inset with white marble highlights. A glass-and-steel square coffee table, the design reminiscent of the desks at LC Leasing, occupied the center of the room, its harsh style softened by a pale-blue throw rug centered between a light-gray sofa and two armchairs.

"Please sit, Detective," Ellen Crawford said. "Can I get you anything?"

Hank sat in the armchair that faced the hallway that led from the foyer to living room. Crawford had been involved in something shady and Hank had come alone, so he wanted a clear line of sight if someone else approached. Propping his crutches against the side of the chair, he shook his head.

"Mrs. Crawford, I'm afraid I have bad news," he began.

"What sort of—? Oh, no! Has something happened to Lamar?" She sat on the sofa, leaning forward, knees pressed together, her hands worriedly clutching the material of her dress. "Some kind of accident?"

"No, he—"

"His illness? Is he in the hospital?"

"What do you know about his illness?" Hank said. "And his treatments?"

"Cancer," she said with a curt nod. But then the floodgates opened on her repressed concern. "It had spread through his body and hadn't responded to any traditional treatment. He had contacted... specialists—alternative practitioners—about some sort of progressive treatment— he wouldn't give me details. Honestly, I thought he was making it up, lying so I wouldn't give up hope. He said he'd keep the details to himself so I wouldn't worry. But I knew insurance wouldn't cover it. And he said it might be dangerous, but that he had no other options. Did he have—some sort of reaction, a side effect?"

She spoke so quickly, Hank had a hard time interrupting her.

"I don't think any of it helped," she continued. "He

would have brief spurts of energy, but nothing…"

"He never told you the names of the alternative practitioners?"

She shook her head quickly. "Some of the… ingredients might have been illegally imported. He said they could get in trouble—that *he* could get in trouble—but he wanted to protect me. Have you—was he arrested?"

"No, ma'am," Hank said. "Your husband… I'm afraid he took his own life."

"Wh—what? No!" She made fists and pressed them against her mouth so hard her knuckles turned white. Then, her body trembling, she gasped for air. "Why? Oh, my God, what happened?"

"I'm so sorry for your loss."

"Mom?"

The son, who looked about fifteen years old, hurried down the hallway, rushed to his mother and stood beside her at the sofa. She clutched his hands in hers, sobbing as she pulled him down beside her.

"Kurt, it's your father… he's… he…"

"He what?" Kurt asked. "He's—he died?"

"Yes, Kurt. He… took his own life."

"Mrs. Crawford, your husband took his life to protect you and your son."

"You were there? When it happened?"

"Yes," Hank said. "My partner and I were questioning him"—Hank took out his phone and displayed a photo of the flyer—"about this flyer? Does this mean anything to you?"

She looked at the image on the phone briefly and shook her head. Leaning past her to check it out, Kurt frowned and dropped his chin to his chest.

"What is it?" Ellen asked.

"That's what we need to find out," Hank said. "The

people associated with that flyer scared your husband so much that he took his own life so they wouldn't come after you and your son."

"This makes no sense," Ellen said, her voice raw from choking back sobs. "Lamar was deathly ill. He… he probably only had a month or two left. Why would he do this? Without—without saying goodbye."

"We need to find the people responsible," Hank said. "Could your husband have kept records here, in the house? On a computer? Or a Rolodex? Something with the names, addresses or phone numbers of the so-called specialists?"

Head hanging low, one hand clutching at the fabric of her dress, the other clutching her son's hand spasmodically, she spoke in a strained whisper.

"No computer records. No written records. No recordings. He said he couldn't have any evidence here. To protect us from prosecution. And it was all for nothing…"

Hank fought to overcome the feeling of intruding on the family's grief. He remained respectfully silent as Ellen Crawford tried to control her emotions. Beside her, her son throttled his own reactions, but a single tear slipped down the side of his cheek. Then Kurt stood up and ran out of the room.

After he left, Ellen looked up at Hank, her eyes red-rimmed, and said, "How?"

"How?"

"How did he…?"

"Gun," Hank said. "Hidden in a desk drawer. It happened so fast, we couldn't…"

Hank chose to spare her the details of the actual suicide, but wanted her to know that he would have stopped it if he'd had the chance. It seemed obvious that he would have intervened, but by telling her that much, she would know her husband hadn't suffered.

Grabbing his crutches, he lurched upright and caught his balance.

"I wanted you to know before word got out," Hank said. "You'll need to go down to the Medical Examiner's Office"—he avoided using the word "morgue," which felt too raw—"to identify him."

She nodded.

"We want to catch these guys," Hank repeated. "If you find anything, or remember anything about them, give me a call."

He handed her his card, which she placed carefully on the glass coffee table, almost as if it were fragile.

"I'll see you out," she said.

"Again, I'm sorry for your loss."

As Hank navigated the few steps leading down to the driveway, he couldn't help wondering if mother and son were both Geiers as well. If so, Nick would have seen them woge during their emotional outbursts. Though Hank knew of the Wesen, they remained, for the most part, undetectable by him, as a normal human. Unknown unless they chose to reveal their nature. They hid in plain sight. And when Hank dwelled on that simple fact too much, he had to admit that it spun the needle on the creepy meter up into the red zone.

Human or Wesen, though, the Crawfords had to deal with all-too-common grief.

Ellen Crawford stood by the front door, clutching a wad of tissues to her red, runny nose, and waited until the detective had exited their driveway. Then she took a deep breath and exhaled forcefully.

"Those bastards!" she exclaimed.

"Mom?" Kurt came out of the kitchen after she'd closed the front door and stood beside her.

Without looking over her shoulder, she reached back toward him with one hand, which he clasped and squeezed.

"We knew he didn't have long," she said. "But they shouldn't have put him at risk of exposure."

"He said it was his only chance," Kurt said, his eyes red and swollen. "That it might be dangerous. But he shouldn't have banned us. It was our right to participate."

"They lied to him," she said bitterly, and woged briefly into her Geier form. "Took advantage of his desperation. They made him do their dirty work. And forced him to…"

Kurt took a step forward and hugged her.

"I never wanted to participate," Ellen said thoughtfully. "So I didn't argue with him." Finally, she looked over her shoulder at him, and saw some of Lamar's determination in his eyes. "But now? Now I wouldn't mind knowing all about it."

"He can't stop us now." Kurt woged briefly.

"No, Kurt," she said. "Not alone. It's too dangerous."

"I know," Kurt said softly, disengaging from the hug to walk back into the kitchen, several papers clutched in his hand.

Lamar had wanted to protect them. And she would keep Kurt safe. Her son had agreed with her, but perhaps too readily. She recalled the steely glint of resolve in his eyes and shuddered.

The address on the flyer from the Homestead Food Co-op's bulletin board led Nick to Portland First National Bank, close to six miles away. As soon as he saw the table in the outer lobby, riddled with flyers and business cards, he knew what to expect. Five copies of the circle-and-triangles flyer were stacked on the left back corner of the table.

He grabbed one, walked into the bank and was immediately greeted by one of the tellers. Again he asked if people needed permission to leave flyers or business cards on the table. And again, the answer was no, but this time his luck changed.

A woman in her mid-fifties wearing a peach pantsuit approached him from a bullpen area with several desks and a copy machine. She introduced herself as Charlotte Blumstein, the branch manager.

"Can I help you?" she asked.

Nick identified himself and said, "You have a security camera trained on the entrance?"

"We do."

"How long do you keep the footage?"

"It's digital," she said. "We store it for ten days before overwriting it. Next month we plan to upgrade our storage capacity and keep thirty-one days."

"Are you familiar with this flyer?"

"No," she said. "I'm afraid I barely notice the stuff on that table anymore."

"I believe it's been in circulation for a week," Nick said. "No more than two. I'd like to review the footage for that camera, see if I can get a shot of whoever left it there."

"No problem. Follow me."

She took Nick to a cramped office in back with a small desk supporting a large flat-screen monitor that displayed eight black-and-white live video feeds from the interior and the exterior of the bank, including one over an ATM machine, another angled toward the drive-through lanes, and one facing the front door from inside the bank. The branch manager sat at the desk and clicked through a program that showed archive footage for that one feed.

"Start with the earliest and work forward," Nick said.

"Ten days ago?"

"Why not?"

"Okay," she said with a resigned you-know-best tone

in her voice. "Ten days ago starts… now."

Nick watched for a minute or two. "Can you play it at a faster speed?"

"Yes," she said, followed by a couple clicks. "This is double speed."

Customers showed up on the feed, seemingly in a hurry; most bypassed the table, but a few stopped and scanned the items on the table before continuing into the bank.

After a lull with nobody entering, Nick said, "Faster?"

She clicked again. "Four-times speed."

People fast-waddled into the bank, while others fast-waddled out. The procession continued. One man stopped and placed a stack of a dozen business cards on the table before entering. A few minutes later, someone ripped a phone number tab off the bottom of a for-sale flyer.

"Faster."

"Eight-times," Charlotte informed him.

People darted in and out of the bank, like fish in a fast-moving stream, too fast to make out features and, sometimes, not even gender.

"Pause!" Nick said. "Back up."

A gray-haired man looked over the table, then set down a stack of flyers. With the footage at normal speed, Nick could tell the flyers were white pages, with large type and no drawings.

"Speed it up again."

After a couple minutes, Nick offered to take over the controls. Charlotte gave him the basics on operating the program and left him alone in the office. The speed was so fast, Nick simply stared at the table as a focal point—almost mesmerized—and waited for any hesitation in movement that indicated somebody was either looking at the table, dropping off flyers and business cards or taking any from the table. After a while, he increased the speed so that he watched activity ten times faster than normal, and had to refrain from blinking for so long his eyes burned.

When he thought he needed a five-minute break, he paused the playback, took out his phone and called Hank. He answered on the third ring.

"Hey, Nick," Hank said. "Any luck?"

"Still following breadcrumbs," Nick said. "Get anything from the widow?"

"She said Crawford kept her and the kid in the dark," Hank said. "Told them he was involved in something illegal and potentially dangerous. Apparently he left no written or digital record in the house to avoid incriminating them."

"Hard to believe he kept no records."

"I know," Hank said. "But he had his work computer wired to self-destruct. Makes sense he'd leave nothing incriminating at home. But I'll get a search warrant."

Nick told him about reviewing the security camera footage.

"We could do that in shifts," Hank suggested. "Or get the techs down there. Let them come up with an algorithm or something to scan for interaction with the table."

"For now, I'll keep at it the old-fashioned way," Nick said. "Since I'm tied up here, I was hoping you could check on Monroe."

"Something up?"

"Texted him a copy of Crawford's flyer. Now that we know it's Wesen-related, I thought Monroe might be able to shed some light on it. Maybe something in one of his old reference books. I called but he's not answering his cell or home phone."

"Okay, I'll head over to his place."

Nick thanked him, disconnected, and directed his nose back to the digital grindstone.

Although the drive-through lanes opened early and

stayed open late, the lobby ran on a nine-to-five schedule. All the cameras, however, ran twenty-four hours a day, which meant Nick could skip ahead in the time stamps from closing time each evening until the next day's start of business.

During the next two hours, the branch manager checked on him a couple times, to see if he needed a cup of coffee or anything else, but he declined, never looking away from the screen.

In the third hour, while reviewing footage from eight days back, he spotted something. Backed up and played it again at normal speed. The timestamp showed 4:15 p.m. when the man came in. Tall and broad across the shoulders, wearing a black hoodie, black gloves and dark sunglasses. One gloved hand clutched several mottled pages the right shade. Without hesitating, the man pushed some business cards aside and placed the flyers in the same spot where Nick had found them.

Gotcha, Nick thought.

His satisfaction was short-lived. Nick paused the image and stared, looking for something useful. He tapped a finger beside the mouse. Clicked "Resume." And, as he'd seen at the accelerated frame rate, the man turned on his heel and exited the bank without coming into the main lobby. He scanned backward until he found the frame where the man set down the flyers, the only moment where any portion of his face was visible to the camera.

"Find something?" Charlotte said, startling him.

"Got the guy," Nick said. "Not much to look at. Adult Caucasian male, possibly Hispanic. Can you zoom in on his face?"

She leaned down and glanced over his shoulder.

"It would be a digital zoom. Pixelated."

She demonstrated, zooming in and turning the face

blocky as the computer attempted to guess at what the larger version should look like without having the actual data to display the image at that size. The zoomed-in image was worse than the distant one.

"Should I print it out?" she asked.

"Yes," Nick said. "The non-zoomed version." He doubted it would help identify the suspect, but it might help eliminate other suspects at some point. He also requested all the footage to pass on to the computer techs at the precinct, in case they could identify someone who had picked up a leaflet. It was a longshot but he figured it was worth a try.

After thanking the woman for her help, Nick took his security feed printout and a copy of the bank flyer with him. He started the Land Cruiser, checked the address at the bottom of the bank's version of the flyer and drove across town to the next breadcrumb.

CHAPTER TWENTY-FIVE

Monroe prepared dinner, chopping green beans, boiling brown rice and broiling two veggie steaks. Decker hovered around, glancing from one pan to the next and clucked his tongue.

"What?" Monroe asked.

"Something is missing," Decker said. "Trying to put my finger on it."

"Let me guess," Monroe said. "Meat?"

"Got it in one!" Decker exclaimed.

"Don't knock the veggie steak until you've tried it," Monroe said. "This could open a whole new world for you—a meat-free existence along with the inner peace we talked about."

"Not sure I want to face a new world sober, brother," Decker said. "Got any beer?"

"Some microbrews," Monroe said. "Check the top shelf. I should have a few bottles from Hair of the Dog."

"Made with real dog?" Decker said, standing with the refrigerator door open. "Yes, I might go there."

"It's beer," Monroe said as he monitored the sizzling veggie steaks. "No actual dogs were involved in the brewing or bottling process." He tried to work out a kink in his neck. Despite meditating—briefly—he found it impossible to relax around Decker. The house had become so quiet that Decker's voice was the only—

He had a head-slapping moment as he remembered he'd turned off his house and cell phones.

"Keep an eye on the stove for a minute" he told Decker. "Don't—don't touch anything—unless something catches fire or boils over."

Monroe hurried to the other room. *But, really,* he wondered, *what could Decker do to the meal? Burn it?* Not like he had any actual meat in the fridge the man could toss in the pan. Unless Nick had bought...

He grabbed his cell phone and powered it on before returning to the kitchen. Immediately, he saw a one-word text from Nick—"Recognize?"—with an attached image. Monroe squinted at the small image but all he could make out was a circle and some writing beneath it, so he sent the image to his wireless printer.

"Everything okay?" Decker called.

"Back in five seconds," Monroe said absently. He grabbed the printed image from his printer's output tray and returned with it to the kitchen, where he set it on the table. Nick wanted to know if he recognized it, but the image meant nothing to Monroe and, with dinner at risk, he decided to check it properly later.

"I kept the house from burning down," Decker said as he backed away from the stove and took a swig from the microbrew's IPA. "Now what?"

"You could set the table," Monroe suggested. "Put out plates, a couple glasses and flatware."

"Flatware?" Decker said. "You don't eat with your hands? You know, sometimes I shove my face right into the plate and rip the meat from the bone with my teeth alone."

"No bones here," Monroe said evenly. "So you can stick with a knife and fork."

Decker was silent as Monroe finished cooking and turned off the burners. He glanced over his shoulder and saw that Decker hadn't made a move toward the cabinets to retrieve plates and glasses.

"What?" he asked.

Decker looked at him and pointed to the flyer. "Do you know what this is?"

"No. Should I?"

Decker shrugged. "Looks like some kind of puzzle, but I'm stumped. Maybe that circle is supposed to be the sun. Where'd you get it?"

"Nick—Detective Burkhardt—sent it," Monroe said. "Part of a case or something."

"Why send it to you?"

Monroe frowned, not wanting to open the Wesen can of worms.

"He's trying to figure out what it means. Guess he thought a second set of eyes might help. Plates?"

"Oh, yeah, right," Decker said, setting down his half-empty beer bottle. After opening a couple cabinets, he located the plates and glasses and set down two place settings on opposite sides of the table, facing each other, adding the flatware last. "I know you went to a lot of—"

The doorbell rang.

"Sit," Monroe said. "I'll get it."

"But…"

As Decker's voice trailed off, Monroe answered the door and found Hank on crutches on his front door stoop. Alone. Monroe leaned out a bit and looked left and right.

"Hey, Hank, is Nick…?"

"Nick said you weren't answering," Hank said. "Asked me to drop by."

"Come in," Monroe said, swinging the door open and stepping aside so Hank could maneuver inside. "I had my phones turned off. Meditation session."

"Oh," Hank said. "Didn't know you were into that."

"I'm not, usually, although I have tried it in the past a few times, but today I had a—"

"Who's your friend?" Decker asked, approaching. "Ah, another cop."

"Detective," Hank corrected.

"Hank Griffin," Monroe said. "Nick's partner. Hank, this is Decker, an old friend of mine. We've been... catching up."

"And meditating?" Hank asked.

They shook hands briefly.

"Gave it a shot," Decker said. "Bit *too* relaxing for me."

"Sometimes 'relaxing' is just what the doctor ordered," Hank said.

"Speaking of doctors," Decker said, indicating the crutches with a sweep of his hand. "Hope that's not too serious."

"Torn Achilles."

"Ouch!"

"Few days away from the cast coming off," Hank said, shrugging. "End in sight."

"Sure," Decker said. "But until then, something like that must put you off your game. No chasing suspects on foot, am I right? Can you even drive?"

"I get around all right," Hank said, clearly wishing to drop the topic. He turned to Monroe. "Nick sent you a photo. Have you had a chance to look at it?"

"I have, but only for a minute or so," Monroe said. "It's in here." As he walked to the kitchen, Hank and Decker followed him. "I had my phones turned off during meditation and forgot to turn them back on before I started cooking dinner."

Monroe grabbed the printed copy of the flyer photo and looked it over again, the circle surrounded by triangles and the address at the bottom.

"Nothing's ringing any bells. Decker thought maybe the circle represents the sun. I'm not familiar with the address on the bottom but maybe that will help the cause."

"Nick's tracking down addresses."

"There's more than one?"

"More than one version of the flyer," Hank said. "Each one's the same except for a different address. That address took Nick to a market, where he found another one, which took him to a bank. Not sure where he's headed now."

"I wish I could help, Hank," Monroe said, shaking his head as he continued to look at the image. "I got nothing. But I could, you know, look into it later."

"Appreciate it."

Monroe set the flyer back on the table and saw the two place settings, awaiting the food cooling in the pans on the stove.

"Hank," he said. "I'd like to offer you a meal, but I wasn't expecting company, well, other than Decker, that is. I could split my veggie steak with you, if…"

"No need," Decker said. "I started to say earlier, I need to bug out. Hank's welcome to my veggie steak."

"But I cooked—Decker, we planned to—" Monroe's frustration began to rise again. Decker flaking out yet again. Why he let his friend continue to disappoint him, he couldn't say. But, clearly, it was time for Monroe to let go. No regrets. "Okay, man. I'm sorry you can't stay."

"It's something I really need to take care of, brother," Decker said. "Completely slipped my mind until I grabbed the plates. Unfortunately, the… temptation of fake meat doesn't trump what I gotta do, you know?"

"Okay."

"We're cool?"

Monroe offered his hand. "Eyes forward, full bore…"

"No regrets," Decker said and shook his hand. "Ain't it the truth, brother?"

This time Decker's grip was firm, but without the dominance display. Monroe walked him to the door, watched him stride down the walk, closed the door behind him and shook his head.

Finally, it was over. No more classes or exercises. No more pep talks. No remaining calendar commitments. Monroe had probably seen Randall Vail Decker for the last time. But he truly had no regrets. He'd said goodbye to the man—and the time he represented in Monroe's life— long ago.

"So, Hank," Monroe said, walking back to the kitchen. "Looks like the numbers worked out. Veggie steaks for two."

Hank looked over at the stove dubiously. "Actually, I need to get back to the precinct, some reports to fill out and loose ends to tie up, before I call it a day."

"Oh," Monroe said, his disappointment obvious.

"You could save it for Nick," Hank offered. "Heat it up later?"

"I'm sure Nick has something planned with Juliette," Monroe said. "But that's okay, I have a healthy appetite and can manage two veggie steaks—again."

Nick pulled onto the parking lot of the Rosedale Community Center and double-checked the address on the bottom of the flyer he'd brought from PFNB. He had the right place— and it was open late, no doubt for evening activities.

Inside the building, he found an expansive main room with a high, canted wood ceiling, scattered tables and chairs, and an information desk that faced the front entrance. Each end of the main room connected to additional rooms visible through glass walls.

He noticed a cork bulletin board against the near wall and veered in that direction. Again, he found several copies of the circle-and-triangles flyer hanging on the cluttered board and took one. But the address at the bottom of the flyer looked familiar. After a moment, it came to him. It was the library's address.

He'd reached the end of the line.

He approached the information desk, staffed by two middle-aged woman engaged with their computer displays. A banner hung over the curved desk advertising free Wi-Fi. Others pamphlets mentioned various exercise classes, and rules for use of the pool and a gym.

Nick identified himself to the closer of the two women and asked if she knew anything about the flyer. The other woman scooted her chair next to the first and they both examined it. Then shook their heads. Nick also discovered they had no formal approval process for hanging flyers.

Between the corkboard, plastic wall racks, one long table with stacks of neon paper, and the information desk itself, the place was a sea of flyers, pamphlets, newsletters and business cards. Nobody asked permission. When the quantity became too heavy, they tossed expired event information first, followed by items that looked particularly old. The community center had no surveillance equipment, but Nick hadn't looked forward to the idea of spending several more hours zipping through days of footage only to see the concealed figure pop in, pin flyers to the board, and hurry out, while revealing nothing identifiable about himself.

Nick really had come to a dead end.

He drove back to the precinct with the grainy image of the large man in a hoodie and sunglasses. The net result of a day's worth of investigation.

* * *

Back at the precinct, Nick swung by his desk to check for messages, saw that Wu had stopped by while he was out, and checked in with Captain Renard, showing him the security camera image of the hooded figure and the four versions of the circle-and-triangles flyer.

"Anything to connect the four locations to the murders?"

"Library, supermarket, bank and a community center," Nick said and shook his head. "Other than places that let people leave information for others, I don't see it."

"No chance those places are involved?"

"Community center... possibly," Nick said. "The others seem unlikely."

"We need something to connect Crawford and the flyers to the murders," Renard said. "Nothing incriminating on the flyers themselves."

"Something on Crawford's computer," Nick said. "I'll get an update from the techs. Barring that, we may need a search warrant for Crawford's residence."

"Hank mentioned it," Renard said. "Let me know if you need me to run interference."

Nick returned to the conference room with the burial site boards and long table piled with missing person folders. Hank sat on one side of the table taking notes. He looked up when Nick entered and said, "Checked with Monroe. Nothing registered. Got the impression he'd research it later."

Before Nick took a seat, Sergeant Wu arrived and stood in the doorway.

"Good. Got you both together. Checked with computer techs. Most of the data on the hard drive is encrypted or corrupted by the partial wipe, so it's slow going. So far, nothing incriminating."

"Something is definitely there," Nick said. "He had that computer ready for wiping the second anybody discovered his involvement in the murders."

"There are leasing records, information on various business sites, copies of contracts, but nothing criminal—other than some of the rates they were charging."

"The restaurant equipment is key," Nick said. "Crawford had no intention of opening that restaurant. They need to focus on any names or addresses or activity related to those orders, other than the orders themselves or the supplier."

"Any mention of the driver by name?" Hank said. "Crawford claimed to have never met the man. Prior knowledge would be a red flag."

"I'll check with them," Wu said. "But at this point, corruption and encryption are bogging down information retrieval."

"What about Nancy, the receptionist?" Nick asked. "She might have a copy of the encryption key or at least know where Crawford kept it."

"They asked her," Wu said. "She denied any knowledge of it. They also checked her hard drive, which wasn't encrypted, and came up empty. Looks like Crawford kept her in the dark."

"Same with his own family," Hank commented. "No idea about the flyers or the so-called specialists treating his illness."

"What about Rio?" Nick asked. "Crawford indicated this happened before, a long time ago in Rio, and that he participated. That's why they contacted him."

"Right," Hank said, remembering that part of the conversation. He picked up the phone and called the Crawford residence. As it rang, he placed the call on speaker.

After a half-dozen rings, a woman answered—Ellen Crawford—her voice a bit raw. "Hello."

"Mrs. Crawford, this is Detective Griffin," Hank said. He apologized for the intrusion during a difficult time. "As I said earlier, I want to find the people who drove your husband to this desperate act."

"Yes," she said. "Yes, of course. How can I help?"

"Your husband mentioned something about a trip to Rio," Hank said. "Rio de Janeiro, I assume. Do you recall that trip?"

"Lamar mentioned that he had been to Rio on vacation once," she said. "But that was long before we were married. As far as I know, he traveled there alone."

"Do you know when that trip occurred?"

A few moments of silence. "I'm not sure," she said. "More than twenty years ago."

"Did he bring anything back? Pictures? Souvenirs? Anything?"

"I haven't seen any photos from that trip," she said. "That was at least three homes ago. If anything remains, it might be in an unopened box in the attic. But my husband isn't—wasn't sentimental about that kind of thing. I doubt he would have carted that stuff from house to house. But, if you want, I could check."

By the tone of her voice, she dreaded the idea of rifling through musty old boxes of her husband's forgotten belongings. Considering what she had to deal with in the present, Nick couldn't blame her.

Hank cleared his throat.

"This could be important," he said. "If you're not up to it, I could swing by—at a convenient time—and check those boxes for you."

"No, that's okay," she said, resigned. "I'll check for any unmarked boxes in storage."

"I'd appreciate that," Hank said. "And, again, I'm sorry for your loss."

"Thank you," she said and disconnected.

Hank set the phone in the cradle and shook his head. "Not promising."

"I'll report back on the techs," Wu said and left the conference room.

Nick looked up at the two side-by-side bulletin boards with the photos and names of identified victims.

"Few more identified from the second site," he commented. "Any leads?"

"Been on the phone, notifying next of kin," Hank said. "And checking again with whoever was last to see them alive. Nothing. If they'd seen anything suspicious at the time of the abductions, it would have been noted in the files."

Nick spread out the four versions of the flyer. Each had an address to a location where another copy of the flyer could be found. He had a hard time believing that any of the four public locations hosted nefarious activity during business hours or after hours. The symbol *had* to mean something to someone.

And there was one place he hadn't checked.

Hank noticed Nick staring at the flyers and said, "Wild goose chase?"

"We're missing the significance of these," Nick said, gathering up the flyers. "One place left to check."

"Aunt Marie's trailer?"

Nick nodded. "You coming?"

"Got a few more calls to make."

"I find anything, I'll let you know."

As Nick walked out, Hank picked up the phone again.

CHAPTER TWENTY-SIX

Nishimura Koji sat slumped against the basement wall, the iron collar heavy around his neck, his right eye swollen where he'd been elbowed by his abductor in his attempt to escape.

He'd left work after finishing the evening shift at Office Silo, an office supply chain store, but never made it to his car. He hadn't seen his kidnapper since he'd been dumped in the basement with the other chained prisoners. But a different man had come to the basement on several occasions, dragging one of them away to protests and screams. A massive man wearing some kind of hellish, horned mask to terrify them.

As the hours passed, and the manacles and chains securing his wrists and ankles clanked with each slight movement, Nishimura began to feel as if he were trapped in a nightmare and couldn't wake up. The sodden gag in his mouth was rancid, and the odors permeating the basement were nauseating.

And yet, in the distance, coming from rooms above them, he heard the strains of classical music playing, each note drifting downward like pristine snow over a cesspool.

If he paused in his movements, he could distinguish the harpsichord and cello, a viola and a flute.

He'd had a girlfriend who'd loved classical music and she'd dragged him to various concerts over the course of their eighteen-month relationship. Since he was infatuated with her—for a time, anyway—he went to the concerts, listened to the CDs in the car and the playlists on her iPod blasting from her Bluetooth speakers. After ten minutes or so, he convinced himself that he was listening to Bach's Brandenburg Concerto No. 5. He hadn't heard it in over a year—since his girlfriend had ditched him, rather than continue a long-distance relationship while she attended college.

Now he had the crazy idea that she'd escaped the living nightmare in which he found himself trapped, carried away on musical notes far from danger, as if she'd anticipated this outcome. Illogically, he became mad at her—like a nightmare-induced grudge—for abandoning him to this fate.

An equally irrational idea occurred to him, that if he could somehow make his way to the source of that pleasant music, he would leave this hell behind and return unscathed to the real world. Maybe even see Gillian again. He could move to the East Coast. Ithaca, New York, wasn't so far away in the grand scheme of things. He fell into a dreamy daze, transported by the music, a faint smile on his face as he considered the changes he would make to take control of his life...

Minutes, possibly hours, passed before the basement door opened and the steps creaked. He was startled out of his reverie as the horn-masked man came to collect another victim.

But this time he came for Nishimura.

* * *

Upstairs, the elegant ground floor—featuring rooms with coffered ceilings and glittering chandeliers—had been turned into several dining rooms. Most of the guests milled about as candlelight reflected off their champagne flutes and wine glasses, chatting amiably. Classical music played in the background, piped through speakers concealed throughout the house, as they waited to be served their evening meal.

The men wore bespoke suits or dinner jackets, the bejeweled women evening gowns fit for a red carpet lined with paparazzi and celebrity gossip columnists. But nobody would mistake those gathered for celebrities, though a few might have been considered stars in Fortune 500 boardrooms. While those in attendance enjoyed the finer things in life, they also enjoyed anonymity.

For some in the Silver Plate Society, this was their second feasting ritual. A handful of those present had enjoyed two previous feasts. Of that number, two sat in wheelchairs, needing assistance to navigate the host's sprawling house.

Though the members exuded a sense of extravagant celebration, they also exchanged bittersweet knowing glances when Host escorted nonmembers, who had responded to the open invitations, to the back room. Empty Chair days meant that the feasts were winding down. And many of those present this time would not live long enough to attend the next official gathering.

The classical music faded and a bell clanged three times. Conversations gave way to an expectant silence.

A portly older gentleman in a chef's hat and jacket wheeled out a large serving cart filled with covered silver dishes and silver serving trays. Though everyone addressed him as Chef, his current role in the society, most members knew his unspoken name: Oscar Cavendish.

With a series of dramatic flourishes, he lifted the

covers off the dishes one by one, announcing the menu as he did so, so the participants could choose their courses for the evening.

"For your dining pleasure, I present Greek heart topped with capers, rocket greens, a fried egg, and a bordelaise sauce. Enjoy this one with sweetbreads in an offal croquette."

He revealed the next dish.

"Or choose Korean tongue marinated in soy sauce and sugar, deep fried with garlic and pepper."

Someone asked, "Adult or juvenile?"

"Both of these dishes come from hearty adults," Cavendish said. "For those preferring juvenile cuisine, let me turn your attention to this next dish, Russian kidney served with a light arrachera sauce. And next we have…"

After uncovering the specials, Cavendish placed them on the long banquet table so the guests could serve themselves. In the middle of that table, two severed human hands with painted fingernails had been arranged palms up to support a woman's severed head. The head and hands served as a decorative centerpiece. The woman's flesh and organs were not, however, featured on the evening's menu.

The remainder of Sheila Jenkins' dismembered body had washed up in a tidal pool.

"Meat?" someone called from the vicinity of the nonmember room.

"Ah, for those of you skipping our organ specials tonight, we will have rib roast, sirloin, porterhouse and rump roast platters coming up shortly, adult and juvenile, in a variety of ethnicities, including Greek, Korean and Russian, with more savory choices coming later this evening. One and all, please enjoy your meals as we savor the last days of this quarter's festival."

With that, Chef received a polite round of applause

from the members, and somewhat of an uncouth whistle from the nonmember contingent. Chef smiled, bowed slightly, and returned to his kitchen.

As the formally attired participants edged toward their preferred meal choices, they woged in delight, one after the other, almost in a ripple effect. The majority revealed themselves as Geiers, with a smattering of Coyotls and Schakal, with even greater Wesen variety in the nonmember section of the house.

A short time later, one woman said to another, "Have you tried the Greek heart? It's to die for!"

"Well, somebody certainly did!"

The first chuckled, delighted. "I heard they collected a whole family."

"Maybe the others will turn up in the later dishes," the second said optimistically. "Certainly on the meat platters."

"The young are so sweet and tender," the first commented. "It would be a crime to waste a single morsel."

"Don't know about you," the other whispered conspiratorially, "but I skipped breakfast and lunch so I could gorge myself tonight."

He drove the speed limit, stopped at red lights, and signaled his turns to avoid any hint of law breaking. They got Al Capone for tax evasion. He had no intention of getting nabbed for reckless driving.

As he approached the designated location, he signaled this one last turn and drove carefully into the dark alley. The hood of the white van gleamed under the sickly pallor of one weak light bulb over the rear door of some unidentifiable business. But the scant illumination succumbed to the surrounding darkness within a few feet of the door. A fading island of light.

The van's headlights cast twin cones of brightness

directly ahead in the suffocating darkness, but could not banish the shadowy edges of the confined space. On the other side of the alley, he noticed a battered Dumpster, overflowing with refuse. As the van slowed to a stop, a dark silhouette stepped out from behind the far side of the Dumpster, raising a shielding forearm as he neared the headlight beams.

Conscious of the possibility that he'd driven into a trap, the driver scanned the other man's silhouette for any telltale signs of a firearm. Knives and hand-to-hand combat he could handle. Bullets flying out of the darkness were another matter.

He leaned out the side window and addressed the other man.

"You alone?"

"Of course," Ray Swartley said. "Ron's in jail."

The brothers worked as a team, but that didn't rule out the possibility of accomplices or hired guns.

"And you got away," the driver said. "Good for you, Ray. You want a gold star? I'm fresh out."

"No, I'm not—I asked you to meet me because… I need your help."

"My help?" the driver asked. "Why should I help you?"

"You know why."

"Do I?" he said menacingly.

"You know…" Ray glanced around the alley, as if somebody might overhear him. "For looking the other way."

"You were paid to look the other way, Ray," he said. "Your brother, too."

"It's gone," Ray said sheepishly.

"What's gone? Your money? How is that my problem?"

"The cops confiscated it, along with our pills," Ray said. "And they pinched Doc Filbert. I lost the money, the pills, and my source."

"Again, Ray, how is this my problem?"

"I need some money," Ray said. "To bail out Ron. Once he's out, we'll run. You'll never see us again."

"You've already been paid, Ray," he said. "I'm not a bank. Or a soft touch. And I'm not your friend. We conducted a business transaction and that transaction is over."

He shifted the van into reverse, but Ray reached out and grabbed the doorframe.

"C'mon, I don't need much money," Ray wheedled. A sign of his desperation, Ray woged into his Reinigen form, his rat-like features twitching. "You know Ron and I would never talk. We'd never tell anybody you buried those bodies in the vacant lot. And once we leave town, the cops won't even be able to find us to ask."

"Glad to hear you would never talk, Ray," he said. "Because we had a deal. I paid you well to keep your damn mouth shut."

"Yeah—but—only thing is, with Ron locked up, the cops, they're gonna put pressure on him to make a deal," Ray said. "Hell, you know they're gonna offer me a deal if I tell them what I know. Maybe one of those witness protection things. They'd hide us away good, and all we'd need to tell them was who buried those bodies."

"Changed my mind, Ray," the driver said. "I'd like you to deliver a message to your brother."

"Sure. What's the message?"

He grabbed the automatic he'd placed on the car seat under his leg, pointed the barrel out the window at Ray— whose mouth dropped open in surprise—and blew a hole through his throat.

The round ripped through Ray's spine and ricocheted off the side of the Dumpster. Ray stumbled backward in a collapsing, uncontrolled stutter-step, and flopped to the ground, staring up into the evening sky as he bled out in the smelly alley.

Tossing the gun on the passenger seat, he backed out of the alley in a smooth, cautious arc, then drove away, signaling as he switched lanes, traveling a couple miles per hour under the speed limit.

Aunt Marie's trailer was a treasure trove of Wesen lore and weapons to combat them, but after flipping through several old tomes and illustrated journals, Nick had found nothing specifically dealing with the circle-and-triangles symbol.

Many different types of Wesen had been known to eat human flesh and organs, or employ specific human body parts as ingredients in various remedies. Which helped explain why Lamar Crawford had colluded with the Wesen responsible for the bare bones murders. He must have clung to the possibility that they could whip up a cure for his fatal illness with spare parts from the humans they butchered.

Aunt Marie's journals listed various species of Wesen who might consume human flesh and organs, and discussed those who believed that sliced-and-diced or liquefied or powdered human organs possessed magical healing abilities, but he found nothing related to the symbol on the flyers. Nick was missing a bigger picture, a conspiracy of silence about something that happened every twenty years, possibly less often.

In addition to researching the symbol, he'd checked for references to Rio and found nothing other than the usual Grimm hunting and killing instructions with notations about potential dangers and difficulties. In other words, more of what he'd been accustomed to reading in these pages.

With a sense of futility, he left the trailer, locked it behind him, and drove from the lot to Monroe's house. Though the Blutbad hadn't recognized the symbol immediately, he had his own arcane reference materials for research. And, unless something turned up there, Nick would have to wait for somebody to break the code of silence about the cannibalistic event, or hope a witness to one of the abductions came forward.

Meanwhile, judging by television, print and radio coverage, the press was having a field day raking the entire Portland Police Department over the coals for ineffectual investigative methods. Multiple murders, the remains of abducted tourists found in shallow graves, and not a single viable suspect had been brought in for questioning. Captain Renard parroted the official line of "pursuing multiple lines of inquiry," a response only marginally more substantial than "no comment."

Somehow, the cannibal aspect of the murders had not leaked to the press, but that revelation could not remain secret indefinitely. And once that lurid detail hit the airwaves, panic would immediately follow. Nick dreaded the idea of conducting a murder investigation in the middle of a media circus. But, without a new lead to crack the case, that scenario was unavoidable.

Worst of all, Nick faced the real possibility that the murderers would skip out of Portland before he found them, as they must have done in Rio all those years ago, and who knew how many times before that. Whatever event was happening in secret would end soon, and the cabal would pack up their cleavers and meat saws and disappear for two or more decades, to start all over again, in some other unsuspecting city.

I can't let that happen.

CHAPTER TWENTY-SEVEN

When Nick arrived at Monroe's house, the Blutbad was already deep into researching the image on the flyers. The old books spread across the table looked like a re-enactment of Nick's last hour or two inside Aunt Marie's trailer. But Monroe's books had been passed down along Wesen rather than Grimm family lines, most of them probably the former property of Monroe's grandfather, a real old school Blutbad.

"Anything?" Nick asked. "I struck out at the trailer."

"Sorry, Nick," Monroe said. "If I had found anything, believe me I would have called or texted or something."

Nick paced the room, feeling as if the answer hung suspended in the air in front of them, just out of reach, that they were one intuitive leap away from solving the mystery. *Connect the right pieces and the confusing image will shift into focus.*

"Talk it out," Monroe said. "Go over what you know."

Nick nodded, willing to try any new approach that might jar some tidbit loose.

"Two shallow grave sites, the most recently used site discovered first, by accident, when a father and son stumble upon human remains while geocaching. Otherwise, we might not have known about this until… it was over." Nick stopped pacing and corrected himself. "No. The mountain bike kids discovered the second site accidentally too."

"Which points to what, sloppiness on the part of the murderer?"

"That's what I thought," Nick said. "But Crawford indicated that this big event was winding down. Maybe the murderer figured he'd be long gone, along with the other conspirators, before the bones were ever found."

"So… expediency?"

"Right," Nick said. "And his miscalculation leads to the discovery of the remains, giving us a small window to catch those involved before it ends."

"Go on."

"The ME discovered that the bones had been boiled, that flesh had been cut from the bones with knives and a meat saw, confirming the cannibal aspect of the murders."

"So people are abducted, cooked, and, probably, fed to others."

"He started with tourists," Nick continued. "People who might not be missed for days or weeks. But the more recent dumping ground contained the remains of locals."

"Acknowledging the shortened timeframe for discovery."

"And Crawford, before killing himself, clearly indicates more than one person is involved, that it's part of a bigger conspiracy. The flyer links him to the second site, where I recovered a piece of an identical flyer."

"Identical except for the addresses."

"Right. Gloved guy in a hoodie and sunglasses drops the flyers at four locations, each with an address that points to one of the other locations. I located all four addresses. A closed loop."

"Four locations above reproach," Monroe said.

"At least three of the four, anyway," Nick said. "These conspirators might meet at the community center."

"But it's unlikely they would be, you know, chowing down on human flesh in a community center."

"Maybe it's used as a meet-and-greet or a place to organize their... activities for later," Nick said, trying ideas out loud to see if any made sense.

"So Crawford reveals this conspiracy," Monroe said. "But he doesn't participate. He's helping them for a cure."

"Which they never deliver," Nick said. "He realizes too late they lied to him, and kills himself to protect his family."

"That's a big commitment," Monroe said. "Shoving a gun in your mouth and blowing your brains out."

"He had, at most, a month or two to live. Once he accepted the fact that the promised cure was never coming, he sacrificed that time to keep his family safe."

"I'm just saying, two months or not, that's a hardcore exit," Monroe said. "If he was desperate enough to do something that drastic to keep his family safe..."

"What did he know?" Nick said, nodding. "Techs are combing through his computer—"

"Which he nuked before biting down on his gun."

Nick sat down at the table. "He knew the identity of some of them," he said. "And he knew what was happening. He placed that restaurant equipment order for them."

"Nick, if they are killing and eating so many people," Monroe said, a bit awkwardly, knowing that Blutbaden could easily be involved in the murders, "they would need a restaurant-sized setup. Think about it: they are butchering humans, storing meat and cooking, I'm guessing, a lot of meals."

"Crawford's restaurant was a front," Nick said. "He placed the equipment orders knowing full well the shipment would be hijacked. The driver was collateral damage."

"Or an appetizer," Monroe said solemnly.

"The killer has been abducting various races and ethnicities, both genders, children, teens and adults," Nick said. "But typical serial killers often have an identifiable victim type. Variety seems important to this one."

"Nick, he's not picking the victims," Monroe said. "He's fulfilling orders. It's the cannibals or the cook who is requesting the variety."

"Many meals," Nick said, nodding. "If this really is a rare event, they'd want to… sample many types of human meals."

"Let me see those flyers again," Monroe said, reaching across the table. He spread them out like a poker hand made up of very large cards. "They're not exact."

"Right. Each one has a different address."

"No," Monroe said. "Something else."

Nick circled around the table and looked down at the four pages.

"You're right. The circle and triangles are redrawn for each version." He stacked the four sheets and held them up, close enough to an overhead light that he could see through the pages. Each circle and surrounding series of triangles beneath the first page looked like ghost images. He took away two pages, and the difference became clear. Then he switched to the other pair to confirm his findings. "Look at that," Nick said, pointing. "On each page, one of the triangles is out of whack."

Monroe took the flyers and spread them across the table again.

"Decker—my old friend you met when Juliette dropped you off—he thought the drawing might be the sun," he said. "Circle and rays coming off it. But the acute triangles all face inward, toward the circle. If you were drawing the sun, wouldn't the rays point away from it?"

"You'd think so," Nick said. "And on each page, the triangle closest to southwest—imagining the circle as a compass—is turned to the side."

"Nick, that's an invitation."

"An invitation to what?"

"Hold on," Monroe said, grabbing one of the books nearby with decayed binding. He flipped through it and stopped when he saw a semicircle illustration on a page. Spaced evenly around the semicircle were three acute triangles, the middle one pointing away from the semicircle. "That circle is not the sun," Monroe said as he tapped the illustration. "It's a table, surrounded by chairs. The chair facing away is called the"—he traced some lines of text in German with his index finger—"*Leeren Stuhl.* The empty chair."

"An empty chair?"

"That's the invitation," Monroe said. "There's an empty chair waiting for you—well, not you, of course, but anyone who figures out what the invitation means. It's starting to come back to me. I think my grandfather used to talk about—the man was incorrigible—about this old world— and, by old, I mean, really old world—tradition among a secretive group of Wesen who would host an elaborate traveling feast where the main course was 'long pork.'"

"Human?"

Monroe nodded, abashed. "Supposedly it lasted a whole month. Very hush-hush. Never the same city twice. And rare! One of those once, maybe twice in a lifetime happenings, like a solar eclipse or the appearance of some named comet. Anyway, my grandfather always dreamed about finding an invitation close to home and sneaking off to enjoy the, uh, festivities. Of course, I thought it was a myth. Some kind of Wesen fairy tale. Mostly, I thought my grandfather made it up."

"Does that book say anything else?"

Monroe skimmed the entry. "Not much," he said. "Membership is hereditary and members generally don't speak about it to nonmembers. Ah… here it says they call themselves the Silver Plate Society. Sounds very upper crust and snobby, in a, you know, cannibal sort of way."

"Silver," Nick said. "Like a silver anniversary?"

"Every twenty-five years," Monroe marveled, nodding. "That sounds about right. Say you attend at twenty-five years of age. Maybe you go again at fifty. But, seventy-five? Assuming you're still alive, you might not want to fly across the globe for a month-long gorging fest."

"And this time, the gorging fest is in Portland."

"Lucky us."

"It is an event for them," Nick said. "You're right. Judging by the number of victims we found, they are gorging nonstop for the entire month. If they wait twenty-five years for this and may not live to see the next one, they won't want to waste a day."

"A fair assumption."

"And if they are using industrial-grade restaurant equipment," Nick continued. "This is not a mobile pop-up restaurant. They are in a fixed location."

"What are you thinking?"

Nick opened his mouth to reply but his cell phone rang, cutting him off. He checked the caller ID and took the call.

"What's up, Hank?"

"Patrol unit found Ray Swartley."

"Is he talking?"

"Not unless it's from beyond the grave," Hank said. "Somebody shot him in the throat, blew out his spine."

"Gotta run," Nick told Monroe. "Figure out how to accept the *Leeren Stuhl* invitation. I want *you* in that empty chair."

Monroe followed Nick to the door, shaking his head. "Seriously, Nick, that's not funny."

As Nick hurried to his car, he called back to Monroe, "Think like your grandfather!"

"Still not funny."

Classical music continued to play softly throughout the feast house. A Rachmaninov Piano Concerto segued into Beethoven's Symphony No. 9 as Chef wheeled out another serving cart, this one loaded with uncovered cuts of meat on silver serving trays, each labeled with a card to indicate ethnicity and age.

"As promised, ladies and gentlemen," Chef said, "I present to you the finest rib and rump roasts, along with sirloin, T-bone and porterhouse steaks, all seasoned to perfection. And, in a little while, I will have additional organ dishes for your dining pleasure."

Polite applause met his pronouncement and—from the nonmember section—a few raucous cheers and indelicate whistles. None of the members seemed to mind. The last days always had more of a carnival atmosphere, restraint abandoned as Host instructed Chef to empty the larder. However, the nonmembers, unbeknownst to them, were observed during the *Leeren Stuhl* days by both members and Host, evaluated for potential membership. The most uncouth were forgotten, but those who participated with a measure of decorum and respect would find themselves taken aside before the festivities ended and offered membership in the society.

Once Chef had transferred the serving trays from his cart to the buffet-style tables and backed toward the kitchen, Host stood up and held his palms up for attention, temporarily placing the collection of savory meats off-limits.

A tall, tanned, distinguished looking man in his mid-sixties, he had a full head of cotton-white hair, matching moustache and beard, and wore a black tuxedo with a powder-blue bow tie to match the color of his twinkling, amused eyes. As a tenth-generation member of the society, he had embraced with gusto his first invitation to host. Members knew him as Graham Widmark, though none would refer to him by name during his time as Host.

"Your attention, ladies and gentlemen of the Silver Plate Society, and invited *Leeren Stuhl* guests," Widmark said in a booming voice. "We have a late arrival this evening, the son of a member—recently departed—who wishes to begin his membership, officially, with us here tonight. His family has been part of our select group for seven generations." He raised his right arm toward the crowd, hand extended to direct their attention, and said, "Please welcome our newest attending member of the Silver Plate Society!"

From out of the gathering, the youth emerged and stood by Widmark.

Applause greeted his introduction.

A nervous smile on his face, he gave them an awkward little wave of acknowledgment, embarrassed by the attention. Then he looked down, hooking his thumbs in the hip pockets of his jeans.

"Welcome, my boy," Widmark said, one arm wrapped around the boy's shoulders. "Good to have you!"

"Thanks," Kurt Crawford replied.

CHAPTER TWENTY-EIGHT

"Somebody's cleaning up loose ends," Hank had said on the way back from the dark alley where Ray Swartley had been silenced for good.

"We're running out of time," Nick had replied. "And leads."

Nick had called ahead to have Ron Swartley pulled out of lockup for questioning again. Now the detectives stood outside the interview room. Hank paused on his crutches as Nick glanced down at the glossy eight-by-ten photo, a copy of the crime scene photo of Ray's head and shoulders, the bullet hole in his neck garishly visible. They wanted the photo for its shock value.

"Whoever did this didn't care if we identified Ray," Nick said. He indicated the closed door with a slight nod. "Is this a mistake?"

"The killer wants Ron to know about the hit on his brother?"

Nick nodded. "Clear message to Ron: Keep your mouth shut."

"Or else," Hank finished. "You said it yourself. We're running out of leads. Ron's not talking anyway. He sees this, maybe he decides he needs protection. And we offer it, if he cooperates with the investigation."

With no other viable options, they walked into the interview room.

Ron sat on the opposite side of a metal table, handcuff chain through the bar welded to the tabletop. Though he lacked the imposing physical dimensions of the Mordstier and seemed sullen and resigned rather than aggressive, they had no idea how he'd react to the news of his brother's death. In addition to restraining the Reinigen, Nick hoped the handcuffs reminded Ron that he was helpless and that that feeling, even if it worked only on a subconscious level, raised the level of his anxiety. If he thought he had no way out, Ron was more likely to tell them what he knew.

Hank elected to stand, supported by his crutches, rather than sit down next to Nick facing the prisoner. Nick stared at Ron, who nervously ducked his head down to rub his stubble-covered chin against his knuckles.

"Got bad news, Ron," Nick said, holding the photo in his hands, facing away from Swartley. "About your brother."

"Ray? What about him?"

Hank leaned forward. "Somebody decided he'd look better with a hole in him."

"What?" Ron looked from Hank to Nick to the back of the photo. "This some kind of cop mind game?"

"No game," Nick said and slapped the photo down on the table between them.

It took a stunned moment for Ron to register what he was staring at, that the lifeless eyes, the bloodless face, and the ruptured and distorted throat belonged to his brother.

Woging, Ron jerked backward, reflexively trying to escape. His handcuff chain snapped taut against the metal bar, trapping him within view of the photo. He sagged back in his chair, as far as the handcuffs and the bar would allow, staring off to the side rather than confronting the evidence of his brother's grisly death.

"Turns out you were the lucky brother," Nick said. "Getting caught."

"Good or bad," Hank said. "Luck runs out eventually."

"Tell us who did this to Ray," Nick advised, "and we'll talk to the district attorney. See that you're protected."

Ron sat still, not speaking or reacting.

"You don't want to end up like Ray," Hank said with a little nod toward the photo Ron continued to studiously ignore. "Shot dead in a dark alley, rats nibbling on your face."

"Nasty way to go," Nick commented.

"I don't know who they are," Ron said quietly, almost too low for them to hear, "or where they are."

"Tell us what you do know," Nick said.

"You know what I know," Ron said. "People died. The bodies were dumped in the lot."

"Bones," Hank said. "Not bodies."

"Same difference," Ron said. "Dead is dead."

"Who shot your brother?"

"How should I know?" Ron said angrily, rattling his chain. "I been locked up in here the whole time. But when I get out, I'll find the bastard and kill him myself."

The last statement reeked of false bravado. Pale and trembling, Ron seemed afraid, very afraid of what he'd become involved in and the enforcer who had snuffed out the life of his brother. Shock had been replaced by naked fear. Ron realized he was in over his head and he was withdrawing.

"Last chance, Ron," Nick said. "You're going down for the illegal narcotics, assault and battery. You don't talk, we can't help you."

"Nobody can help me but me," Ron said quietly, in the manner of a new personal mantra. "Got nothing else to say."

True to his word, Ron sat in silence until they left.

The detectives returned to their desks, checking for any updates or messages. Nick had a message from Juliette, wondering how much longer he'd be at the precinct. They updated Captain Renard on Ray's execution and Ron's silence. With no leads to go on, pressing or otherwise, they decided to call it a night.

Ellen Crawford sat in the dark, on the wing chair that faced the hall leading to the front door. Waiting. Only after the African American detective called her with additional questions had she noticed Kurt's absence. She'd thought he'd retreated in grief to his bedroom. But she should have known better. She should have remembered the steely determination in his eyes, the *Leeren Stuhl* flyers clenched in his hand.

After she hung up on the detective, she'd called up to Kurt's room, to have her son go into the attic, gather the Rio photos along with Lamar's journal about his feasting holiday, and burn all the evidence before the police showed up with a search warrant. That's when she discovered that Kurt had slipped out without telling her, leaving her to burn the box of Rio evidence in the fireplace herself—and worry about him. Because she knew instantly where he had gone—without planning or preparation.

She'd set certain wheels in motion, but her plan required patience. Kurt had reacted impulsively, running off to the feast. First she'd lost her husband because of the Silver Plate Society and now she had to wait, helplessly, hoping that they wouldn't kill Kurt on sight. All she could do was wait, and worry.

Anxious hours passed…

Finally, the deadbolt clicked, the doorknob turned and the door eased slowly open, as if Kurt were merely sneaking in after breaking curfew. He slipped into the foyer and closed the door gently behind him, locking it before continuing down the hall.

"Where have you been, young man?"

Her stern voice had the desired effect. He flinched, stopping in his tracks as his eyes adjusted to the darkness.

"Mother," Kurt said, and walked toward her.

Once he entered the living room, the ambient light spilling down from the moon and stars in the clear night sky bathed his excited features in a wan glow.

"Mother," Kurt said again, kneeling before her and taking her hands in his, "they want to meet you."

As he approached his house, Hank sighed.

Finally, another long, frustrating day over.

Not for everyone, though. He shook his head in sympathy as he passed the Riveras' place—a few doors down from his home—and noticed the plumber's van at the curb. Sign on the side panel read BUSTED FLUSH PLUMBING.

On top of everything else, please spare me plumbing emergency hassles.

Hank parked his Volkswagen CC, struggled out of the driver's seat, hopping on one good foot until he reached through the open window and retrieved his crutches, once again regaining his three-legged balance.

Surprised the guys aren't calling me Tripod.

Getting from the car to his doorstep, unlocking the front door, working his way into the house and relocking the door behind him was almost the end to his daily struggle navigating the world on crutches.

By the end of the day, his underarms ached, his neck and shoulders were stiff and his hands were cramped and sore. He'd taken to sleeping downstairs rather than ascend a flight of stairs as one extra challenge to bookend his day.

Meanwhile, he counted the days until the cast came off, grateful to be in the home stretch.

Standing in the foyer of the dark house, he whipped off his lanyard and badge and placed them on the table near the front door. Next, he unclipped his holstered sidearm and placed it on the table, along with his cell phone and house keys. His thoughts preoccupied with the day's events, culminating in the discovery of Ray's body and Ron's refusal to give up any information about the killer or any of the conspirators, Hank absently reached for the light switch by the door and flicked it up—

Nothing happened.

He flipped the switch down and up again. Still dark.

Must have blown a damn fuse, he thought, already visualizing the hazards he'd encounter on his way to the circuit breaker panel in the dark, on crutches, hoping he didn't break his neck in the attempt.

"Son of a bitch," he whispered in the darkness and sighed audibly.

As he turned on his good heel and prepared to swing forward on the crutches, he noticed a rustle of movement in the darkness, a darker shape with weight and substance moving through the open space toward him. Alarmed, he reached back for his gun—

—a jolt of pain struck his chest.

His jaw clenched violently and he lost control of his limbs.

A brief feeling of vertigo seized him. He slipped sideways, the crutches flopping out from under him as 50,000 volts convulsed his body. He struck the floor but had only a disconnected sensation of the impact.

Before the shock and disorientation of the Taser attack had completely passed, a figure loomed over him, gun in hand.

"You're the last one," he said. "A place of honor at the table."

When the man kneeled down beside him, Hank recognized his face.

His mouth needed a few seconds to relearn how to speak. And he gulped air like a fish out of water before croaking out a single word.

"You!"

The man's hand was a blur of motion, the butt of his gun racing toward Hank's head—

His aching head greeted his return to consciousness.

He squeezed his eyes shut against the throbbing pain, willing the discomfort away, as if it had the nebulous tenacity of a bad dream. Alternately, he hoped unconsciousness would reclaim him. But the longer he waited, the worse his head hurt and the less likely sleep or stupor would claim him. Instead, he sat up—

—and heard the rattle of chains. He felt the pull of their weight on his wrists. He opened his eyes, or tried to, and experienced a new throb of pain, along with a fresh surge of nausea, which he forced down as he became aware of the gag in his mouth. With his good heel, he pushed himself back against the wall and, finally, felt the iron collar bolted around his neck. Grimacing, he forced his eyes open to take in his surroundings.

A long dim room, cloaked in shadows, housing a dozen other huddled figures, male and female, chained to the walls, occasionally readjusting their awkward positions with listless movements. *Starved, dehydrated or drugged*, he guessed.

As he listened to their distraught whimpering and moans, another possibility occurred to him: hopelessness.

They're resigned to their fate.

He tried to recall what had happened to him, how he had wound up in what appeared to be an underground room chained to a wall with other prisoners. He remembered Ron, refusing to talk, driving home, the Busted Flush Plumbing van, fumbling for his keys at his own door then… everything after that was a blur. Had he opened his door and gone inside? Had someone crept up behind him?

A Taser! He remembered someone attacking him with a Taser. A mild concussion could explain the memory loss. But knowing what happened wouldn't free him of the chains tethering his neck, wrists and ankles, or the gag stuffed in his mouth.

After a few minutes and despite his pounding headache, his eyes adjusted to the relative darkness. Some of the prisoners closest to him stared, but even those who had shed their gags said nothing to him. As he worked on pushing the gag from his mouth, to ask them what they knew about their captor or captors, he realized that he recognized some of the faces silently watching him.

For a moment, he wondered how that was possible. Then it came to him in a flash. The missing person folders. Some of the missing people were very much alive, down here, with him, waiting to be eaten by cannibal Wesen.

And now Hank himself was among the missing.

CHAPTER TWENTY-NINE

Dominik Koertig arrived at Portland International Airport at 10:10 AM on American Airlines Flight 2027 out of Chicago's O'Hare Airport. Barrel-chested, he sported a meticulously trimmed beard and wore a tailored overcoat. He had passed the entire flight in complete silence, preparing himself for his upcoming ordeal. If any of his fellow passengers had considered lobbing a conversational gambit his way, one glance at his dour demeanor squelched the idea.

He took his aluminum briefcase from the overhead storage bin and—since he had no baggage to claim—proceeded directly through Concourse D and caught a taxi into the city of Portland, a thirty-five-dollar fare to the Pearl District, plus a five-dollar tip when the cabbie dropped him off at the entrance to the Paragon Hotel.

He stopped at the concierge desk to pick up his reserved room key and took the elevator to the fifteenth floor. Unoccupied, Room 1502 had been reserved for him the prior day and had received a maid's attention. When he crossed the room to a businessman's table, he spotted the stack of flyers printed on faux parchment paper, as expected. Beneath the four flyers, he found a folded map of the city.

Koertig sat down in the nearest of two padded chairs and reached under the table. His fingertips skimmed across the table's underside until he found the loaded 9mm automatic taped there. Beside the gun, he found three extra magazines, similarly secured. He ripped the tape free, opened his briefcase and placed the gun and extra ammunition in the padded interior. From the briefcase, he took a pen and legal pad and wrote down the four addresses. Then he opened the map and noted the location of each address.

Checking his wristwatch, he calculated how much time he had before the festivities began. Of course, given the exact location, he wouldn't need to wait long hours to crash the party, but he required a full house to complete his task, so he would go the *Leeren Stuhl* route.

He took out his cell phone and called his local contact. Since he had time to kill, he would gather as much information about the participants as possible. Knowledge of the players might prove crucial before the night was over.

When his contact answered the call, he skipped pleasantries and said simply, "Tell me everything you know."

After his late night at the precinct, Nick spent the morning alone reviewing the missing person case files in the precinct conference room. A few more sets of human remains had been identified, mostly through dental records, and the pattern continued to hold.

The second site featured the remains of tourists—with Alex Chu, Chinese male, early thirties, traveling up the West Coast on a road trip—while the Claremont Park site had been the final resting place for two other missing locals—Nakamura Reika, Japanese female, twenty-two, employee at a Pearl District bridal shop, and Esperanza

Rios, Mexican female, thirty-six, school cafeteria employee—reinforcing the notion that the killer had stopped scouting tourists in recent weeks and had instead chosen locals, possibly based on their ethnicity and age.

Nick made a few calls to relatives, informing them that the remains of their loved ones had been found, giving them closure, if nothing else. He would have liked to tell them he had their killer in custody and that person would never see the light of a free day again. Instead, he had to tell them the PPD was pursuing all lines of inquiry and was hopeful of an arrest soon. The meaningless words stuck in his throat.

After a few hours with his head either buried in case folders or pressed to a telephone receiver, Sergeant Wu arrived with an update from the computer techs.

"They found a bunch of commercial and residential rental properties on Crawford's computer along with fishy leasing agreements."

"Fishy?"

"The names on the contracts appear fake, either aliases or stolen identities. Almost seems like insurance fraud, but there aren't any claims. I checked with Crawford's carrier."

"Residential addresses?" Nick asked. "I thought Crawford dealt strictly with business leases."

"That's another part of the fishiness," Wu said. "The addresses don't exist."

"What?"

"Techs think they might be in code."

"Fake names and fake addresses?"

"That's what they tell me," Wu said. "I took a sample, to check. All phony as a three-dollar bill. Are two-dollar bills phony again? Or still legal? You never see them in circulation anymore. Hey, where's Hank?"

Nick looked across the conference room table at the

empty chair. Hank hadn't stopped in for as long as Nick had been there.

"He's not at his desk?"

"Passed it on the way in," Wu said. "Unoccupied."

"He hasn't called in," Nick said.

He took out his cell phone and called Hank. After ringing several times, the call went to voicemail.

"Hank, it's Nick. Give me a call when you get this." He looked at Wu and shook his head, perturbed. "Let me try his home phone." He dialed again and this time the call was directed to an answering machine. He left a similar message and disconnected. "This is not like him."

"He's on crutches," Wu said, considering. "Maybe he had an accident."

Nick started to imagine Hank climbing stairs on crutches, a nasty fall. Hank could have called an ambulance, or might still be lying in pain in his house, unable to reach a phone. Or could he have followed up a lead on his own and run into trouble...?

Rather than continuing to speculate about what might have happened, Nick said, "Have a uniform swing by his place."

With concern for his partner's safety placed on low boil until he had more information, Nick attempted to turn his attention back to the missing person case files, but soon gave up on that avenue of investigation. He had to assume the abductions happened without the presence of a witness and that the victims were chosen for what they were, not who or for any other traditional motive.

What he really needed to figure out was the location of the month-long feast.

He spread out the four different flyers on the desk, glancing from one innocuous address to the next. Then he went in search of a map of Portland and pinned it up on the Claremont board, which required less space for victims. One by one, he drew an X over the address on each flyer. Of the four locations, the community center might function as a meeting place for the Silver Plate Society. He supposed the time had come to stake out the location, to wait and see if any unusual meetings took place there. Figuring out what constituted an unusual meeting without attending each and every one on the premises was the problem.

And time, the lack of it, was a major problem.

As he stood there, slapping the barrel of a ballpoint pen against his palm, he said, "Residential properties."

And then he remembered another case, a body washed up in a tidal pool. The body of Sheila Jenkins, an employee at a property management company, head and hands removed to thwart identification. At the time, the case hadn't fit the profile of the bare bones murders. But, since then, the bare bones case had included a suicide cover-up and an execution. What if Sheila Jenkins had been a loose end? The bare bones killer had buried the bodies in shallow graves to buy time until the feasting month ended. What if the same stalling tactic applied to Sheila's execution? Keep her role unknown or at least obscured until it was too late to matter.

Nick hurried to his desk and grabbed the Sheila Jenkins file, picked up the phone and dialed the extension for the computer forensics department.

"This is Detective Burkhardt. There's another computer we need to check and cross-reference with Lamar Crawford's. Yes, this is related to the bare bones murders." Nick read the address for Forrester Cade Realty, Sheila's place of employment. "See you there in fifteen minutes."

Located in the Pearl District, Forrester Cade Realty's office stood between a luxury spa and a trendy art gallery, and its workmanlike aesthetic suffered in comparison. The interior featured modern furniture and fixtures, similar to those at LC Leasing, Inc., but the walls and doors had been painted with bright and bold colors, adding a warmth that had been lacking in Crawford's workplace.

Nick arrived before the computer tech and introduced himself to Noel Forrester, one of the partners—Robin Cade, the other partner, was vacationing in Italy—and explained that he was working the Sheila Jenkins case and needed access to Sheila's computer and written records. Forrester oversaw the small staff of leasing agents with an amiable air. With his silver hair, ruddy cheeks and ample girth, he would've been a natural as a department store Santa Claus.

If the man had something to hide or had any involvement with the Silver Plate Society conspirators, he could have stonewalled Nick and demanded a search warrant, but he wanted Sheila's murder solved as much as anyone and immediately agreed.

"Anything you need," Forrester said. "Let me know."

At that moment, a tall, hunched man with curly black hair and round glasses, wearing a green-checked shirt, jeans and brown loafers stepped into the office and looked around as if startled by his surroundings. He carried a black messenger bag, the strap slung casually over one shoulder. When he spotted Nick, he made a beeline toward him.

"We a go?" he asked.

Nick nodded. To Forrester, he said, "Gary Popa, one of our computer guys."

Forrester introduced himself and shook Gary's hand.

Gary glanced at Nick. "Where's the workstation?"

"Follow me," Forrester said, leading them past several occupied desks to a low-walled but roomy cubicle in the back right corner of the office. "So you think Sheila had prior contact with the person who murdered her?"

"Either she knew her murderer," Nick said. "Or she knew something the murderer wanted kept secret. That's our working theory."

"Suppose that makes sense," Forrester said, rubbing his jaw thoughtfully. "As much as a senseless tragedy like this *can* make sense."

Gary sat at Sheila's desk and reached for her keyboard.

"You'll need this," Forrester said, leaning over the desk to write Sheila's username and password on a sticky note.

Gary took the note, thanked him, and started typing.

"You know, Sheila was full of energy," Forrester said to Nick. "Never complained. Always willing to go the extra mile, take on any challenge. I miss... I miss seeing her around here. Sometimes I come in the office and look over here, at her desk, expecting... Then it hits me again."

"I'm sorry for your loss," Nick said.

As Forrester started to walk away, Nick tapped his arm.

"We may need to take the computer back to the precinct for analysis."

"That's fine," Forrester said absently. "Her client files are backed up. Don't really care about a piece of hardware. What's it worth? Couple thousand, tops. If it helps catch Sheila's killer, you can keep it."

"You'll get a receipt," Nick assured him. "And it will be returned."

"Just let me know if it helps you catch the bastard," Forrester said and wandered away absently, shaking his head.

Nick's cell phone rang: Wu.

"Burkhardt."

"Nick," Wu said, a note of alarm in his voice. "Somebody broke into Hank's place. Back door was jimmied."

Nick walked away from the tech's rapid keyboard clacking. "What?"

"And Scarpelli says Hank's missing."

"Missing? How does he know—?"

"He found Hank's gun, cell phone, keys—and crutches—on the floor in the foyer. And Hank's car is out front. All patrol cars have been notified to be on the lookout for him."

"Are you there now?"

"On my way."

"I'll meet you there." Nick turned to the tech. "Gotta go. You okay here?"

"I'm good," Gary said. "I can take this tower with me?"

"That's what the man said," Nick replied. "Call me soon as you find anything."

Nick hurried to his SUV, and raced to Hank's house.

Unsure what he hoped to find at Hank's place, Nick checked everything the junior patrolman and the crime scene unit had already examined. As Hank's partner, Nick hoped he might notice something the others had missed.

He started with Hank's VW CC. Doors were locked. No sign of a struggle in the car. After the Swartley interview, Hank had left the precinct alone. Nick had watched him drive off the lot from his Land Cruiser. If he'd planned to stop anywhere before home, he hadn't mentioned it to Nick.

Wu came outside and met Nick as he approached the house.

"Crime scene is dusting contact points for prints," Wu said. "Back door—point of entry and, probably, exit— has been wiped down. Prints on the front door, probably Hank's. We'll know later."

"Neighbors?"

"Scarpelli and Billbrough are canvassing nearby houses," Wu said. "No reports of gunfire or any altercation in the street. One neighbor"—Wu checked his notes—

"Ted Malone, saw a plumber's van outside a house across the street. So far, nobody on the block called a plumber last night."

"Don't suppose Malone got a plate number."

"No," Wu said. "Had no reason to be suspicious at the time."

Inside Hank's house, Nick noted Hank's firearm, phone, keys and crutches scattered around the floor, near an overturned table by the front door. Nick tried to imagine the sequence of events: Hank struggling into the house on his crutches, setting down his gun, phone and keys on the table. Then he fell or... he'd engaged in a struggle.

"Any blood?" he asked a tech kneeling nearby.

"Negative for blood," the man said. "But the foyer light bulb is missing."

Hank had come home to a dark house, on crutches, unable to turn on the lights, caught unprepared for his attacker...

Nick walked toward the back of the house. No signs of a struggle beyond the entry point, but a couple items of furniture had been bumped or pushed aside to clear a path to the rear door, where the lock had been jimmied. Through the back door, Nick examined the ground: a few partial prints leading toward the back door, more definitive prints leading away.

"Only one set of prints," Wu said.

"Hank was unconscious," Nick said. "If he was awake, he'd have struggled. We'd see evidence of that inside or out here." Nick followed the footprints. "His assailant didn't drag him out to the van though. No heel drag marks."

"He carried him?"

Nick nodded. "The depth of the prints increases on the way out. His weight basically doubled. Strong enough to carry Hank to the van. Twenty, maybe thirty seconds, from back door to the van. Over so fast, nobody witnesses the abduction."

"Why Hank?"

"Good question," Nick said.

They'd worked the case together. But Hank had interviewed Crawford's family alone. Was the killer keeping tabs on them? Lamar Crawford had certainly feared for his family's safety. But Hank had returned to the precinct with his information. If the killer thought he'd uncovered something, why not grab him before he could tell anyone else?

Or had Hank returned to the Crawford residence to follow up on the Rio photos? Nick doubted that. After the phone conversation, the widow had planned to check for the photos herself. And if Hank had found information crucial to the case he would have phoned Nick, not retired for the night.

"Makes no sense. Grabbing a homicide detective," Wu said, "inside his own home."

"His guard would be down," Nick said. "Caught in the dark, ambushed."

"But why Hank?" Wu repeated.

During the course of the investigation, Hank had become known to the killer, apparently observed by the killer, even before the abduction. Why Hank? Nick closed his eyes and imagined the two bulletin boards in the conference room, filled with the names and photos of the recovered victims. Various ages, both genders, multiple ethnicities. Greek, Korean, Japanese, Russian, Hispanic, Vietnamese. A vast variety of victims for the cannibal Wesen to devour. There had been an African American woman, too. But as far as Nick could recall, none of the victims had been African American and male.

Until now.

CHAPTER THIRTY

Frustrated with waiting for the crime scene test results at Hank's house and the tech results from Sheila Jenkins' computer, Nick returned to the precinct to re-examine, yet again, the accumulated evidence in the conference room.

He'd placed the Portland map on the Claremont Park board before he'd left and he continued to stare at it and the four Xs he'd drawn to mark the addresses listed on the four flyers. He turned his head to the side a bit, stood up and grabbed a red marker from the narrow tray. Leaning over, he drew lines to connect the four addresses. Connected, they formed a rectangle. He picked up a blue marker, proceeded to draw a curving shape to connect all four points and managed a rough circle, almost an ellipse.

Maybe the round shape was an analog for the circle on the flyers.

He recalled the one triangle that faced away from the circle, the *Leeren Stuhl*, or open chair, and wondered if the equivalent spot on the map circle marked the location of the feast. He grabbed a legal pad and wrote down the approximate address of that southwest point on the circle.

At that moment, he heard quick footsteps behind him.

At first he thought Wu had come with news on Hank, but as he turned he saw that it was Monroe, with an anxious look in his eyes.

"Nick, we're running out of time before—where's Hank?"

"Taken," Nick said gravely. "Killer grabbed him at his house last night."

"The killer? The bare bones killer? As in, the Silver Plate Society killer?"

"Yes, I believe so," Nick said. He approached Monroe and lowered his voice. "I believe Hank was taken, in part, because he's African American. For the menu variety."

Monroe looked up at the board, the photos of the victims. "So they haven't—they didn't take a—?"

"Not a male. Not until Hank," Nick said. "I have to hope he's still alive."

"The *Leeren Stuhl* days are almost over," Monroe said. "The empty chair invitation is the last week. Judging by how long the flyers have been in circulation, there's only a day left—two at the outside. Once it's over, these guys vanish for twenty-five years. Scattered to the four corners."

"I'm well aware that the clock is ticking."

"Right. But I wanted to—this is even worse than I thought, because if Hank is the, if it's the last day, then that means that he's…"

"Spit it out, Monroe."

"Once I knew the Silver Plate Society was responsible for the—for everything, I went back and checked for references about them and, it turns out, the last day of the feasting month is reserved for the *Straffe Kette Abendessen*, the 'Tight Chain Supper.'"

"Do you know what that means? Exactly?"

Captain Renard walked into the conference room.

"I do," he said. "It's the live meal."

"How do you—?"

"Finally heard back from some of my own sources," Renard said. "Various rumors and myths about the Silver Plate Society, embellished over the years by urban legend and blatant exaggeration, but some things kept turning up, and the Tight Chain Supper was among them."

"But a live meal means…"

"He's chained to a table, alive and awake," Monroe said. "And they cut into him with knives and claws and, well, cannibalism doesn't get much more hardcore than that."

"If that's happening tonight," Nick said, "We've only got a few hours to find him…" *Before it's too late,* he finished silently.

Sergeant Wu approached, rapped his knuckles on the doorjamb.

"Got something."

Nick, Renard and Monroe gave him their undivided attention.

"Just got off the phone with Gary down in Computer Forensics," Wu said. "The same phony residential addresses and names that they turned up on Crawford's half-nuked hard drive, he's also found on Sheila Jenkins' computer."

"Fake addresses and IDs get us nowhere," Renard said.

"True," Wu said. "But Sheila Jenkins was not as security conscious as Crawford. No encryption. No self-destruct program. Apparently, Crawford—who dealt only with business leasing—knew Sheila. He contacted her to arrange some premium, short-term, and secret residential leases, luxury homes, high-end condos and apartments."

"Short term," Nick said. "As in one month?"

"Give or take a week," Wu said, nodding. "Crawford convinced her the clients were celebrities who demanded anonymity and were willing to pay a premium for it."

"Celebrities?" Monroe asked. "Really?"

"Based on her notes, that's what Crawford told her.

Business had been slow and, with substantial security deposits in hand, she didn't ask a lot of questions."

"How does this help us?" Renard asked.

"In one of her personal folders, Gary found a file called 'Celebrities' which, it turns out, is a translation key to the phony addresses. Beside each phony address is the actual address of the property."

"Warrants?" Nick said, glancing at Captain Renard.

"We've been waiting for a break on this case," Renard said. "The DA has a judge on standby. We've got probable cause. They'd move fast. But with a kidnapped police officer at risk in a murder spree, we've got an emergency exception." He turned to Wu. "How many addresses?"

"At least a dozen."

"Teams of two, minimum," Renard said. "Let's hit as many addresses simultaneously as possible. Go!"

Wu rushed off to start making arrangements for coordinated raids, while Renard returned to his office to update his superiors. Monroe caught Nick's arm on his way out of the conference room.

"Nick, the feast won't be at any of those rental homes," Monroe said. "You're looking for a secluded location, with an official host. That's where they'll have Hank and any other kidnap victims who are still alive."

"I realize that," Nick said. "But if we catch any members of the society, we'll have them take us to that location."

"The Silver Plate Society has survived for hundreds of years," Monroe said. "Maybe longer. Even if you catch them, they won't talk."

"Oh, they'll talk," Nick said as he hurried out. "Believe me, they'll talk."

They spent the next two hours raiding spacious rental homes, luxury condos and apartments. Nick partnered with Wu for backup. They personally checked three of the addresses, and faced one disappointment after another. Each location showed signs of recent habitation and more recent abandonment. Dishes in the sink, an occasional tipped over trashcan, closet doors open, hangers spilled across the floor, and, under one bed, a forgotten pair of red Manolo Blahnik sandals. The contents of a few trashcans had been burned in place.

Other teams recovered some articles of clothing, coffee, alcohol and bottled water, but few food items. Nick imagined they wouldn't eat anything much more than what was being served on the cannibal menu and would always plan to arrive at the feasting location with a hearty appetite. They'd waited twenty-five years to indulge themselves on human flesh. No sense filling up on the bread basket.

Unfortunately, none of the teams recovered anything identifiable to any particular individual. The members of the Silver Plate Society had traveled to Portland under false identities. Maybe Crawford's computer had a key to convert the false identities to real, prosecutable names, but if so, the techs hadn't found it.

When Nick had a moment away from Wu, he called Monroe to tell him the raids had been a waste of time, too much time. The crime scene techs would dust the rental properties for prints and swab for DNA on any items left behind, but identification remained a longshot unless some of the cannibals were already in the system.

"Nick, if they've abandoned those rentals, today must be the last day," Monroe said. "From what I've read, they'll gather together at the feasting location, a farewell celebration, like closing ceremonies."

"How could they know we were coming?"

"Could be the last day timing," Monroe said. "Or…"

"Or what?"

"Or they've been told Hank's a cop," Monroe said. "And they're covering their tracks as a precaution. In a way, this is good news."

"Good news?" Nick asked, incredulous. "How?"

"I'm just saying, they won't forfeit their last day," Monroe replied. "This is it for them, Nick, the big finish—the *pièce de résistance*—after which they'll go their separate ways for twenty-five years. So no, they won't deprive themselves of their last glorious day of feasting. The *Straffe Kette Abendessen* is highly anticipated by these guys. It *will* go on as planned. And if they're saving Hank for that last 'tight chain' meal—"

"Then he's still alive."

"Guaranteed."

"For how long?" Nick asked, dreading the answer.

"That's the bad news," Monroe said. "Hank's running out of time."

Nick took the Portland map from the Claremont Park board to Monroe's house. He set it on the table, hoping that between the two of them they might come up with the location for the cannibal feasts. Above the map, he laid out the four flyers. Monroe stood beside him, hands stuffed in the front pockets of his light cable-knit sweater, frowning in concentration.

"If these flyers are the invitation," Nick reasoned, "the guests need to find the banquet. But each address leads to one of the other addresses. And none of them are the banquet location."

"They're a set," Monroe said. "You need all four."

"That's why I marked the locations on the map."

"And you made a red rectangle," Monroe said, "and a blue—kinda—circle."

"I thought maybe the circle matched the circle drawn on the flyers," Nick said. "Converting it to the map and the open-chair triangle as the location."

"What's at that location?"

"Near as I can tell," Nick said. "A soccer field."

"So, unless it's underground," Monroe said. "Probably not a cannibal resort."

"No," Nick said. Moving the circle from the flyer to the map had seemed like a good idea at the time, but it led nowhere.

"I remember reading something about the invitation," Monroe said, walking around to the far side of the table and picking up some of the old books and journals he'd been checking for details on the Silver Plate Society. He had a series of sticky notes attached to more than a dozen pages. He leafed through two books before opening one of a more recent vintage. "Here it is. 'When Open Chair arrives, make your invitation and partake in our feast.'" He looked at Nick and shook his head. "I thought the open chair *was* the invitation."

Nick looked at the map for a moment.

"I've been focusing too much on the information we lacked—or thought we lacked—rather than on what we know."

Monroe returned to Nick's side of the table. "You have an idea?"

Nick took the red marker out of his jacket pocket.

"This rectangle..." he said as he uncapped the marker. "If you connect the four points, top left to bottom right and top right to bottom left—" Nick drew an X inside the rectangle "—it sort of looks like the folds of paper on the back of an envelope. An invitation."

Monroe tapped the intersection of the two lines. "And 'X' marks the spot."

Examining the nearest cross streets on the map, Nick said, "I know that place. There's an old shopping center there. And a used car lot on the other side of the street."

Monroe was shaking his head as Nick talked.

"What's wrong?"

"They'd want something more refined, Nick. Something secluded and maybe a bit scenic. That place is low-rent commercial. Probably an eyesore."

They stood together in silence, Nick conscious of the ticking clock. Each minute that passed put Hank at greater risk. They had no idea what time the 'tight chain' feast would begin. Once they started cutting into Hank with knives and claws—Nick couldn't let it get that far.

"What are we missing?" Nick wondered aloud.

The *Leeren Stuhl* was planned to bring nonmembers to the feast. Nonmembers were on the outside, looking in. They would need to figure out how to get to the damn feast.

The flyers held the answer—they *had* to.

Each flyer led to the location of another. The four addresses had to show the way. A complicated code would defeat the purpose of the open invitation. If it was too hard to figure out, nobody outside the inner circle would come. And they had gone to a lot of effort to spread the flyers around town, hiring a hooded and gloved man to run around and put them in place.

"It's there," Nick said, pointing at the X. "It's the only thing that makes sense."

Monroe jumped on his computer and brought up a mapping site, zooming in on the location marked by the center of the X and then accessing photographic street views. Rotating the street view through the full 360 degrees, he confirmed Nick's memory of a shopping center and a used car lot, along with a bowling alley and an audio equipment store. Nothing remotely upscale.

"No way, Nick. Not here."

Nick looked over his shoulder. He noticed a bus stop shelter near the intersection.

"That's it!"

"No, man, I'm telling you, these guys are into upscale—"

"Not the banquet," Nick said. "A pickup point."

Monroe thought about it for a moment. "Ah… a chauffeur! That makes sense."

"But how?" Nick wondered. "How do they contact the chauffeur? No phone number on the flyers."

"Not how," Monroe said. "When."

"Same problem," Nick said. "Or does it run every thirty minutes, like a shuttle at Disney World?"

Monroe picked up one of the flyers. "The open chair location on the circle," Monroe said. "It's not southwest. The circle doesn't represent a compass. It's a clock face."

"Which would make it… seven o'clock."

"Picked up at seven," Monroe said. "Dinner wouldn't be until eight o'clock. Maybe later. But not before."

"Hank has until eight o'clock."

"Not that we'd want to cut it that close," Monroe said. "Okay, 'cut' was a poor word choice, but yeah, eight o'clock is a safe bet."

Nick checked the time and experienced a stab of anxiety, bordering on panic. Hours wasted with so little time left before Hank became the main course at a cannibal party.

"That gives us less than an hour to get in position for the pickup."

"Us?"

"Well, you," Nick said. "I assume the invitation is Wesen-only."

"Me?"

"Yes, you're accepting the *Leeren Stuhl* invitation." Off Monroe's panicked expression, Nick added, "Don't worry.

You don't have to eat any flesh. And I'll be following you all the way—at a discreet distance."

"Okay, sure," Monroe said nervously. "Absolutely nothing could go wrong with that plan."

CHAPTER THIRTY-ONE

With a nervous Monroe in tow, Nick stopped at Juliette's house to pick up Hank's belongings, where he'd left them after the crime scene team finished with them. Juliette heard him pull up and greeted him at the door with a kiss, then trailed after him as he purposefully crossed the room. Her coat still on, pocketbook on the sofa, she must have arrived moments before him.

"Good, you're here," she said brightly. "I left a couple messages. I finally got us reservations at Escapade, that new restaurant I've been wanting to… Nick, what's wrong?"

"I'm sorry, Juliette," Nick said. "Tonight's no good."

"Tell me," she said, touching his arm. "I want to help— are those Hank's crutches?"

Nick had stood the crutches in the corner, and placed Hank's sidearm, shield and personal effects in a large manila envelope in a drawer, which he recovered, checked and closed again.

"Hank's in trouble."

"Did he fall? Is he in the hospital?" she asked, placing herself in front of him. Ever since she learned about his responsibilities as a Grimm and about the existence of

Wesen, she refused to be left out of any conversations on those subjects. She'd been kept in the dark so long, she was determined not to let it happen again and create a gulf between them. "Did he reinjure his heel?"

"No," Nick said. "It's worse than that. Much worse."

"I don't understand."

"Monroe's in the car," Nick said. "Captain Renard is meeting us here."

"Where is Hank?"

Nick sighed. He'd told Juliette the answers to all of her questions but there were some details about Wesen culture—the consumption of human flesh and harvesting of human organs—that remained unknown to her. And sometimes truth was best absorbed in small doses. She'd been accepting about everything in his Grimm life so far, but could she handle knowing about Wesen cannibal dinner parties? He thought it prudent to save a full explanation for when time wasn't so critical.

"Hank's been abducted."

"What? Who? I mean how—why?"

Setting down Hank's stuff, Nick caught her upper arms in his hands, a calming gesture.

"We've been working the bare bones murders," Nick said, proceeding cautiously.

"Yes, I know," she said. "I've been following the news reports about the two sites with shallow graves. It's awful."

"Hank got too close to the perps—the people involved."

"There's more than one killer?" Juliette asked, startled.

"We don't know," Nick said. "But we suspect others are covering up the murders."

"And they're Wesen?"

"Yes, definitely."

A car horn beeped outside. Renard.

"Is Hank—? Have they—?"

"We think Hank is alive—for now. But we need to act fast," Nick said and gathered Hank's items. "Gotta go. But I'll explain everything later."

"Call me!" she said, following him to the door. "As soon as you know Hank's safe, call me!"

Nick promised to call her and nodded to Renard who stood waiting beside Nick's Land Cruiser. Obviously they couldn't involve Wu in a Wesen takedown. But at some point, they might need to call in reinforcements. For now, to ensure Hank's survival, they had to approach the cannibal Wesen discreetly.

Nick slid the crutches into the back seat with Monroe, who still hadn't warmed to the idea of going undercover with a secret society of Wesen cannibals. Not by a longshot.

Renard rode shotgun and Nick took the driver's seat, tossing the manila envelope on the corner of the dashboard. Nick checked the clock.

"We should arrive ten to fifteen minutes before the pickup."

"You're sure about the place and the time?" Renard asked.

"Hope so," Nick said. "Hank's life depends on it."

Traffic cooperated. They arrived fourteen minutes before the scheduled pickup time, assuming the open chair position on the circle represented 7:00 p.m.

Nick parked on the street, outside the strip mall parking lot, with an excellent line of sight in every direction. They expected somebody to pick up the Wesen who had accepted the invitation, but the mode of transportation remained a mystery. A stretch limousine would look garishly out of place in the rundown commercial district. But the Wesen driver could easily pull up in a taxi or an airport shuttle, even an old school bus, without attracting undue attention.

270

Monroe had remained quiet during the drive, but after Nick parked the Land Cruiser he became agitated, sighing and scrubbing his moustache and light beard with an open palm.

"Nick, I want to help. I do. I consider Hank my friend too. I'm just saying, with your captain here, don't you think he might make a better *guest* at this banquet—and a much better undercover operative? Experience has to count for something—oh, no offense, Captain. I was referring to your police experience, not cannibal experience."

"No offense taken," Renard said, scanning left and right, mirroring Nick's vigilance.

"Won't work," Nick said, without taking his attention away from the road. "Captain Renard is too high profile. After the televised press conferences this week, his face has been all over the airwaves in Portland. Too risky."

"Right—you're absolutely right," Monroe said. "Okay. It's fine. I can do this."

"You can do this," Nick said. "We've gone over it. You're prepared. Take the ride. Stay calm. We'll follow you to the site."

"Okay. I'm ready."

Nick passed folded copies of the flyers over his shoulder to Monroe.

"In case they ask how you found them."

"Right," Monroe said nervously.

"Wait, I recognize that woman," Nick said, pointing toward the corner of the intersection. A middle-aged female walked beside a teenage boy. "From the photo on Crawford's desk. That's his wife, Ellen, and her son, Kurt."

"They're headed toward the white van near the bus stop," Renard said.

"Hank's neighbor noticed a plumber's van near his house last night."

"This one's plain white," Renard said. "Ford Econoline. Already parked there when we pulled up."

Monroe watched the woman and her son, followed the direction of their path toward the waiting van.

"Hmm," Monroe said. "That looks familiar."

Ellen Crawford and her son stopped beside the driver's side door. The driver turned toward them expectantly. Mother and son woged briefly, revealing Geier features to their driver. At the same moment, the driver woged, displaying a fierce Blutbad visage before reverting back.

"Oh, no!" Monroe said, gripping the back of Nick's seat. "This is not good."

"What?" Nick asked.

"The driver," Monroe said. "That's Decker."

Nick stared, leaning forward over the steering wheel, trying to catch a better glimpse of the driver.

"You're right. It's him."

"Who's Decker?" Renard asked.

"Monroe's friend," Nick said.

"Old friend," Monroe said. "From another time in my life." He looked at Nick, alarmed. "What now? Nick, he knows me! I can't go through with this."

Renard shifted in his seat to face Nick directly.

"Are we overlooking the obvious here?" he asked. "Arrest Decker. Force him to take us to the location. Even if that requires putting a gun to his head."

"Too risky," Nick said, shaking his head. "Hank has an hour, two at the outside. If Decker calls our bluff, Hank dies and the Silver Plate Society scatters in the wind. Lost for twenty-five years."

"Who said I was bluffing?" Renard's jaw was set, unwilling to compromise, but unable to refute Nick's logic. And killing Decker meant losing any chance of finding Hank in time.

"Nick's right," Monroe said. "This society has stayed secret, its members hidden, for hundreds of years. We can't risk Hank's life on the slim chance that Decker will cooperate. Knowing him as I do, I doubt he'd talk. He's more likely to dig in his heels and enjoy the challenge of frustrating us until it's too late." He heaved a resigned sigh. "Unfortunately, I am the best option."

He stepped out of the SUV, brushed the creases out of his trousers, patted the pockets of his cable-knit sweater and nodded.

"Okay, I'm ready."

Nick leaned out of the window. "Are you sure about this, Monroe?" he asked, concerned for his Wesen friend. The plan hadn't changed, but the risk level had. An anonymous ride as an open invitation guest had seemed simple enough. But with Decker involved, Monroe was no longer anonymous. "We could wait and follow the van without you."

"We talked about this," Monroe said. "If I'm on the van and you lose it, I can find a way to call you once I arrive at the location. If I'm not on the van and you lose it, you lose Hank. And any chance of stopping the Silver Plate Society for at least twenty-five years."

"But he knows you," Nick said. "He knows you're reformed. You're the last Wesen who'd want to attend this… party. You'll have to convince him you've…"

"Fallen off the wagon," Monroe finished. "It happens, Nick."

"Yes, but can you sell it?"

"Let me worry about that."

He's right, Nick thought. They had no other choice. Either Monroe convinced his old friend that he'd lapsed in his reformed lifestyle or they would have to roll the dice with Renard's suggestion, a gun to Decker's head. Given both options, Nick had more faith in Monroe's gambit.

"Good luck," Nick said. "We'll be right behind you."

"Not too close," Monroe said. "If he spots the tail..."

No need to finish that statement. Hank's life depended on Decker driving the van to the banquet site. Any delay or misdirection on his part and Hank would pay the ultimate price.

As Monroe walked casually toward the white van, Nick glanced at the dashboard clock. Two minutes to seven. Unconsciously, his hands tightened their grip on the steering wheel. All he could do now was follow the van and hope the plan worked.

Throat dry and heart racing, Monroe checked his wristwatch as the second hand approached twelve. Almost seven o'clock. Glancing left and right, he quickened his pace. Nobody else approached the white van. Decker could pull into traffic at any moment. Monroe turned the corner, mentally preparing his story. He'd spent the last few days trying to convince Decker how to lead a reformed lifestyle and failed miserably. Now he had to flip the script.

All week I've told him he never has to eat meat again, Monroe thought. *Now I have to convince him I'm dying for a porterhouse steak. Well, not porterhouse in the traditional sense of the dish, but...*

Monroe took a deep breath to calm himself.

Not even close, he thought, nerves jangling. *Okay, work with the nervousness. Tell him, I'm jonesing for some meat.*

The van's engine rumbled to life.

Monroe hurried forward and called out, a little too loudly, "Room for one more?"

Decker turned, looking out the window, and did a double take.

"Monroe? What in the ever-loving hell are you doing out here, brother?"

"Decker?" Monroe said, again too loudly, feigning surprise. "I had no idea you were part of this?"

"Part of what, buddy?" Decker said, tugging down the brim of his battered, black leather confederate cap. "I'm just out for a drive with a few friends."

Stalling for time, Monroe pulled the folded flyers out of his trouser pocket.

"I finally figured out what these are. My grandfather always talked about finding an invitation."

"Your grandfather, huh? Quite the hellion," Decker said. "Nothing at all like you, Monroe. You color inside the lines, brother."

"You know me," Monroe said hastily. "My history."

"Yes, your *history*," Decker said. "Past tense. I know all about the present-tense Monroe and—gotta be honest with you, brother—he's no fun. At. All." He put the van in gear. "Now, if you'll pardon me, I'm running late."

"Wait!" Monroe said, catching the doorframe. "Don't you see, Decker? All week I've been trying to change you, but it's made me realize what I've been missing, what I've been denying myself. My grandfather knew the truth. This… society thing, it's a once-in-a-lifetime opportunity."

Decker shrugged. "More or less."

"Who knows if I'll ever get this chance again?" Monroe said. "I'll probably never know where the next one happens. Maybe on the other side of the world. I mean, think about it, Decker. If you live my lifestyle and you wonder if you'll ever fall off the wagon—and it's bound to happen, right?—what better time than now, what better excuse—than *this*!"

Whether from desperation over Hank's plight or some long-suppressed desire to walk on the wild side again,

Monroe had almost convinced himself he wanted to join the diners in a final night of cannibalistic revelry.

"Please," Monroe said. "I *need* this."

Resolute, Decker stared at him for the longest time, then a grin split his face. "First, lift your shirt and give me a three-sixty."

Monroe complied; Nick expected the driver might check for a wire. "Okay?"

"Hop on board, brother," Decker said. "It is glorious."

Monroe nodded, fumbled with the door latch before yanking it open. Three people sat on the second row bench seat: the Crawfords, and a lightly bearded man with ramrod posture wearing an expensive overcoat, dark trousers and black boots. Monroe glanced behind the bench seat and saw only storage space with a small scattered stack of large magnetic signs advertising phony businesses.

"In the back?" he asked.

"Nonsense," Decker said. "My good buddy rides shotgun. But make it snappy. We're burning daylight."

Monroe slammed the side door shut and hurried around the front of the van, wondering briefly if Decker would run him down. He climbed into the passenger seat and slammed the door shut, staring straight ahead so he wouldn't be tempted to glance toward Nick's Land Cruiser.

"Ready."

"Not so fast," Decker said. "You're forgetting something."

Monroe looked down, then glanced over his shoulder.

"Of course, safety first." He yanked down the seatbelt and, with a trembling hand, poked the tongue at the buckle a couple times before he heard the lock engage.

"Safety first," Decker said. "But cell phones second. Our party, our rules. Everybody goes off the grid for the evening." He held out his hand expectantly. "Tell me you aren't carrying a cell phone and I'll perform a full body cavity search to make sure we're being truthful with each other. So hand them over, folks. And make it quick."

Nick had anticipated this. Of course they'd want to avoid cell phone tracking and any possibility of photographic or recorded evidence. Monroe reached into the pocket of his vest where he'd placed his cell phone and surrendered it. Decker ejected the sim card with practiced ease, using a straightened paper clip affixed to his keychain.

"Next!" he barked.

One by one, the passengers handed over their phones and Decker removed the sim cards, stuffing the tiny chips in his trouser pocket. He tossed the phones in the glove compartment.

"Don't worry. You'll get them back on your way home tonight."

"Lead the way," Monroe said, belatedly realizing how stupid he was for uttering that particular phrase. "Obviously, I mean, I'm looking forward to this evening in a mouthwatering, stomach-grumbling way. Licking my Blutbad chops."

Decker looked at him and, despite the fixed grin on his face, his eyes remained cold and wary. *He takes his chauffeur duty seriously,* Monroe realized. *Jokes about the feast are falling flat. Worse, my rambling is making him suspicious.*

"Sorry," Monroe said. "This is a big step for me."

"One last thing," Decker said, leaning forward slightly to reach under his seat.

Monroe tensed. In that instant, an image flashed through his mind: Decker pulling out a gun and shooting him right in the middle of his forehead. Monroe never suspected Decker's role in the Silver Plate Society. And what was the exact nature of that role? More than cannibal and chauffeur? Could Decker have butchered and buried all the victims in Nick's bare bones case? Just how dangerous was his old friend? Monroe forced himself not to recoil or flinch—and almost sighed audibly when he saw only black cloth come up in Decker's hand.

"Put these over your heads," he said, tossing hoods over the seat to the three other passengers. "Everyone except Monroe."

"Why not him?" Ellen Crawford asked suspiciously.

"He's an old buddy," Decker said. "I trust him. Besides, he's visible up front. How will that look out on the highway? A passenger wearing a hood over his face? The goal is to not draw attention to our little shindig. That's why I'm driving this crappy old van and not a stretch limo for you folks." He waved his index finger in a horizontal circle, like a baseball umpire signaling a home run. "C'mon, people! You want to party, you wear the hoods!"

Overcoat man nodded once, slipped the hood on. Ellen nodded to her son and they both complied with Decker's directive.

"Satisfied?" Ellen asked, her voice a bit muffled by the cloth.

"Indubitably, dear lady," Decker said. "And congratulations, folks. You've made the last run of the last night. So let's rock and roll!"

He shifted the van into gear, checked the side view mirror and pulled out into light traffic. Monroe also checked the mirror, ostensibly backing up Decker's caution, but actually he hoped to see the Land Cruiser enter the flow of traffic behind them. With so few cars on the road, Nick would have to hang back, way back, to avoid detection.

Decker began to whistle a series of classic rock tunes. After a few minutes of this, Ellen Crawford said, "Must you?"

"Excuse me, lady?"

"Is the radio busted in this crappy van?"

"We got us a firecracker," Decker said, chuckling. "Guess some folks get irritable when they're hungry." He turned on the radio, hit a preset which delivered a dose of death metal, and cranked up the volume. "Better?"

Ellen fired back, "Immeasurably."

Decker slapped the steering wheel, laughing heartily.

"Don't look so glum, Monroe," Decker said after a sideways glance. "You'll remember this night for the rest of your life."

Monroe nodded, feigning as much enthusiasm as possible with a queasy stomach and virtually bleeding ears. Hunching a bit in his seat, he glanced surreptitiously in the mirror again, hoping for the slightest glimpse of Nick's Land Cruiser. No such luck.

In a crowded van, headed for a cannibal's feast, Monroe was completely alone.

CHAPTER THIRTY-TWO

In the hours since his captivity began, Hank had managed to remove his gag, but had little to show for his work trying to loosen the freakishly large eyebolt to which they had chained his iron collar. The ungainly bolt looked as if it had been forged by a medieval blacksmith—and for all Hank knew, it had. The collar seemed of more recent vintage, perhaps Civil War era. Both were crude but effective.

The eyebolt itself had been welded to a metal plate, which had four heavy duty bolts at the corners screwed into the concrete wall. Rather than a single point to stress, he needed to place back-and-forth pressure on the entire plate. If he could work enough play into those four points, he might then wedge his chain in the gap between plate and wall and wrench the plate free. But even if he succeeded in freeing himself from the wall, he would need to drag the collar chain and heavy metal plate with him, in addition to the wrist and ankle chains. With twenty pounds of chain and metal in tow, his chance of making a stealthy escape was practically nonexistent.

Once he'd removed his gag, he told the other captives he was a Portland PD homicide detective working on the case and that his partner and the entire police force would leave no stone unturned to rescue them. As the hours crept by with no sign of a police raid, their initial excitement waned. And they finally sank back into their hopeless state of resignation when the man they called the butcher—a horn-faced Wesen reminiscent of a rhino—collected one of their number, an Indian woman named Nisha Nadeem, who kicked and screamed as the butcher dragged her from the basement.

Hank flung himself against his chains, straining to block the large man, to engage him somehow and stop him before he could leave with the woman, but he couldn't come close enough to his path to even warrant the Wesen's attention.

"Let her go!" Hank yelled. "Take me instead!"

The butcher paused, glanced dismissively at Hank and said, "Your time is coming, hunter. Soon."

Hunter? What the hell's he talking about? I'm no hunter.

Without another word, the butcher ascended the stairs, dragging the hysterical woman with him. The door slammed shut with an ominous clang of metal, followed by the click of a deadbolt falling into place.

At that moment, Hank realized the Wesen was overconfident. He'd met little, if any, effective resistance culling his "livestock" from the chained herd and had no doubt the routine would continue until they were all dead. That overconfidence was a weakness Hank could exploit—given the opportunity.

"There's nothing you can do," Alice said miserably, as if reading his thoughts. "Doesn't matter you're a cop. He's a monster. You see that, don't you? One by one he takes us away and butchers us. Then, upstairs, they eat us."

"She's right," said Philippe Brosseau, a young man across from Hank. "One time, he left the door open... just enough that we could hear the... the chopping sounds."

"I'll think of something," Hank said. "Help is coming."

"Look at you," Alice said bitterly. "You're chained, same as us. No different. And nobody knows where we are, or they'd have come already. Face it, Detective Hank Griffin, we're all going to die here. Even you."

"Shut up, Alice!" Philippe said, lashing out with his leg and kicking an overturned slop bucket. "You're not helping."

"Nobody can help."

Hank watched the iron-bound wooden bucket rolling toward him. He hooked his good foot through the metal handle and pulled it toward his hands. The butcher fed the captives slop every few days and usually collected the buckets afterward. But he was so sure of his own dominance over the dejected humans, he'd become careless.

For the rest of the night, Hank worked on breaking the bucket down into its constituent parts. He slammed it against the wall, battered it with his manacles, and stressed it with an application of his chains. One of the slats cracked and broke free, forming a crude wooden stake. The iron bands might be useful as levers against the metal plate bolted to the wall, but he concentrated on filing the narrow end of the stake down, rubbing each side against the rough concrete wall, sharpening the point.

An opportunity. That's all he needed.

While music played upstairs, Hank worked on the pieces of the bucket. As the early morning hours approached, the other captives—sensing they were safe from selection for a while—dozed off, one by one, falling into fitful, nightmare-laden sleep. A few of them screamed during the night.

In the morning, exhausted, Hank hid the stake under his sprawled body, along with one of the iron bands, and permitted himself a nap. But he shouldn't have bothered. Anxiety followed him into a light sleep that ended each time the horned face of the butcher leaned over him and said, "Time's up, hunter!"

Hank startled awake repeatedly, clutching at his hidden weapon, only to come to his senses and realize the image had been a fractured nightmare. Twice during the day the butcher came, first taking a middle-aged man who had slipped into a state approaching catatonia. The butcher tugged his slack body out of the room. Minutes later, he came back for a college-aged woman who kept screaming, over and over again, "No—no—no!"

Both times, Hank yelled at the butcher, insisting the butcher take him and not his chosen victim. The first time, the Wesen ignored him, but the second time, he paused long enough to say, "I'd cut out your tongue, hunter, but they want to hear you scream."

Hours passed in frustration. Hank had promised these people he would help them, but he was powerless unless the butcher came within arm's reach. Forced to bide his time, Hank continued to work on the bolts of the metal plate that secured his collar chain.

With the approach of evening, the butcher came for another visit. The deadbolt turned. The door handle squeaked and the door opened, sending a shaft of cold light into the dim basement.

Hank grabbed his collar chain and pulled with all his might. Concrete dust sifted down from behind the plate and he sensed some give in the bolts, but not enough to pull free. If he had the chance to attack the butcher, he must keep in mind that his range was limited by the collar chain. If the initial attack failed, the butcher had only to take one step back to render Hank powerless again.

The Wesen stood in the shaft of light coming from the hallway that led to the slaughtering room.

"I have some good news," he said, turning so that his

gaze passed over the ten remaining captives, including Hank. And that's where he stopped, while staring at Hank.

Here it comes, Hank thought, slipping his hand under his side. The crude weapon remained hidden, but ready.

"The good news for you, hunter, is that you bypass my table and tools," he said, his deep voice sounding like stones rolling in a barrel. "This is Last Night. And the special honor of the *Straffe Kette Abendessen* is yours. Eaten fresh."

"Doesn't sound like good news to me," Hank said.

"A matter of perspective," the butcher said, shrugging with amusement. "As for the rest of you, the good news is that you will not, unfortunately, be eaten by the guests."

Alice sat up, leaning forward until she winced in pain and clutched her ribs. When she spoke, her voice was a little breathless, but held a new note of cautious hope.

"You'll—let us go? Let us live?"

The butcher shook his head. "Unfortunately, you're spoilage."

"What is that? What does that mean?" Alice said. "Tell me!"

Hank had a feeling she wouldn't like the answer. They were all witnesses, and dead witnesses tell no tales. As the butcher strode toward him, Hank tensed, clutching the wooden stake out of view. A dozen coarse splinters stabbed his palm and fingers but the needles of pain helped him focus.

"I leave it to our own hunter to explain spoilage to you, Alice," the butcher said as he removed an antique keychain from a front pocket in his bloodied apron. "He'll give you a practical demonstration. All of you." He lowered himself on one knee next to Hank, keychain in his right hand. "But this hunter's time has come."

Hank had been waiting for the butcher to fumble with

the key and the lock to attack, in the moment the larger man was distracted. That's when he intended to drive the stake into the butcher's throat, a fatal blow. What he hadn't counted on was the butcher's first move.

The Wesen's left hand clamped over Hank's forehead, the muscles in his forearm and biceps bulging as he prepared to shove Hank's head back against the wall to stun him.

Hank had an instant to react before the back of his head struck the wall. With the butcher's neck blocked by his massive, raised left arm, Hank had no choice but to drive the stake under the ribs, where the old wood had the best chance of penetrating flesh.

A split second after the makeshift stake stabbed into flesh, Hank's head banged into the wall, dazing him. His arm numb, he lost his grip on the stake, which had snapped in half after sinking less than an inch into the Wesen's tough hide.

Hank grabbed the round iron band and attempted to brain the man, but his uncoordinated movements were ineffective.

He fought for consciousness, only vaguely aware of the crude collar slipping free of his chafed neck. The butcher then hoisted Hank's body in the air, throwing him over his shoulder in a fireman's carry. The room spun beneath Hank, causing a surge of nausea that forced him to close his eyes to hold it at bay.

But moments later, he slipped deeper into darkness and couldn't find his way back.

As they drove away from the heart of Portland, traffic became even lighter, forcing Nick to drop back farther and farther from the white van. Decker left main highways for country roads, turning seemingly at random and doubling back to his southwesterly direction. He'd made this run before and had a procedure designed to discourage tails. Make enough random turns and the same car stays behind you, chances are the driver is following you.

Nick couldn't risk being made by Decker. The man could pull into a rest stop, allowing time and Hank's life to slip away. He had to err on the side of caution and hope that, if Decker slipped free, Monroe would contact him and Renard and guide them to the cannibal house.

"Heard from the FBI field office," Renard said, as all around them drivers began to switch on their headlights. "Word is, they're taking over tomorrow. You and I and the rest of the department will be on support detail."

"Tomorrow none of this matters," Nick said solemnly, convinced that this was the last night. If they failed to apprehend the members of the Silver Plate society in the next hour or two, they would have to wait twenty-five years for another chance. "One way or another, this ends tonight."

Renard nodded.

Nick adjusted his tight grip on the steering wheel and locked his gaze onto the distant van's taillights. As the minutes ticked by, they began to look like all the other taillights in front of them. Cars changed lanes, flashing turn signals, and then a speeding semi almost sideswiped them as the driver abruptly crossed into their lane. Nick slammed on the brakes, then swerved around the truck and accelerated. When he emerged in front of the semi, his gaze darted left and right.

He'd lost sight of the van.

Monroe fought off his nervousness, allowing himself only occasional glances at the side view mirror, never once spotting Nick's Land Cruiser, but confident in the detective's ability to maintain a tail on a suspect.

Don't worry, Monroe, he reassured himself. *They teach that stuff in Cop 101.*

But his anxiety increased, like an itch he couldn't scratch. Decker took a circuitous path, exiting and returning to the interstate highway, then switching to country roads for a while.

Monroe restrained himself from asking about Decker's random course for fear of raising or renewing Decker's suspicions about his motive for accepting the invitation. But the answer seemed obvious. Decker either suspected someone followed them or simply drove in the best way to expose or lose a tail.

Each furtive glance in the mirror revealed fewer cars behind them. With only indistinguishable pairs of headlights to mark them, Monroe had no idea if any particular pair belonged to Nick's SUV.

He faced the possibility that he was alone, without backup.

Decker chuckled.

"What?"

"Remember when I saw the flyer on your table and asked if you knew what it was?"

"I didn't know," Monroe said, honestly. "Not at the time."

"My first thought was, 'Monroe's a damn hypocrite! Lecturing me on the finer points of vegetarianism and yoga, and the bastard's coming to the meat banquet.'"

Monroe shrugged. "I decided to find out," he said. "When I realized it was for the big feast my grandfather always talked about… I had to know what it was like."

"If you had asked," Decker said, "I could have given you the whole set. Spent last week leaving them around town."

"Is that why you were at Shemanski Park Market when I bumped into you?"

"Shemanski? No, I drove Chef there. He wanted to check it out. Who knows why. Nobody in the society wants fresh produce. As a garnish, maybe? But those people prioritize the meat, the flesh, and the organs. They can eat a tomato or a squash whenever the hell they want."

"So, you're more than a chauffeur for them?"

"Chauffeur? Ha! Driver. Errand boy. Wet work," Decker said, ticking off each job on his fingers. "They call me Fixer."

"Wet work?" Monroe asked nervously. "By that, you mean…?"

"Getting my hands dirty for the cause," Decker said, chuckling again. "Aside from the free meals, I enjoy that stuff the most."

Monroe's hands were suddenly clammy. Casually, he wiped them on his trousers and tried to maintain steady breathing. Decker had basically admitted responsibility for the bare bones murders in Portland. And somehow Monroe had to seem okay with that knowledge.

"So, on the news, the chopped-up bones. That was you?"

"It's more complicated than that," Decker said. "Mostly, I deal in… procurement. Butcher does the draining and chopping. But sometimes, they need me to… fix leaks. Ha! Maybe they should call me Plumber." Laughing, he jerked his thumb toward the back. "Already got the signs for it."

"Leaks?"

"Yep. And some who poke their noses where they don't belong," Decker said. "We had this one bitch, thought she was finding rental homes for celebrities and poked… Well, let's just say that curiosity killed that cat. Once you know a person can't be trusted, you deal with that person. Permanently."

Decker suddenly swerved off the country road onto a

dirt road that seemed to appear out of nowhere in a heavy tree line.

"Ladies and gentlemen, we have arrived at our destination. Our very own private soiree."

The van rumbled over a lumpy one-lane dirt road, tires crunching over pebbles on the gentle incline of a winding private driveway. After the shocks had a thorough workout, Decker braked to a stop, about a hundred feet from a house at the top of the hill, windows aglow, surrounded by dark woods.

"You three in back may now remove your hoods, leave the van and make your way up the remainder of the driveway," Decker said. "You'll be greeted at the door."

Monroe peered into the night at the sprawling log cabin home. Twin lines of rental cars ran along either side of the house, some with luggage strapped to the roofs. Members, apparently, knew the secret location, while nonmembers had to decipher the flyers and wear hoods to attend the gruesome festivities. Absently, Monroe reached for the door handle, but Decker caught his other arm.

"I'd like a moment in private, brother."

"Okay," Monroe said, nodding and forcing himself not to ramble.

Decker waited for the Crawfords and the man in the overcoat to walk toward the house, then looked at Monroe, a strange glint in his eye.

"Let's talk outside."

Once out of the van, Decker called Monroe over to the driver's side.

"I have something to show you before you get the grand tour inside."

"Okay," Monroe said again, trying not to let panic creep into his voice. He had a bad feeling that nothing about the situation was "okay."

Decker led him a short distance off the narrow dirt road, closer to the trees.

"Hope you left a trail of breadcrumbs?" Monroe said, hesitant to take one more step along the scant trail threaded between the dark and looming trees.

"Hell, you must think I'm an idiot, Monroe," Decker said, shaking his head in disgust. He pulled an automatic from the back of his waistband and pointed it at Monroe's chest. "This is as far as you go."

CHAPTER THIRTY-THREE

Hank awoke first to the insistent throbbing of his head, but then he became aware of the pleasant sound of violins—Vivaldi's *The Four Seasons*—playing all around him, and he tried to forget his own discomfort to focus on his present surroundings. The occasional clinking of wine glasses struck discordant notes above the bed of music, prodding him to remember, along with the indistinguishable susurration of a dozen overlapping conversations. Not until he opened his eyes and squinted against the painfully bright light shining down on him from an elaborate chandelier did the pieces fall into place: the basement dungeon; human captives chained to the walls, dreading the moment when the house butcher came for them; and the butcher himself, a rhino-like Wesen with a large horn in the middle of his face, and a shorter, bony protuberance above that, in the middle of his forehead.

He remembered the Wesen butcher shoving his head against the wall and before that, his promise that Hank would be eaten alive. Then Hank became aware of his arms stretched over his head as he lay on his back. He tried to sit up and heard the rattle of chains a second before the play in them ran out. Ignoring for the moment the formally dressed partygoers milling around him, he glanced up toward his restraints. They'd stretched his arms apart and chained his wrists to iron rings that passed through angled beams of wood that came together under his body. Lifting his head, he confirmed that his ankles had been secured in similar fashion. He'd been spread-eagled over an X-shaped table. In addition to the chains at his extremities, a two-inch-thick padlocked iron band looped around his waist and the center of the table.

Hank thrashed side to side, trying to topple the table, to no avail. Leaning sideways and craning his neck as much as possible, he looked down and noted the table's wide base. The center of gravity was too low for his tipping strategy to work. In a crowded room of seemingly civilized people, he was completely helpless, a lamb to the slaughter.

"Help me!" he yelled. "Someone! Think about what you're doing!"

A man in his late sixties wearing a crimson tuxedo turned and looked down at Hank, smiling.

"Oh, believe me, we think about this. For twenty-five years we think about this. I wore red for the occasion!"

"You're crazy!" Hank yelled. "A bunch of freaking psychos!"

A few men in tuxes and women in evening gowns deigned to glance at him, appearing uniformly amused by his outbursts, but none offered assistance or even a reply. Hank couldn't goad or shame them into helping him. His defiance was only a source of amusement. Futilely, he pulled on the chains binding his wrists, pulling them first one way and then another, seeking some give in the iron rings or the wood holding them in place.

A bell rang, three times in a row.

A hush fell over the crowd.

Is this it? Will they cut into me now?

A portly old man wheeled out a serving cart and someone whispered, "Chef's last offering before our main course?"

"Ladies and gentlemen," Chef said. "While it is soon time to enjoy the *Straffe Kette Abendessen*—our tight chain supper—please allow me to present for your delectation, and to whet your appetites this evening"—he lifted the lid off a serving dish which Hank, mercifully, couldn't see—"Bone marrow topped with French escargot and herb breadcrumbs to give it a delightful crunch. With this, ahem, Brosseau Marrow Special"—several knowing chuckles, whereupon Hank remembered the name of the French youth he'd been unable to save—"I offer toasted house-baked baguettes and grilled lemon wedges."

Polite applause followed Chef's announcement.

Another man strode up to Chef's side and slapped his shoulder appreciatively.

"Thank you, Chef! This has truly been a marvelous month of gustatory delights!" More applause, this time with much more enthusiasm. "It is my duty, as Host, to bring our month-long festival to a close this evening with the *Straffe Kette Abendessen*. And tonight, I've selected a special meal for tight chain, a hunter who has become our prey." Applause and whistles of approval. "A member of the local constabulary, this man sought to find and arrest you, the members of our very discreet society, and put an end to our festival tradition. Well, I say, his loss is our gain." He waited for the umpteenth round of sick applause to fade. "And our victory will make the raw meat all the sweeter. So, in a few minutes, we shall close our festival with tight chain. But, a word of caution for our first-timers, who have witnessed only decorum thus far. This last meal gets messy!"

Boisterous laughter and cheers erupted around Hank.

Chef returned with his serving cart, but this time, he'd brought out a gleaming assortment of carving knives. Hank heard one tall, hunched woman in a sparkling, ankle-length gown say she preferred tearing into raw flesh with bare hands and claws. "So much more sensual that way!"

Jaw clenched, Hank bucked and pulled against the chains until his muscles trembled with unrewarded effort. Finally, he dropped back, exhausted and panting, and wondered if he'd descended into one of the levels of hell.

At that moment, Hank watched as Ellen and her son, Kurt, approached the host. Ellen leaned forward and whispered in his ear. The host nodded.

"You!" Hank yelled at her. "You're involved in this freak show?"

Ellen looked toward him but avoided his accusatory gaze, while Kurt looked downward, avoiding eye contact with everyone in the room.

Crawford protected his family from this sick bunch, Hank thought, confused. *And she joins the psycho party...? Was she involved all along?*

"Everyone, your attention please," the host said, arms raised. "Our last meal is postponed for just a few minutes. I need to speak privately with the Crawfords about a business matter, then I will join you all for the final celebration. In the meantime, please sample the bone marrow special. Thank you for your patience."

Hank watched the three of them leave and wondered if the widow expected a final payment—a death benefit—for her husband's services. From everything she'd said, and everything Crawford had admitted, his family had been kept in the dark. *She shouldn't even know about this place.* At this point, Hank assumed everyone had been lying.

* * *

Ellen Crawford followed Graham Widmark up the stairs to his second-floor office, Kurt close to her side. On the second floor, the classical music and dinner conversation faded and Ellen's nerves became frayed. She'd taken a chance coming to this place, but she had wanted to see for herself, despite the danger.

Widmark walked behind his large mahogany desk decorated with a brass banker's lamp and stood there, motioning them to sit in the two wingchairs in front.

"I'm glad you came, Mrs. Crawford. I've planned this event for years—my first time hosting Silver Plate—and it would not have been possible without the contributions of your husband."

Ellen and Kurt approached the chairs but neither sat. Widmark, too, remained standing.

"Lamar wanted no part of this," Ellen said bitterly.

"And yet, I was delighted when his son, young Kurt here, decided to join our feast last night." He looked at Kurt and smiled. "You slipped out before I had a chance to say goodbye, young man. I hoped you enjoyed your meal."

"I didn't eat any of it," Kurt said. "I only wanted to see this for myself."

"No shame in that," Widmark said. "Not everyone has the stomach for a participating membership. How about you, Mrs. Crawford? Have you sampled any of Chef's specials this evening?"

"Not at all," Ellen said. "And I have no intention of starting now."

"Regrettable, but I understand," Widmark said. "You are in mourning. Now, as to the matter of the additional payment you requested for Lamar's efforts on our behalf…" He leaned forward, opened the right desk drawer and reached inside. "I'm afraid that's not possible."

"I don't want your blood money, you bastard!"

"You misunderstand," Widmark replied. "You see, neither you nor your son will leave here tonight. Had you not come to me, I would have had Fixer pay you a visit tonight. To keep our society secret, we are forced to take extreme measures."

Ellen pulled a steak knife from the left sleeve of her gown and brandished the gleaming blade in her right.

"Every last one of you will die tonight!" she said angrily, almost frothing at the mouth as she woged. "Grab him, Kurt!"

Kurt rushed around the side of the desk, but froze when Widmark pulled a handgun from the open drawer and leveled it at his chest.

"No!" Ellen yelled, attempting to draw Widmark's deadly attention away from her unarmed son.

Behind her, the door burst open and she had time to glimpse the Dickfellig in a bloodstained butcher's apron a moment before his thick forearm clamped around her throat. As he applied painful pressure, her vision dimmed, dancing with dark spots.

"Please, don't hurt my son," she begged Widmark, but her voice came out as a feeble croaking sound. She'd had one goal. Kill the host. And she'd failed. Now her son would pay the price for her failure.

A gun at his back, hands clasped behind his head, Monroe walked deeper into the woods lining the unpaved driveway of the Silver Plate Society's banquet house, knowing each fateful step brought him closer to his own death.

Decker had him stop at a deadfall.

"Good a place as any to end our friendship," Decker said. "It's all good, though. I'm returning you to the forest, brother."

"Why?"

"Because you can't be trusted with this secret."

"No," Monroe said as he slowly turned to face his former friend, careful to keep his hands behind his head in the nonthreatening posture. He needed to stall, to give Nick time to catch up and stop Decker and the rest of them. "Why take the classes? The Pilates, t'ai chi, the meditation, all of it? Why bother? If you're part of this meat festival, you had no intention of reforming."

"I was surprised to see you at the market," Decker said. "Thought you'd come to town for the feast, but then I remembered you live here. But I wasn't buying the reformed act. Thought it was a cover. The wolf in grandma's clothes. Keeping a low profile, above suspicion. If you didn't know about Silver Plate, I couldn't tell you. So I wanted to see if you were for real with the reformed nonsense. And the more I learned, the more pathetic you became." Decker chuckled in a self-deprecating way. "Fool that I am, I thought I could tempt you to return to your roots. No such luck. The more you tried to get me to reform, the more convinced I became that I was wasting my time with you."

"Obviously, I felt the same," Monroe said. "Wasting my time with you."

"So, imagine my surprise when you turn up at my pickup point," Decker said, smiling. "For one hot minute, I thought, 'He's come around, at last.' But the more I thought about you and those cop friends of yours—and those ridiculous classes—I couldn't believe it. Either you were collecting evidence for your detective buddies, or you were hoping to lead them to our doorstep. If you could have seen how jumpy you looked in the van. The mighty wolf transformed into a rabbit! Well, this is the end of the road, Rabbit. You should thank me for ending the pitiful existence your toothless life has become."

"You could let me go, for old time's sake," Monroe said, nervously. *Face it, Nick's not coming. Decker must have lost him on the way here.* "Promise I won't tell anyone about any of this."

"Like I said before, brother," Decker replied. "Can't trust you. They call me Fixer for a reason. I clean up loose ends. And, unfortunately, you are a loose end."

Decker extended his hand, aiming down the dark barrel of the automatic.

Taking an involuntary step backward, Monroe stumbled, almost fell.

Decker adjusted his aim—

—as a dark figure darted out from the trees behind him, reached around and sliced deep into his throat with a dagger.

Stunned, Decker toppled forward, blood gushing from the fatal wound.

The dark figure—the man from the van who had worn the tailored overcoat but now wore only a black tunic, black trousers and black boots—woged, revealing himself as a hound-like Hundjager. After wiping the dagger on the back of Decker's jacket, the man shoved it into a sheath hidden in his left boot. He pried Decker's automatic from his lifeless hand and removed his own gun from a holster in his right boot.

"Leave now, Veggie Wolf—or die with the rest of them!" he growled at Monroe. With an automatic clutched in each hand, the Hundjager darted back into the trees in the direction of the sprawling house above.

Monroe patted his sweater pocket and panicked when he found it empty. Then he realized he'd put Hank's phone in his pants pocket—given to him as a spare by Nick in the Land Cruiser long before he'd left to board the van—and dialed Nick's number.

Nick picked up almost immediately and confirmed they'd lost the tail, but they were tracking Hank's cell phone GPS and expected to arrive momentarily.

"Hurry, Nick," Monroe said. "There's a Hundjager here and he plans to kill everyone."

Monroe sprinted across the woods, backtracking the path he'd taken with Decker until he reached the unpaved driveway. As he looked toward the county road, the Land Cruiser turned into the driveway, headlights off as it rumbled across dirt and gravel, halting inches from the white van's rear bumper.

Nick and Renard jumped out of the SUV, guns drawn, and followed Monroe as he raced toward the expansive log cabin home.

In the distance, they heard a bell ring three times.

CHAPTER THIRTY-FOUR

The man called Chef by the guests in the cannibal house wheeled his serving tray lined with carving knives beside Hank's X-shaped table. He raised his hands and the background music faded. Immediately, all conversations stopped and everyone gave him their undivided attention.

"Ladies and gentlemen," Chef said. "After twenty-five years of anticipation and planning, the time has finally come for us to conclude our festival with the *Straffe Kette Abendessen*."

Those holding wine or champagne glasses raised them. Others clapped or cheered. A few chanted, "Tight chain supper!"

"Wait!" Hank said. "The other one—your host—he said to wait."

"These people have waited long enough!"

Cheering erupted. Hank saw one elderly man, hands clasped together under his chin, actually lick his lips.

Chef picked up a knife with a serrated six-inch blade, grabbed the bottom of Hank's V-neck sweater and sawed upward to the collar. He repeated the cutting motion on Hank's shirt, mostly to rip the buttons free, and exposed

Hank's chest.

More than a dozen cannibal Wesen edged closer.

A wide-eyed man, who might have been a stockbroker or a bank manager, leaned toward Hank's torso and said, "Should I use a knife or"—he woged into Geier form, holding claws up for Hank to see—"or simply rip a hunk of flesh off with my bare hands? The latter, I think. It's a night for the old ways."

"Get away from me, you sick bastard!" Hank gasped.

The man's clawed hand darted out and raked a narrow furrow in Hank's chest, then he brought the tip of the claw up to his tongue and tasted the blood. Hank thrashed, snapping his chains back and forth, but with no real hope of freeing himself. *If I get my hands on any of these Wesen psychos, I'll rip off their damn fingers and shove them down their throats!*

Chef raised an arm, blocking the man from a second strike.

"Now, now, sir! I haven't given the rule or the word yet."

"The only rule is, no individual feeding frenzies," Chef said. "When you get a hunk of meat or fistful of organ, you step back and allow the next guest his or her turn. That way everyone gets a taste before we reach loose chain. Understood?"

They all nodded, but their eyes stared hungrily at Hank, at the line of fresh blood trickling down his side.

Hank had his doubts that they would restrain themselves, but he also understood that "loose chain" meant the moment he went into shock from pain or blood loss—or died.

Chef held up one hand.

"For those who prefer blade to the claw, I've laid out an assortment of carving knives. Please take one and let me know if we need more."

Several people near the serving cart hefted knives, while those on the other side of Hank's table held out their hands and waited for someone to pass them a blade, handle first.

"After the triple-bell sounds, you may begin," Chef instructed. "Health and circumstances permitting, I hope to see you all again in twenty-five years!"

With that, he lowered his hand—

—and the familiar bell rang, three times.

Despite Chef's admonition, a feeding frenzy began. Men in tuxedos and women in evening gowns rushed forward, woging en masse, pushing and shoving indiscriminately to get the first hunks of Hank's living flesh.

A gunshot rang out.

Hank saw the carving knife slip from Chef's hands before he saw the bullet hole in the center of the man's forehead. Blood trickled down either side of Chef's nose before he toppled over. The cannibals recoiled from the unexpected death among their own ranks. Several shouted in fear.

Whipping his head around, Hank located the shooter: a man dressed in black, an automatic handgun raised in each hand. A moment later, the man fired both guns, dropping one cannibal after another. Before the mass of Wesen around Hank could disentangle themselves and scatter, the man-in-black's shots fell with deadly accuracy, reminding Hank of the old expression, shooting fish in a barrel.

Next Hank heard a crash from farther away and guessed that someone had kicked in the front door.

"Portland Police!" Nick's familiar voice shouted into the panicked crowd. "You're all under arrest."

Ellen Crawford flinched at the sound of gunfire. For a split second, she thought Widmark had shot Kurt. But she recovered her wits quicker than Widmark or the

Dickfellig who throttled her. They hadn't expected gunfire to interrupt their festivities.

She swung her right arm backward, with all the force she could muster, and drove the tip of the steak knife into the right eye of the butcher. Releasing her, he stumbled backward through the open doorway, into the hall.

Another gunshot rang out, this one much too close.

Her gaze flicked toward Widmark and saw the savage expression on his face, before she looked to the left—and screamed. Kurt staggered backward, crashing into the wall before sliding down into an awkward sitting position. A look of agony twisted his face as he peered down at his hands, clutching his stomach, covered in blood.

As soon as Nick raised his foot to kick in the front door, he heard gunshots from inside. Monroe had told him about the Hundjager armed with two automatics who'd vowed to kill everyone in the house. And Hank was in the house, along with an unknown number of abductees. With the tight chain supper and a murderous Hundjager on the loose, they'd run out of time for subtlety.

Nick burst through the doorway first, gun raised in a Weaver stance. Renard followed and shifted to the right, Monroe to the left. Before Nick could register the layout of the rooms on the first floor, the members of the Silver Plate Society rushed toward him, most of them wielding knives of various sizes, eyes wide with panic.

"Freeze!" Nick shouted, his finger tightening on the trigger.

"Nick!" Hank's voice called, from another room.

"Stop them," Nick yelled over his shoulder. "I'll get Hank."

An old man in a rumpled midnight-blue tuxedo lashed out at Nick with a carving knife as long as his forearm.

Nick dodged the blow and clubbed the man on the back of the head with the butt of his gun.

Captain Renard shoved a woman in a glittery silver gown carrying a thin silver knife back into a chair, knocking the chair over, and her with it.

Monroe woged and slammed a young man with a knife into a hutch, smashing the glass doors.

"Hank!" Nick called.

"In here," came Hank's reply.

Nick veered down the hall to a main dining area, and registered the bizarre tableau in an instant.

A woged, ambidextrous Hundjager shot an old woman cowering in a corner, hitting her in the back of the skull. When the gun's slide locked open, signaling an empty magazine, he tossed the gun away.

Nearby, Hank lay spread-eagled on an X-shaped wooden table, chained at wrists and ankles, a locked iron band wrapped around his waist. His shirt had been ripped open and blood ran down the side of his bare chest.

Nick stood in the doorway, but the room had another door in back, through which some of the guests had slipped out, unnoticed by the Hundjager. But he spotted Nick, pivoted, and fired with his other automatic.

Nick had jumped back at his turning motion and felt bits of drywall spray his face as the bullet ricocheted past his head.

Abruptly, the Hundjager lowered the barrel of the gun to Hank's face—

From upstairs, they heard a woman scream—

Startled, the Hundjager looked up—and retreated to the rear archway, shooting defensively at Nick to provide his own cover fire.

Crouching low, Nick crossed into the room and fired two shots at the Wesen. But he couldn't risk pursuit, as that would leave Hank chained and helpless.

"Glad you made it before they served the entrée," Hank said. "Now get me the hell off this cannibal table."

Nick glanced around the room. "Keys?"

"The hell should I know?" Hank asked. "Improvise!"

Nick located the padlocks on the iron rings securing his partner to the table. He chose the safest angles and fired bullets into each lock, then wrenched the locks from the rings. The final lock held the iron waist band in place. Hank still had manacles and chains on wrists and ankles, but they were free of the table.

After helping Hank to a standing position, favoring his casted foot, Nick retuned his shield and sidearm.

"Prisoners in the basement," Hank said. "They plan to kill them all."

"Can you manage?" Nick asked. "I have your crutches in the car."

"No time," Hank said. "Go! I'll guard the basement door. Prisoners' keys should be in the butcher's room."

Despite Dominik Koertig's insistence that she stay clear of the house, Ellen Crawford had come to the Silver Plate Society feast. Worse, she'd brought her son with her. Between her and the police raid—led by a Grimm, no less—the operation had spiraled out of control. But all was not lost. Simply a few more tasks on his to-do list.

While the police were preoccupied with the surviving banquet attendees, he ascended the stairs two at a time and sprinted along the upstairs hallway. The butcher, a hulking Dickfellig in a bloodstained apron, lay in the hallway, moaning, fingers wrapped around a knife protruding from his right eyeball. A fresh bloodstain had spread across his abdomen. At the moment, he represented no physical threat.

Koertig stood over him, aimed his automatic at the good eye, which widened at the sight of the gun barrel, then disappeared when he fired. The butcher's head jolted backward with the bullet's impact, bits of scalp, skull and brain matter rupturing outward on the hardwood floor.

Ejecting the spent magazine, Koertig pulled a fresh one from his pocket and slammed it home, pressing the slide release to cock the gun.

Turning on his heel, he entered the upstairs office and looked left to right. Kurt Crawford lay unconscious, propped up against the wall. Ellen Crawford, her face drawn and pale, mascara-streaked with spent tears, had one arm wrapped around him. Her chest was covered with her own blood, which had begun to pool around her. A broken desk lamp sat on the floor beside her, also streaked with blood. Slumped in his desk chair, Widmark stared at him, stunned, blood gushing from a scalp wound that seemed to have been inflicted by Ellen with the broken desk lamp.

"You'll kill them all?" Ellen asked, her voice strained. "As promised?"

"Everyone," he said, walking toward Widmark. "This ends here, Host."

"Who—?"

Koertig raised his weapon and fired at the old man's forehead in one smooth motion. The chair rocked backward then came forward, and Widmark's body fell face first on the desk, exposing the ruin of the back of his skull.

Koertig walked across the room and stood over the Crawfords.

"I'm sorry," he said to Ellen. "Everyone."

He fired two more kill shots.

From the ground floor, he heard shouting, screams,

gunshots and general pandemonium. He doubted the society members would allow the police to arrest them, part of their rumored "death before disclosure" oath. But he would make sure that option was denied them.

He left the office and stealthily descended the stairs. He had to attack swiftly, without warning, for maximum effect. As soon as the dinner guests came into view, he opened fire, taking headshots to conserve time and ammunition.

With Hank waiting in the kitchen at the top of the stairs, Nick descended to the basement and found a locked metal door at one end of a hallway, an open slaughtering room door at the other end.

As he approached the open doorway he heard faint sounds: the clink and clank of metal. Pausing at the threshold, he took in the horrifying scene: an open walk-in cooler with a headless and gutted human corpse hanging from a hook, a winch rigged to a gambrel in the center of the room, trails of dried blood leading to a drain in the corner. But he couldn't see the source of the metallic rustling.

Gun high, braced with the palm of his left hand, he moved forward, sweeping the sights of his gun right—*nothing!*—to left—a large man in a white apron, his back to Nick, standing at a butchering table covered with severed body parts, an assortment of carving knives, and a meat saw. The Wesen used the flat side of a meat cleaver to sweep chunks of human flesh and bone into a large bucket he'd positioned beside the table.

Getting rid of evidence? The thought flashed through Nick's mind.

"Freeze! Portland Police!" he shouted.

The man froze, as instructed, still clutching the cleaver.

"You are not permitted here!" he said.

"You're kidding, right?" Nick said. "Party's over. Drop the cleaver, butcher!"

"I am Sous-Chef," the man said indignantly. "Not Butcher!"

"I don't care," Nick said. "Drop the damn—!"

The sous-chef moved fast for a big man. Instead of dropping the cleaver, he flung it backward, spinning sideways with deadly accuracy, right at Nick's head.

With no time to duck, Nick deflected the heavy blade with his raised gun. The cleaver ricocheted off the open walk-in cooler door, but Nick lost his grip on the Glock.

Before he could track it, the Wesen—woged to reveal his Schakal nature—charged him, wood-handled meat hooks gripped in both hands.

Nick unleashed a waist-high kick, driving the heel of his shoe into the man's solar plexus. The Schakal's forward momentum increased the severity of the blow. He staggered backward, wheezing.

"First, I kill you, Grimm," he snarled hoarsely. "Then the livestock."

Nick darted to the side, scooped up the cleaver and faced his opponent in a wary stance, balanced to duck either way.

He didn't have long to wait.

The Schakal bull-rushed him again, alternating overhand swings with the meat hooks. Dodging the blows, Nick ducked right, then leaned to the left. A whistling meat hook snagged his jacket. Nick smashed the butt of the cleaver into the back of the Schakal's elbow.

Bone cracked and the Schakal roared, doubled over in pain. With the cleaver in a double-handed grip, Nick swung the blade as if it were an axe and he was chopping wood. His arms met momentary resistance at the Wesen's spine, but the stroke was powerful and the sharp blade burst free with a spray of blood.

The Schakal's head spiraled down to the floor and rolled to a stop beside the winch. The lifeless body toppled over—the neck spurting blood for several seconds—and sprawled awkwardly beneath the gambrel.

"Nick?" Hank called from the top of the stairs.

"Everything's under control!" Nick yelled back, breathing heavily.

Circling around the mess, Nick located an old iron key ring hanging from a peg on the wall.

Quickly, he unlocked the door at the far end of the hallway. There he found nine survivors—five men and four women—all chained to the walls, in various states of exhaustion. Upon his arrival, several cowered in fear.

"Don't—please don't kill us," pleaded one woman, favoring her ribs. "Please!"

"It's okay," Nick said. "I'm Detective Nick Burkhardt. My partner, Hank Griffin, sent me to rescue you."

"Is he—is Hank still alive?" the woman asked, incredulous.

"Yes," Nick said, offering a reassuring smile. "And you're all getting out of here."

He took the key ring and, one by one, unlocked their collars and chains.

Monroe and Renard had succeeded in herding the formally dressed cannibals, along with a few in casual clothes, away from the exits. Most sat on or near sofas and chairs, or leaned against tables.

Renard had shot and killed one murderous Geier, armed with a machete, with two rounds in the chest. That got the attention of the others, who dropped their weapons and seemed resigned to their arrest.

One indignant man spoke of his high-priced attorney

on retainer, and proceeded to convince the others that the man could legally extricate them all from "this unfortunate situation." Monroe wondered if that was legalese for a mass-murdering cannibal gathering. In the distance, he heard approaching police sirens. Renard had called for back up as soon as they'd gotten the crowd under control.

Renard heard something and called, "Nick!"

At that moment, the Hundjager opened fire, and the society members panicked anew. One after another, they dropped, most with instantly fatal head wounds. Flipping a banquet table on its side, Renard ducked behind it and returned fire, but he had a bad angle.

Monroe, on the far side of a coatrack, stood beyond the Hundjager's line of sight as the man stepped off the bottom of the staircase, killing everyone in his path. He strode into the room to take out a woman crouching beside a coffee table, then an old man cowering behind a gold settee with a fleur-de-lis pattern.

Monroe woged and charged the Hundjager.

He felt a spike of panic as the man's arm swung around, the barrel tracking toward him in the blink of an eye. Diving under the sweep of that arm, Monroe knocked down the Hundjager.

They both struck the hardwood floor and rolled in opposite directions. Monroe sprang to his feet, but the Hundjager beat him to it and aimed the automatic at his chest. The second time that had happened to him in the last ten minutes.

Monroe froze.

A gunshot roared.

Flinching, Monroe reflexively clutched his chest.

But he hadn't been hit.

Renard, now with a clear line of sight, had shot the Hundjager in the side, below the right armpit, spinning him around. The Wesen assassin staggered back a half-step, fighting for balance.

Renard fired again, drilling him in the center of the chest. Another stagger-step backward, before Renard fired a third time.

The bridge of the Hundjager's nose exploded in a crimson plume of blood. His body teetered for a long moment, then collapsed at the foot of the staircase.

Monroe looked around in a daze at all the dead bodies, society members and nonmembers, unable to find a single survivor. Then he heard a rush of noise coming from the kitchen.

Nick heard Renard call, "All clear!"

"Let's go, people," Nick said.

He strode from the kitchen, gun against his thigh, leading the bedraggled group of human survivors toward the front of the house. Hank brought up the rear, hopping awkwardly on his good foot but smiling in genuine relief.

Outside, sirens whooped. Red and blue lights flashed through the front and side windows. The chatter of police radios filled the night air.

Nick surveyed the collection of sprawled bodies and busted furniture—a macabre festival in utter ruin—looked back at the human survivors and then, pointedly, at Renard and Monroe.

"It's over," he said.

The former captives probably thought his words referred to their ordeal alone, but Renard and Monroe recognized their greater meaning. The Silver Plate Society was over. In twenty-five years, only the urban legends would remain.

EPILOGUE

Once they had completed what seemed like reams of paperwork, giving a decidedly non-Wesen slant to the slaughter and mass executions at the house in the woods, Nick and Hank stopped by Captain Renard's office.

But before Nick could ask the question that had been bugging him, Sergeant Wu slipped past them and spread several newspapers across Renard's desk.

"For your reading pleasure," Wu said, then excused himself, leaving the two detectives alone with the Captain.

The newspapers featured lurid headlines in bold block type: SECRET BANQUETS SERVED HUMAN FLESH; MASS GRAVES EXPOSE CANNIBAL CULT; CAPTIVES FREED FROM "LIVESTOCK" PEN; SURVIVOR: "THEY WERE MONSTERS, WE WERE MEAT"; ROGUE CULT MEMBER SLAUGHTERS REST.

"Who was he?" Nick asked. "The Hundjager?"

"Traveled under a false identity," Renard said. "Prints came back as belonging to Dominik Koertig, matching a second ID and passport we found in his hotel room safe. Quite the world traveler. Listed occupation is contractor. Let's assume that's a euphemism. Best guess? A freelance fixer hired by the Verrat to put an end to the Silver Plate

Society. Not that they'll ever admit it existed. They either found out when word of the flyers circulated or…"

"Ellen Crawford," Hank guessed. "Never thought she was involved. When I saw her at the banquet, she looked out of place. And upstairs, she and her son must have squared off against the host, Widmark."

"Blamed the society for her husband's involvement and premature death," Renard said, nodding in agreement. "Revenge is a powerful motive."

"She sent an assassin," Nick said. "Why go to the banquet?"

"It was personal with Widmark," Hank surmised. "She wanted to kill him herself."

"Frankly," Renard said, "I'm glad none of them survived to get processed through the system. Lets us spin our own narrative. Explaining a cannibal cult is bad enough. And the human survivors, imprisoned in the basement, witnessed little. They believe the butcher wore a fright mask."

"Might hold up with the press," Nick said, "but there's no mask at the site."

Renard shrugged. "Evidence destroyed during the raid."

Nick nodded, trying to take comfort in knowing they'd saved some lives, without forgetting all those who had suffered and perished for a barbaric feasting ritual. Some families would get to experience joyful reunions with their missing loved ones. As for the rest, once the remaining bones were identified they would have closure, if nothing else. Maybe they would find solace in that.

That evening Nick and Hank stopped at a local bar for an after-work drink. When Nick had knocked back the last of his beer, he looked at his partner, sitting on the stool next to him. Hank looked spooked, as if he had just woken from a particularly disturbing nightmare.

"You okay?" he asked.

"Could've been worse," Hank said, taking the last sip of his bourbon and spinning the ice cubes around the bottom of the glass. Smiling, he shook his head. "And my cast made it through in one piece."

"Ever regret having a Grimm for a partner?"

"Not at all," Hank said, pushing the glass away and reaching for his crutches. "In this strange new world, who better to have my back?"

Later, at Monroe's house, Nick and the Blutbad prepared for a double date with Juliette and Rosalee. Nick checked the time and saw they had a few minutes before they needed to head to Juliette's place. Monroe came down the stairs, looking less than comfortable in a brown suit, white shirt and jade-green necktie.

"So Juliette managed to snag a reservation for four at Escapade?" he asked as he tugged and adjusted the knot in his tie.

"Yes," Nick said. "So I'd better recover my appetite in a hurry."

"Completely understand," Monroe said, flashing a sympathetic grimace. "I hear they offer an extensive vegetarian menu."

"That's what I'm told," Nick said. "Are you okay with that?"

"Me? Why wouldn't I be?"

"You weren't tempted?" Nick asked. "To really fall off the wagon?"

Nick retained some residual guilt over pushing Monroe into a close encounter with the cannibal Wesen. He'd really had no choice—it had been their only chance to save Hank and the other captives. But he knew Monroe sometimes struggled to stay reformed, and Nick had chosen to disregard that for the greater good.

"Tempted, sometimes," Monroe said seriously. "But not by that naked barbarism. If anything, I'm more dedicated to the reformed lifestyle than ever."

"Glad to hear it," Nick said.

"And, believe it or not," Monroe added, "I actually enjoy Pilates."

ACKNOWLEDGMENTS

Thanks to Cath Trechman, my editor at Titan Books, for opening the door for me again, this time to participate in another show's universe, and for coordinating everything with NBCUniversal. Also at Titan, thanks to Valerie Gardner, Katy Wild, Natalie Laverick, Helen Bertrand, and Antonio Nilletti. Thank you to Chris Lucero, Alex Solverson, Jessica Nubel, Kim Niemi, Ed Prince, and Lynn Kouf at NBCUniversal.

I'm indebted to Donna Spector, BS, DVM, DACVIM—Veterinary Internal Medicine Specialist at SpectorDVM. com, for helping me with the details of a true diagnosis masquerading as another condition. Any errors that may have occurred in dramatizing the disorder are solely mine.

Additional thanks to Matthew Passarella for helping me build an ad hoc show bible and for sorting pages and pages of character dialogue. This behind-the-scenes organizational effort helped me make my deadline. Thanks to Jeffrey Richards for answering some geocaching questions and offering name suggestions. Thanks to Andrea, the cook in our family, for helping me present the cannibal feasts. And finally, thanks to my son, Luke, for escorting my daughter, Emma, to/from summer drama class so I could write into the pre-dawn hours every night (day?) and not have to worry about setting my alarm clock.

ABOUT THE AUTHOR

John Passarella won the Horror Writers Association's prestigious Bram Stoker Award for Superior Achievement in a First Novel for the coauthored *Wither*. Columbia Pictures purchased the feature film rights to *Wither* in a prepublication, preemptive bid.

John's other novels include *Wither's Rain, Wither's Legacy, Kindred Spirit, Shimmer* and the original media tie-in novels *Supernatural: Night Terror, Supernatural: Rite of Passage, Buffy the Vampire Slayer: Ghoul Trouble, Angel: Avatar*, and *Angel: Monolith*. In January 2012, he released his first fiction collection, *Exit Strategy & Others. Grimm: The Chopping Block* is his eleventh novel.

A member of the Authors Guild, Horror Writers Association, International Thriller Writers, International Association of Media Tie-In Writers and the Garden State Speculative Writers, John resides in southern New Jersey with his wife, three children, a dog and a cat. As the owner of AuthorPromo.com, he is a web designer for many clients, primarily other authors.

John maintains his official author website at www. passarella.com, where he encourages readers to send him email at author@passarella.com, and to subscribe to his free author newsletter for the latest information on his books and stories. To follow him on Twitter, see @JohnPassarella.

GRIMM
THE ICY TOUCH

JOHN SHIRLEY

When a torched body is found in an underground tunnel,
Portland Police Captain Sean Renard takes one look
at the victim's burned claws and assigns the case to
homicide detectives Nick Burkhardt and Hank Griffin.
They soon discover that a criminal organization known
as The Icy Touch is threatening Wesen into joining their
illegal drug-smuggling operation, and brutally murdering
those who refuse. But as Nick closes in on the gang's
charismatic and ruthless leader, the Grimm uncovers an
ancient—and deadly—rivalry...

A brand-new original novel set in the *Grimm* universe.

GRIMM
AUNT MARIE'S BOOK OF LORE

As his Aunt Marie is dying, homicide Detective Nick
Burkhardt discovers he is descended from an elite line
of criminal profilers known as "Grimms", who keep the
balance between humanity and mythological creatures.
As well as inheriting the "gift" from his aunt of being able
to see the creatures' true forms, he also inherits useful
artefacts, including the Book of Lore.

An in-universe book exploring the weapons, potions and
creatures of *Grimm*.

GRIMM

ON BLU-RAY™ AND DVD

BLU-RAY + DIGITAL UV

GRIMM
SEASON TWO

2

GRIMM

Products based on characters and stories from the hit show!

AVAILABLE AT YOUR LOCAL COMICS SHOP

To find a comics shop in your area, call 1-888-266-4226
For more information or to order direct visit
DarkHorse.com or call 1-800-862-0052

BY THE WRITERS OF THE HIT NBC SERIES!

"One of the best adaptations of a TV series ever... 5 out of 5 stars."
- **MAJOR SPOILERS**

"Monsters, exotic locales, terrific heroes, great dialogue, and one perfect story... Overall grade: A"
- **SCIFI PULSE**

"Non-watchers of the show shouldn't hesitate to jump in."
- **UNLEASH THE FANBOY**

"Unique and fresh... A more-than-suitable companion to the hit series."
- **GEEKS OF DOOM**

"Kind of like the TV show... but kind of better!"
- **ENTERTAINMENT FUSE**

GRIMM

VOLUME ONE:
THE COINS OF ZAKYNTHOS TPB

COLLECTING ISSUES 0 THROUGH 5
STORY BY DAVID GREENWALT & JIM KOUF
WRITTEN BY MARC GAFFEN & KYLE McVEY
ART BY JOSÉ MALAGA

COLLECTION IN STORES NOVEMBER 2013 • ONGOING SERIES IN STORES NOW!

DYNAMITE.